BURNING BLOOD

Bonds of Blood: Book II

DANIEL DE LORNE

For Alison, my nonna,
For the stories and everything else

PROLOGUE

XADRAK FLED, BUT ONLY SINARA SAW HIM ABANDON WHAT he'd wrought. Everyone else was too busy slaughtering. The two Ikiri-rai armies clashed in vicious battle and the dirt soaked up their black blood. The clang of blade against blade merged with the angry buzz of sorcery and the screams of the fallen. Her nose wrinkled at the stench of innards and the metallic whiff of life spilled. It would never end unless she dragged Xadrak back—or just his head.

She hacked her way through her enemies, driving her sword into the chest of a demon she'd once known, once called friend, and he collapsed. Her blade, forged of fire-stone and imbued with powerful incantations, came out bloody and thirsty for more. Combat raged all around her, the Ikiri-rai fighting in the air as well as on soil, weapons and magic used in equal measure. Before she'd been forced to descend because of Xadrak's retreat, she had hovered high above, watching and directing her army. They were weary from years of war, but still they fought. Even when they'd thought all was lost.

The turning point had come some months prior. She'd used her invisibility to sneak close enough to fire an arrow at Xadrak's heart, but he'd detected her presence and spun to protect himself. Though it missed its mark, the arrow tore apart a wing joint and damaged the structure so he'd never fly again. She'd nocked another but his followers had surged and forced her retreat. Though the assassination had failed, his grounding had reinvigorated her troops and showed he could be bested.

A spear, shot from above, narrowly missed her wings. Pivoting, she prepared for a second attack, but her assailant was already falling. One of her soldiers rattled his gore-covered axe at her before he winged away to fight another. She continued her hunt.

She reached the edge of the battle as Xadrak scurried into a canyon, scrabbling on foot like the creature he had become. She had never ventured far into the Blighted Lands, this place desolate long before Xadrak had taken them for his stronghold. From here he'd spread out across the nation, drawing the corrupt and the depraved to his cause. They were demons who hadn't been satisfied with the order that ruled Crion, an order she had benefited from as the daughter of one of its leaders. She had trusted it hadn't troubled Xadrak, that what they had shared mattered more than power. Lying in his arms, those beautiful black feathered wings wrapped around her, stroked by a tail as velvet as a brindlelock's pelt, she had believed they were more than enough for each other.

How wrong she had been.

She ascended, soaring high on the hot draughts rising off the desert. Xadrak disappeared into the gorge. He was no longer the demon she had loved. His once sleek and smooth horns were now as twisted and gnarled as his soul. His tail had transformed into a spike that had pierced her brother through the eye, and his fingers were now pointed claws that had ripped open her mother's breast.

Even smeared in viscera, her white body exposed against the sky provided too much of a target. She turned invisible and waited to see what he would do, to ensure no second army prepared to swarm out of hiding and ravage her forces. A quick look over her shoulder at how their crusade fared revealed a battlefield awash with colors as Ikiri-rai challenged Ikiri-rai. Every now and then one plummeted, breaking their bones on the ungiving ground.

So much carnage, but they were winning. Finally, they were winning.

The chasm opened into a bowl, and Xadrak ran to its center where three large, black stones formed an arch. She flew nearer, beating hard against the wind that signaled a dust storm rising from the west. That arch—she'd heard of something like it before. As the memory of its purpose returned to her, the breath sucked out of her lungs, as surely as if Xadrak choked her. She had wanted to capture him alive so he could stand trial, but instead she had to stop him at all costs.

Standing before the arch, he stabbed his sword into the sand. The metal shimmered, cursed with the darkest magic at his command. He raised his arms and summoned the power to open the portal into another realm. The air beneath the arch wavered.

She was too far to disable him with a spell, and if she missed her target and struck the portal, she risked doing much greater damage to this world and the ones beyond. She beat her wings harder, the muscles in her back screaming as she crested the canyon's lip and dipped down. Without the wind blowing, her descent accelerated. She readied her sword to strike Xadrak between his shoulder blades.

The portal opened. He retrieved his weapon and stepped forward. A crimson mist swirled around the metal blade, charged and ready to conquer.

But he didn't enter. Instead he spun and searched the sky. She should have known he'd sense her, that old bond that had once comforted them both now costing her the advantage. He brought up his weapon and his lip curled in a ferocious snarl. With the speed of her approach, he'd strike her as she fell on him, but she was willing to sacrifice herself to secure his death.

She dove, the wind howling in her ears, her teeth clenched and bared, preparing for her final attack. He grew larger in her vision, until suddenly she was there, and her sword plunged through his torso with a sickening thud. But she couldn't stop her momentum and screamed as the acid touch of his blade slid into her abdomen, her strength wavering as it buried up to the hilt. Her invisibility faded.

They were the closest they'd been in a long time, and the shock of seeing his eyes, once beautiful in their darkness but now flaming, severed her from the agony thrashing in her body. Could she have saved him from this? Or was he always this full of hate?

He snapped his razor teeth at her, and as she jerked away from him, they lost their balance and tripped into the portal.

The magic in their weapons exploded and shattered the gateway behind them. Shards peppered her back and a few lodged in his face. They burrowed into her flesh and stung, but then the pain didn't matter. Death's talons latched onto them as they tumbled in between the dimensions. Her mind calmed as it began to die, aware only that at least Xadrak would not make it to the other side still breathing.

They were dragged down. The metal of their swords

shredded to ribbons and disintegrated, slipping out of their bodies and grasps. With nothing to hold them together, they drifted apart and into the gloom.

In the nothingness, she lost her name. She didn't know if she still had form, and soon she forgot why she was there or how she came to be wherever this was.

Then she wasn't falling but floating, floating in a dim world, aware of another.

And before much time passed, or perhaps an eternity had flown by, she was nestled in a warm place, listening to a beat that soothed most of her, but not all. Because with the darkness came the knowledge she wasn't going to be safe for long.

❧ I ❧

BLOOD IS THE KEY TO
EVERYTHING

1390

I

AURELIA JERKED WITH THE CART AS THE WHEELS RUMBLED over each bump in the road. Her muscles tensed as she tried to stay upright, but it was difficult with her hands shackled in front of her and chained to the floor through metal loops. She studied them. If she didn't, she'd be forced to look up and see the faces of the screaming towns-folk of Carcassonne, people who'd once been her kin, as they shrieked for her to burn. If she looked up, they'd be the ones to dance in the flames, and right now she just wanted to get this over with.

An onion punched her in the left breast. Almost as strong as Henri's fist. It stole her breath and she doubled over. More vegetables pelted her, some as hard as stones. Maybe they were. She couldn't stand straight any longer. She'd have to take the remaining distance hunched over, protecting herself as much as possible and holding onto her will.

She could have done away with this in an instant. She could have scorched the earth around her, making a pyre

9

of her own that would blaze through the vile villagers gathered here today to watch her go up in smoke.

Keep calm. This will all be over soon.

She focused on the floor of the cart, then on one plank of wood, then tighter on one small section of its worn grain. The sounds and cries around her muffled. She kept her concentration locked on one tiny, curled knot and poured her whole world into it. The vegetables, the rocks, the missiles continued, but they were as gnats on a summer's night.

The cart lurched to a halt, but she saved herself from tumbling. Calmer than she'd felt in a week, she raised herself upright. With all the majesty she could muster, she regarded the peasants she'd been forced to live among. She fixed her eye on the tanner poised ready to throw a turnip, but it slipped from his hand. The corner of her mouth curled.

She looked at the stake rising out of a pile of dried sticks. They would ignite with the barest of sparks and set her white smock aflame. She swallowed hard. For the first time since her sentencing, she felt uneasy about what was to happen next.

Out of the corner of her eye she spied the two priests in their vestments, moving towards the cart—and her. Their lips mumbled prayers to the Lord, old white-haired Père Laurens with the younger Guillaume beside him, both with their eyes bright and hungry for the spectacle of seeing God's will be done. It had been weeks since their last burning.

One of the guards who'd led her cart untied her from the floor. He grunted, and pulled roughly on her rope, pitching her forward. Hating him for the loss of grace, she wished she were a more vengeful person. The things she could do to him…

Maybe I will when all this is done.

The pelting began again as she was brought to the pyre and led up the steps to the stake. From this higher point she could see the crowd and how it swelled. The square heaved with people. Children on fathers' shoulders. Women with their faces twisted. More of those who had once been her people roared for her execution.

Her stomach ached, not from lack of food, for she'd been provided for, as disgusting as it was, but from the hate surrounding her. She had once been among them and now was cast out forever. She found Simone, Violette, and Marie, but she no longer knew them. Just as they no longer knew her.

The Aurelia they had known was gone; the girl with the raven hair and the brightness in her eyes that seemed a blessing from God, considering she lived with those *men*, her *family*, and with no mother. Well, maybe that explained it. She'd made a deal with the Devil because her mother had run away and left them behind.

She could hear it all, spoken aloud or not. The gossips down the street who'd whispered about her diminished family, the silent stares as she walked past and the chatter starting again when she wasn't quite out of earshot. Her family had always been under suspicion. Now it had been proven justified. Especially now after her brothers' disappearance.

The guard bound her to the stake with her hands behind her back and a rope looped around her neck.

Where were Olivier and Thierry now?

They lived, that she knew, but how did they fare? Drinking the blood of others no doubt suited Olivier, but Thierry wasn't made for such things. She should have kept him close. While she wouldn't want Thierry here to witness this, she couldn't help but long for him.

"Do you repent of your sins?" Laurens asked.

Guillaume waved that ridiculous cross on its long stick in front of her face. She smiled slightly and let Laurens continue with his entreaties.

"Do you repent of your sins, witch, and deny Satan so that God may have mercy on your soul?"

When she gave no answer, Laurens puffed himself up and his words fired at her, foam gathering in the corner of his mouth and spittle shooting from his lips. The man was utterly terrified.

"Witch, you have been tried and convicted under the benevolent will of God. You are a consort of Satan and shall burn at the stake. Repent now and God may have mercy on your soul. Fail to repent and you shall writhe on that stake just as you shall writhe for eternity in the pits of Hell!"

The rough rope grazed her neck as it tightened, ready to take away her breath and leave nothing but an empty shell to cook in the flames. The cross danced in front of her face, with Christ's tortured body hanging limply on it, the crown of thorns cutting painfully into his forehead.

"Bring the flames and let that be the end of it," she said, her voice cutting through the rabble's clamoring.

Gasps came from those nearest her and then a roar erupted once more, baying for her to burn.

"Witch! So shall it be. You are hereby condemned to Hell. May you feel the full force of God's vengeance."

The executioner stepped forward. Henri—master butcher and her father—had volunteered to put his own daughter to the flames. A cynic would have suspected him of doing it to deflect suspicion. She knew he did it to exact his revenge. Yet now the time had come, he didn't hold the torch as confidently as he would have if he were wielding a knife to slaughter a lamb. Gone were the strength and the certainty, his once defiant and staunch posture replaced with a wimpy frame. She wanted to laugh at him, and then she was.

Laughing at those sad, pathetic eyes as he came forward to burn his daughter to death.

Laughing at what she'd let this man do to her and her brothers for so long.

Laughing at how much loathing she had within her.

"She's crazy."

"Evil!"

"Listen not to her cackling."

Henri stood there, two hands grasping the torch when before he would only have needed one. A priest moved to either side of him, each putting an oiled torch into the fire, lighting it, and with a final call to God to have mercy on them, tossed them onto the pyre.

The faggots ignited quickly, and smoke rose to choke her. Heat radiated from below as more sticks burst alight and the branches snapped. Dancing flames leapt at her smock and sweat broke out across her body. She took shallow, rapid breaths.

What if this went wrong?

People punched their hands into the air, chanting for her grisly demise. She couldn't look at them any longer, couldn't even look at Henri. She'd wanted to stare into his eyes until the end, and pour all her fiery contempt into him, to make him burn as she did. But vengeance would have to wait. She needed to concentrate.

Fire scorched her ankles and she groaned at the freezing and burning that blasted her body, threatening to make her cry and scream. Her skin blistered.

Fighting back tears, she closed her stinging eyes. Breathing became harder, the smoke scratching her throat, but she compelled herself to relax and chanted under her breath.

Cool air surrounded her body, holding the flames back. She continued her incantation, opening her eyes to see the fire encase her. The people silenced and, in between the flickering, she saw the disbelief on their faces. She was supposed to be screaming, begging God for mercy, or at least whimpering. Anything except standing there whole.

The priests crossed themselves and clasped their hands. She focused on Henri. His mouth hung open, and his eye twitched. The fire rose higher, cutting off more of her view.

She should end this now.

Not for the first time since the soldiers had dragged her from her home, she wondered if this had been the right way to do things. She'd always tried to avoid a spectacle, preferring to work quietly in the background. Her mother had taught her that. Most times it was better to avoid suspicion and not let her power show.

But just this once, she wanted them to see what she was capable of. She wanted them all to know, especially Henri.

What will Mother say?

She recited a short but powerful spell, and energy rose out of the earth to swirl around her and the blazing pyre. No one but her could sense it or see it. It twisted, creating a cone that rose to a point far above her head. The energy took on form and gathered the flames, bursting into an inferno. People leapt back; some ran. The flames churned, spinning and spinning, a conflagration that heaved like waves on rough seas. The energy then worked on her and she sailed into the air, leaving Carcassonne behind and nothing to show she'd even been there.

II

"Christ's balls!" Hame dropped the bucket, spilling water across the grass. With it went the vision of the burning girl, and he was once more back in the forest, now with wet feet and a return journey to the river to make.

These unprompted visions mocked him, this oracle that couldn't control his Sight.

At least it wasn't a premonition, merely a glimpse of something happening far away—something that *might* be significant. Loic would know.

He grabbed the bucket handle and stalked back down the path to the river. Whenever a vision snuck up on him it only confirmed what he already knew. He was broken. And the pieces within him ground against one another like mismatched cogs in a windmill.

It had been twelve years since his first prophecy. Twelve years since following it across the sea from his home in the Scottish Highlands to find Loic waiting for him and ready to teach.

Twelve years of disappointment.

He clenched his teeth, the pressure boring into his jaw.

No matter how Loic had trained him, how many days and weeks and months and *years* he'd worked, he still had no control over what he saw. The visions tapped him in the head whenever they wished, a game of tag where he was forever "it".

Well, if the visions weren't going to play fair, he just wouldn't play.

He laughed bitterly at that thought, the sound harsh in the quiet woods. He raked his fingers through his unruly hair and grabbed at the roots.

"As if I have any say in it." He released his hair, smoothed it as best he could, and continued on.

Still, he tried to spite his visions. That was why he was out here collecting water. Why, earlier, he had been chopping more wood than they needed. Why he had been sliding boulders around, the bigger the better.

Loic could enter a trance-like state within seconds, recite and remember prophecies while in them, and send his mind out on both the ether and the astral.

Hame, by comparison, may as well have been a mule.

The path to the river was well worn, taking him through trees that had grown alongside him, trees he'd climbed more times than he could count. Back when he'd first come here, they'd been a bit of fun to balance the training Loic put him through. But as the years wore on without progress, they became an escape. Not from Loic's disapproval—he never gave that—but from that look of hope.

Loic kept the faith, even when Hame had lost his.

Reaching the river, he stepped off the bank and plunged up to his knees in the cold, rushing water. The chill shot up his body and swept away that streak of self-pity he hated just as much as his failure. His mind turned to what he'd seen—the girl with the raven hair soaring into the sky. He knew who she was; recognized her power.

He thrust the bucket into the water, scooped it up, and climbed out of the river to return to Loic.

"He'll want to know about this. He sighed. He had a feeling it was going to be important.

III

Henri launched himself clear of the explosion, but others weren't so lucky. Laurens danced around as his cassock burned, even as Guillaume tried to smother the flames. Others cried or screamed as their skin peeled and blistered. People hurried for buckets of water to hurl at the roofs of the crowded houses around the square.

His gaze shifted over the mayhem to the pyre. The fire had extinguished, leaving behind smoldering blackened sticks at its base. The central pole was untouched, the shackles hanging free and whole.

A burst of light and a rumble of thunder overhead turned his eyes skyward. Dark and heavy clouds galloped in. Then came the downpour.

As townsfolk aided one another, he retreated. It wouldn't be long before the people of Carcassonne turned their suspicions towards him and wondered what unholy pact he had forged to produce such a daughter.

Let them cast their stones.

He was Henri d'Arjou and the first to speak ill of him

would fall beneath his fists and taste his butcher's blade. He relished the opportunity. These fools would bleed and die.

Unlike Aurelia.

Unlike his sons.

The rain dogged him. The streets turned to mud, and his boots sloshed in the putrid puddles. He shoved aside a man and woman who were moving too slowly, and she fell in the muck. The man cursed him. He swiveled and stalked back. No one talked back to Henri d'Arjou; not his wife, not his children, not these maggots.

He smashed his fist into the cuckold's face and the man crumbled, falling back over his woman. She screamed, that high-pitched sound that reminded him so of Aurelia when he'd taken her, of Elaine when she'd started acting the slut. He backhanded the woman and knocked her unconscious.

He marched on, noting a few cowering into doorways as he trudged past.

This was all Elaine's fault. That wife of his had been the wicked one. Three children born of her womb had all been tainted. They probably weren't his at all but the bastard offspring of some monster the whore had lain with. How else could their—*her*—spawn be explained? He hurried on, feeling strong after defending himself, but the oily shame of being unable to fight Aurelia's magic dribbled down his back. She'd turned her magic on him that night the boys had attacked and tried to bite him. Her touch had burned, burned worse than any cut, any kick from a heifer. It had burrowed into him, made his bones creak and his skin crackle. He'd doubled over and screamed, but nothing came out, the agony so intense he'd forgotten who and where he was. Only later did he remember what had happened. And then he'd plotted his revenge.

Sodden, he arrived at the door to his house, pushed it open and shut himself inside.

Alone at last.

The house sat quiet. Both rooms were bare and simple. The first had a table, hearth and a straw bed in the corner that Olivier and Thierry had shared—curled next to each other in life as they had in the womb. The second was where he'd slept, and made Aurelia lie with him after her mother had disappeared. For now, he felt safe here, even as the walls shook with the storm's furor. On the table were a candle and his favorite knife, the one he held as he slept, ready to split open anything that came for him.

Three heavy knocks beat at his door, louder than the thunder, so strong that the wood rattled. So strong that his body quaked. His throat jammed as he swallowed.

Three more knocks.

It was probably the soldiers, come to arrest him for sorcery or for thumping that man and his wife. Well, if they wanted him, he'd fight. They weren't going to see Henri d'Arjou quiver in fear. He'd fight every last one of them and beat them all.

Just the soldiers. It is just the soldiers.

His hand tremored as it hovered over the handle. It was someone else's hand, not his—not the master butcher's, not one of the most feared men in Carcassonne. With his right hand bunched into a fist, he turned the handle with his left, pulled the door back and peered through the opening.

A horror waited to come in.

His eyes bulged and his mouth flapped. Sweat mingled with raindrops and trickled down his neck like rats scurrying over him, their sharp nails pricking his skin.

"It can't be."

He tried to push the door shut but it wouldn't close. He rammed his massive frame behind it, and it held for a moment but then it drove him back. *Him!* He turned to the knife on the table, knowing—as unbelievable as it was—he could not hold the door, and he gave it one final shove then lurched across the room. He grabbed the hilt and skidded around the table, using it as some meagre barrier between him and the now-gaping door.

With the knife brandished in front of him, he trembled as his witch-daughter entered, engulfed in rolling flames.

IV

Aurelia suppressed a smile at seeing Henri cower. For all his bulk, all his once-menacing frame, he shriveled to almost nothing. His hands gripped the knife, but soon he'd clasp them in begging prayer.

She floated into the room, illuminating the small hovel she'd once called home. The door slammed behind her.

Light reflected off his wide eyes. "I don't…" he said, before his words failed.

She darted forward, and he scurried into the room where she'd been forced to lie with him. Her stomach churned as her body remembered his thick fingers pinching her skin. Her flames intensified.

She'd put up with it until she'd learned how to stop it. A knife to the ribs would have been quicker, but she'd seen the benefit of having a living being on which to practice her craft. Mother had said to make do with the scraps she'd been left. Find the opportunity in everything. And so she had.

Now Henri had no use, except to suffer her wrath.

He scuttled into a corner, slamming his back into the wall and waving that butcher's knife at her.

"Witch!" he yelled. "You burned at the stake, and now you're burning in Hell."

Only then did she allow herself a smile. "Oh, Father, I had to come back for you."

She opened her hands, releasing fire. With a curl of her fingers, the flames wrapped around his wrists and bound him, forcing him to drop the knife. He grimaced. The smell of sizzling meat made her hungrier for his agony. Still the defiance shone in his eyes, like a condemned murderer spitting on the boot of the executioner.

"Use your magic," he growled, "but I will not suffer the way you shall suffer."

His words roped themselves to her heart like a lodestone and dragged it down into the pit of her stomach. He would never understand what he had done to her. He would never repent or apologize. Wanting those things was nothing but childish fancy. Even so she couldn't let him live. If Mother were here, she'd say Henri was important and should be left unharmed.

But Mother wasn't here.

She cast away her self-pity and steeled herself.

With a flourish of her hands, the flames encased his fists and climbed his arms. He bit his lip until it bled, then in a spluttering cough his mouth opened, and he released a sniveling bellow. His eyes watered and sweat cascaded from his brow.

Her magic kept him upright while he writhed.

"This is what you wanted for me, Father." She drew near.

He threw his head back, trying to avoid her gaze.

"Look at me," she commanded.

His head straightened, and he was unable to avoid her eyes. He shouted, wept.

"It's only right I should want this for you."

She sent a spark to his boots, the leather and his hose catching alight. He danced, trying to extinguish the blaze, then screamed anew as the fire scorched the skin on his feet and legs.

"Mercy!" he screamed.

She held her tongue. She made her face calm, as neutral as stone, while he thrashed. That was how she'd survived, having learned crying and pleading only made him more brutal. Instead she had retreated into herself and waited for him to finish.

Soon the fire devoured him, his clothes burned away, and his skin melted. His hair ignited, and before long he was silent. She thought he was dead but looking into the inferno his eyes held hers and something shimmered across them.

Something knowing.

Something mocking.

Her lips pulled back as the consciousness in his eyes died. In a rage, she released a burst of power that disintegrated the body and extinguished the fire.

Her breathing stuttered. She didn't know how he'd found quiet in that final moment. But there it had been, that condescending look, that triumphant gaze. A ripple started in her belly and expanded out in a wave. She closed her eyes, tipped back her head, and keened. His torture hadn't been long enough, and now he was gone.

I was too hungry for it.

She sobbed. For herself. For her brothers. For an opportunity she'd never get again.

But then she heard something under her cries.

Laughter.

She took her hands away from her face and screamed.

A winged beast, horned, taloned, and tailed, appeared where Henri had been. It wasn't corporeal, but she couldn't deny its glowing presence and the way it pushed against her. It chuckled as it floated towards her, whipping Henri's ashes into a small whirlwind. She scurried back, her fear and its malevolence shoving her, telling her to run —run forever.

Banish it.

She couldn't find the strength, couldn't summon the concentration. Her throat constricted as if he gripped her in those terrifying claws. This thing was worse than Henri, could *do* worse than Henri. Terror sucked on her marrow as the creature towered over her, and she was herded into the other room. She hit the wall, and the air forced from her lungs.

"Now it's my turn." Its voice scraped her bones, and its gnarled hand rose.

She was going to die.

The door shot open, light erupted, and a blazing white pentagram appeared in front of her and repelled the beast. She looked to the doorway.

"Didn't I tell you to leave Henri alone?"

Mother.

Relief and dread rushed through her.

The beast shrieked like a serpent of the deep and struck the pentagram with its fist. It connected with the star and light consumed it. The monster vanished but its howl lingered.

Elaine dispelled the star. "Come on, I hate this place." She turned on her heel.

"How could—"

"Not now," her mother snapped.

She held her tongue, but she would have answers.

Once outside the house, Elaine grabbed Aurelia's hand and pulled her into the ether. She had traveled like this before in her mother's company, but then, the journey had been smooth, going from here to there like an arrow flying to the middle of a target. This time, something was wrong. A wind buffeted them and attempted to throw them off course. The journey was too rapid for normal sight and everything rushed by in a blur.

Her mother tightened her hold and propelled them through with more force to land in the mouth of a cave inside a forest. Aurelia hunched over to catch her breath, feeling as if she'd been dumped then pulled from a river. At least they'd made it out safely.

Elaine placed a hand on her shoulder. "Are you all right?"

She shrugged it off. "I will be."

"How could you be so stupid?"

She reared up to look her mother in the eye. Though Elaine had always been the stronger of the two, Aurelia felt no fear in confronting her. Especially not now.

"If anyone is going to be blamed for stupidity, it's you."

"How dare——"

"You left me alone with that thing. And not just me, my brothers as well. Children! What were you thinking?"

"If you'd followed my instructions, you wouldn't have been in danger," Elaine said through her teeth.

Blood rushed to her ears. "We've always been in danger. The moment you left us behind, you *put* us in danger. It's only dumb luck we weren't killed."

"Aurelia, please, this is not the time." Elaine pleaded with her, but she wasn't asking for forgiveness.

"You don't understand what it was like being there. I wanted something to make the pain go away."

"And did it?"

She looked at her mother, a sharp agony puncturing her chest over and over in time with her heartbeat. "How could it when he's not really dead? When that monster…" The terror and hurt bubbled inside her and she screwed her eyes shut.

I will not cry.

A soft touch scalded her.

"Don't!" she shouted. "I don't want your comfort."

Elaine's hand retreated. "Then tell me what you do want?"

Since she was twelve, she had kept her mother's secret, sealed it with the promise that one day her mother would come for her, and together they would work amazing magic. In the meantime, Elaine taught her when she could, but never stayed long. Even so, she had kept faith as the questions stacked inside her.

Why did she leave her children behind? Why let Henri live when he deserved the worst kind of punishment?

"I want answers. What was that thing, and why was it inside Henri?"

Her mother couldn't avoid it. She'd imprisoned her in ignorance long enough.

V

Freedom! The charred meat fell away, and Xadrak slipped from the clutches of mortality. True, he'd been banished, but now he soared on the winds of the ether.

He rose into the astral, a higher plane where his power increased. The ether mixed the earthly and the astral, balancing one with the other. Being a spirit, he could not hope to rule Earth, but in the astral he was already filling with energy and might.

He would gain dominion here then seek a way to return to Earth in his full glory, horns gleaming, tail thrashing and wings intact. Then he would rule the world, just as he had sought to rule Crion.

A gaze shifted over him, slid down him, examined him. He stopped. There was nothing there, nothing to see, but he knew he was being watched and appraised, as if he were a curiosity.

The gaze circled him, and he responded in kind, sensing it with his mind. It was human, someone with power of a sort, though small compared to what he possessed. Knowing it had been noticed it bounded away, no doubt searching for some burrow in which to hide.

Xadrak released a whisper of his power, near undetectable, and hooked gently into the other mind. The softness of it drained him, being unused to such careful work. Subtlety had never been his strongest trait, even when he'd been whole. Sinara had called him a brindlelock, the six-legged beast that roamed Crion's mountains. They didn't go around the boulders strewn in their path; they pushed through them with their curled horns and massive shoulders. She'd laughed, lying in his arms in the deep valley, the purple grass swaying in the warm breeze. He'd stroked her—

He quashed the memory, and floated after the mind, gradually drawing nearer. He skirted its edges and found a name—Loic—and the mark of another.

Sinara.

This Loic belonged to her. So, she'd made it through as well. And if her minion searched for him, it wouldn't be long before she came within his reach.

Then the bitch would suffer.

VI

"His name is Xadrak."

Aurelia shivered. "So that thing wasn't Henri?"

"Please understand that while he was human, he was harmless." Once spoken, her mother rushed to cover her ill-chosen words. "I didn't mean—"

"*Harmless?* He forced himself on me. On Olivier. He slashed Thierry from ass to neck, and yet you did nothing. What could have been so important to justify leaving us with *that?*" Her eyes stung. This time she couldn't hold back the tears as her mother's callousness struck her heart like an axe.

Arms encircled her and held her tight. She struggled to break free, but she couldn't, and eventually she succumbed to her mother's warmth. For too long this had been all she'd ever wanted, but now her mother's affections were tainted. She sniffed, clawed back her emotions, and pushed her mother away.

"I'm—" Elaine began.

Aurelia cut her down. "Who is Xadrak?"

Elaine opened her mouth to speak but closed it again

and looked at the ground. When she finally spoke, she sounded empty. "Many years ago, there was a war between the demons in a world separate from our own. Xadrak led dark forces but when his army began to lose, he attempted to escape through a portal, pursued by another demon."

"What demon?"

Elaine looked into her eyes. "Me."

Beetles skittered up her body. Remembering the awful beast that had been Xadrak, she summoned a banishing pentagram.

Her mother—the demon—tilted back her head and looked to the cave's roof, shaking her head slightly. "You have nothing to fear from me, Aurelia."

"How can I trust you?"

Elaine stepped towards the pentagram, and Aurelia imbued it with more power. "I am your mother."

"If you are my mother, then Xadrak is my father."

"No, it doesn't work like that. Henri and I are both mortal, but the spirit that inhabits our bodies is demon."

"Even less reason to trust you."

Elaine's shoulders sagged. "Though I have not always protected you, I have never directly caused you harm. There is no need for you to guard yourself from me."

Grudgingly, Aurelia admitted her mother was right. Whenever they had been together over the years, Aurelia learning at Elaine's side to control the power she'd been given, she had been generous. While it now made her feel as if she'd been bought off, she'd not been in danger.

She withdrew the protection.

"What happened when you followed him through the portal?"

"We fought and during the battle it collapsed, sending us to Earth. Here, our powers were forced into human blood and bone."

"Why do you have power and Henri didn't?"

"For a while I was the same as him, but then I started to get flashes of memories that weren't my own. And with the memories came my power."

"And then you left."

She had seen her mother near hysterical back then, weeping when she'd thought she wasn't being watched, and chasing her out of the house when she'd caught her spying. The twins hadn't noticed or, if they had, they didn't let on, but Aurelia had. Not being able to help ease her mother's worries had sat like cow dung in her stomach.

Then she was gone.

And Henri changed.

"I had to find out what it meant."

Aurelia folded her arms, the weight on her belly easing the nausea brought on by the memories. "And did you?"

"Yes, an oracle helped me discover what my path was and how I must finish what Sinara started."

Sinara. Two names for two faces.

"And what's that?"

"To return Xadrak to his realm where he will face justice."

"Then why is he still here? If you knew what he was, why did we have to suffer him?"

"It wasn't the right time. I didn't have all the pieces, so I had to wait. While human, he was without magic. Now that he's a spirit, he's out there, growing stronger and becoming everything he once was."

"And he's going to come for you."

"For us. We're in this together, Aurelia."

Aurelia's heart tried to break through her chest. Elaine wanted her to face the demon *again*?

"I want none of this. Xadrak is your problem."

"A problem you created."

"You blame me for this? An accident of birth is what this is. Everything else is your battle, your fight, and your burden to bear."

Elaine reached for her. "I can't do this without you."

"Why not? I seem to have made this all so difficult for you. You could leave me be and that would be the end of it. You left me once before. I'm sure you can do it again."

Elaine slapped her, knocking her to the ground. Her head swam from the blow. When her vision stabilized, her mother's face was close to hers, her hand near her cheek. She jerked away.

Elaine pulled back her hand. "I'm sorry. Please, Aurelia, I need your help. I worry that it won't be safe for you now Xadrak is free. Help me rid the world of him forever. If not for me, then for yourself."

She had been coping fine without a mother for longer than Elaine knew. She had been the one to care for the house. She had patched up Thierry and Olivier's wounds, her only failing that she couldn't save them from their curse. Her mother had been a fantasy, a dream she now knew could never become reality. Too much had happened, too many scars carved into her flesh. All she could hope for now was some consolation, and to take the only thing her demon mother could still give her: power and freedom.

She pushed herself off the ground. "I'll help you, but I'm doing it for me. You will teach me all you know; I won't be kept blind. And we will work together."

"As you wish," Elaine said, her voice packed hard with grit. "Let's get out of here."

She held out her hand, and Aurelia recoiled.

"Would you rather walk?"

"If it means not having to go through that tempest again, then yes."

Elaine's lips thinned. "I was unsettled before. It won't happen again."

"But what if he's there waiting for us?"

"I'm prepared. Summon the pentagram if needed. It should allow us time to evade him."

"Should?"

"If everything was predictable, we wouldn't be here right now, would we?" Elaine stretched her hand for her daughter to take.

Aurelia was about to argue, her mouth opened and ready to complain, but she thought better of it. And even though she'd won a battle, as the skin of her palm met her mother's, she couldn't fight the way it soothed her.

Xadrak didn't follow them, though Aurelia had been ready to blast the demon with everything she had. Relief swept through her as they landed on a stone ledge overlooking a valley. Elaine's hand ripped from hers, but Aurelia was too fixed on the sight of the mountains to care. Peaks beyond pierced the sky, and below them a lake reflected the deep blue. Her heart swelled at a beauty she had barely dared to dream of.

"Come!" came Elaine's sharp order, shattering her reverie. She turned as her mother disappeared into the darkness of a tunnel in the side of the mountain.

She couldn't match the forceful stride, not knowing what waited for her within, but she stepped into the black anyway. She walked blind for a few steps, each one barely covering a few feet. The gloom was pervasive, sticky, and slowed her down. Then it faded, releasing her, and a glow appeared ahead. The tunnel ended quickly, no doubt a trick of her mother's to guard this place, and when she stepped into the light, she stood inside a chamber with a tall vaulted ceiling. White marble lined the walls and glowing orbs shone from above. Three other corridors led off from this room.

Whenever her mother spirited her away from Carcassonne, they had gone to forests, the seashore, to anywhere but a home. She had often wondered where Elaine lived.

To think that this is now my home.

But for all its magnificence and the power required to create such a thing, she couldn't help but feel suffocated. There were no windows, and no natural light penetrated this deep. She would be spending as much time as she could out on the ledge.

"This way," Elaine commanded as she disappeared down the corridor to the right.

Aurelia hurried after her mother. There were two doors on either side, and Elaine stopped in front of the last on the left. Pushing open the wooden door, she gestured for her daughter to enter.

"This is your room."

Aurelia's steps slowed, suspicious of what her mother had provided. An empty room perhaps? A straw mattress on the floor? Anything would have been better than what she'd come from because here there was no Henri to be forced to lie against. She peered around the doorway and gasped.

Her eyes fell on the bed, a proper one raised off the ground, no doubt a thick mattress beneath the quilt that covered it. And the size!

Forgetting her mother's stare, she stepped into the room, her hand open over her chest as if she fought to keep her heart inside.

Beautiful, lush rugs carpeted the floor. Carved chairs, stained and lacquered to a deep, rich red, sat around a square table. On the far wall, a tall wardrobe that, when opened, revealed clothes of many colors, with a dominance of green, her favorite. She touched the velvet of an emerald dress, the restrained smoothness a delight beneath her fingers. Her throat ached with the lump lodged there. She had never seen such wealth.

Are you so easily bought?

The thought whipped her mind, and she snatched back her hand, closing the wardrobe with precise movements. As she turned around, she glanced over at the dresser, no doubt also stocked with bribes.

Elaine stood in the doorway, eyes of iron, mouth grim. Aurelia nearly said thank you, but she kept her jaw tight. It would take more than a few dresses and a cozy bed for her to forgive.

They stared at each other. The air between them grew cold. Aurelia wouldn't speak. She wouldn't betray her crippling need for comfort, even as the weariness heaved its way into her body and mind. Before, she would have wanted nothing more than to lie with her head in her mother's lap, to feel Elaine's fingers comb through her hair, and send her off to sleep. Now her back stiffened from the sentiment.

"Rest. We will discuss more later." Elaine's lips parted to speak again but she closed them and walked away.

A moment later one of the doors in the corridor opened and locked. Aurelia stuck her head out but couldn't see which one Elaine had entered. Pulling back into her room, Aurelia shut herself in and sagged against the stout wood.

She was alone.

Screams rose through Elaine's chest and throat, ready to roll out of her mouth, but turning the key in the lock was enough to hold back her howling. Denied release, they crashed through her body, freezing her hands in open, shaking claws. Shattering, she collapsed on the floor.

How had she got this so wrong?

She had left Aurelia and the twins behind, believing *she* was the dangerous one. Seeing battling demons inside her head had nearly sent her leaping off Carcassonne's high walls. And when she'd learned the truth, she couldn't kill Henri. A human monster was preferable to the one that would be released at his death. Each of her daughter's cries had stabbed her heart, but she couldn't change the past. Instead she taught her magic, incantations, and spells that she eventually used to keep his grimy fingers off her.

Elaine breathed deeply, noisily, as guilt stung her eyes. She forced herself up and paced the room to help ease her anguish.

Back then she'd believed she'd done the right thing.

Now?

"I'm a fool."

But she was hopeful Aurelia would still help her. She had to be, even when she just wanted to crawl into bed and never wake. Henri's execution had brought them to crisis, and exiling Xadrak to Crion wasn't yet possible. She still needed the key.

And when I get it, what of my sons then? What becomes of them?

She wrenched her head to the right, screwing her eyes shut.

This has to be done. It was what they were made for, Sinara spoke inside her mind.

She used to fight that voice, but the more she denied it, the more it pursued her with memories of strange places and a world that wasn't her own. It wasn't until she accepted they were a part of her that she got some semblance of peace. They gave her purpose and a mission that soothed her need for answers and for action.

But it came at a price, and one a mother should never have to pay.

VII

Hame attempted to make out shapes as he peered into the black above him. Loic's muttering in his sleep nearly drove him crazy, but it wasn't that which kept him awake. It was Elaine's daughter, Aurelia.

While he'd never met her, he knew her mother from her visits to Loic. Even though Loic had named him his successor as oracle, Elaine had barely exchanged more than a few words with him. She was polite, but she knew he wasn't up to the task. He was an apprentice that would never become a master. He could no more control his visions than he could control the weather.

Hame threw back the blanket, sleep scared away completely by the frustration thrashing within him. When he'd returned from the river, Loic had been distracted and unwilling to listen to what he'd seen in the vision, so he'd been left to puzzle it out by himself.

Without stopping to dress, he stamped out of the house, not worried about waking the master.

What use was it to see Aurelia burned at the stake?

A brisk chill shot up his feet when they hit the grass and goosebumps rose over his skin. To warm himself, he jogged into the forest, dim moonlight enough of a guide to the place he knew even better than the hut.

Navigating the rough terrain through trees and over rocks, he arrived at the edge of a circle of old oaks. In the middle of it stood the dolmen—two upright stones with a capstone across the top—that Loic would sit beneath and let his mind drift. No, drifting wasn't the right word. It implied a lack of focus, and if there was anything the oracle had in abundance, it was focus. His mind shot with precision into the astral, directed to whatever point in time he desired, and struck its target.

Loic could have a vision anywhere, but he favored the dolmen. He said the fresh air provided clarity and he often encouraged Hame to sit beneath its shadow, hoping it would activate his control.

It didn't.

Hame walked across the grass towards the looming black stones. His breath quickened as he neared them, hopeful despite his cynicism that this time he would succeed. Because if he didn't try something, didn't continue working on it, he would go mad.

He sat on the flat stone at the dolmen's base. It served as Loic's seat, worn smooth over forty years. His skin shrank at the touch of the cool, polished rock. Once settled and acclimatized, he looked out at the oaks and closed his eyes, seeking a vision.

Minutes passed.

Nothing.

He shut his eyelids tighter before remembering what Loic had said about relaxing, that too much concentration was counterproductive. He breathed, unwound, and turned his focus inward, away from the sashaying of the leaves and chirruping of insects.

The deeper he went the lighter he became, going up while going down. This mental exercise had been one of the first things Loic had taught him. The oracle's delight at seeing him so quickly take to it had been one of the happiest moments of his life. Instead of the fear and worry in his parents' eyes, he was praised for what came almost naturally. His pride had bloomed.

Only to shrivel.

He snatched his mind free of that nettle patch. He drifted into the trance-state, ready to find that which hid from normal sight, and learn why Aurelia was now so prominent in his thoughts.

An image of her formed in his head, her hair darker than the night, her eyes as green as new leaves in spring. She was younger than his twenty-four years, but she was already a woman, with a surety about her that was unlike anything he'd seen. Not that he met many people, and certainly none like her.

With her face fixed in his mind, he groped for the veil between his ordinary daydreams and the visions. Loic told him it was like parting a waterfall. He had to reach into the crashing flow with both hands and create a curtain to walk through. Gloom and darkness lay beyond but in there he would find treasure.

But no matter how hard he tried he couldn't get to the other side. Aurelia was merely a figment.

And he was useless.

He tumbled beneath the pounding water. His chest stretched tight, as he grew desperate to break free and gasp air. Even when he surfaced, the failure hammered inside his ribcage. His eyes snapped open, and he roared until his throat bled.

"Eat something," Hame said. "You're not well."

Loic rocked on his stool, his food untouched. "Do not command me, boy," he barked, and continued rocking.

Hame rapped his spoon on the table. Loic was hardly ever sick, and when he was, it was usually only a sniffle. This? Whatever it was, it burrowed deep, affecting Loic's mind as well as his body. In little more than a day, Hame barely recognized him. His tanned skin was now sallow, and his cheeks—which were usually full and puffed up with good humor—sagged. Deep purple bruises spread beneath his eyes, and his body curled in on itself.

But it was the sounds that came out of Loic's mouth that set Hame most on edge. Whispers, barks, and mutterings, sharp and slurred, exclamations at any time of the day or night; each sound tightened the muscles in the back of his neck.

In twelve years of living with Loic, he'd never been like this.

Hame let his spoon fall and pushed away from the table. He came around to kneel beside Loic, then took the man's head in his hands. His skin was clammy, the touch of it making Hame's stomach churn.

Loic struggled, tried to push him away, but he wasn't strong enough. Instead he reared back, but Hame rose with him and didn't let go. Free of the table, he positioned himself in front of his tutor's face. Loic's grey eyes didn't rest, and instead shifted from left to right. If he could get Loic to focus on him, then maybe he could figure out what was wrong.

Suddenly, the oracle's eyes centered. Hame breathed easy, but his breath halted when he saw them turn black and ringed with crimson. He released Loic, as if he'd been

42

burned. The oracle's eyes returned to how they'd been before, shifting but not seeing, and he shuffled away to his bed. He lay down, faced the wall, and muttered.

Hame didn't move.

What lived inside Loic's head?

The oracle once said possession happened to fools who weren't smart enough to shield themselves. If they took the proper precautions on the astral, they would be safe.

Loic was no novice. Maybe he was mistaken in what he'd seen. It could have been a vision made flesh. Maybe he was seeing what Loic saw while in a waking trance.

But the sucking void in his gut told him the awful truth. There was another being in Loic intent on destruction. If he were in control of his ability, he could try reaching into Loic's mind and banish whatever festered inside. But he was a failed oracle.

Loic's muttering slowed, dropped to barely a whisper. Moving closer, Hame could make out a phrase Loic repeated as it gained strength and clarity. He reached out a trembling hand and touched his tutor's shoulder.

Loic spun, latched on to his wrist, and pulled himself up. Desperation flared in eyes that Hame recognized.

"Get Elaine!"

Then Loic passed out.

Hame shook him, growing ever rougher and more frantic, but Loic didn't wake. He slumped on the edge of the bed, resting his hand on Loic's chest as it rose and fell in sputtered gasps.

The knowledge crashed down on him that his teacher —his friend—was going to die because of his uselessness. The only way he knew how to reach Elaine was by touching her mind, as Loic was sometimes able to do, but it was something he'd never attempted.

Yet looking down at Loic's unconscious and twisted figure, he had to try.

And he had to succeed.

VIII

DESPITE THE COMFORT OF A REAL BED AND THE EXERTION of the day before, Aurelia woke feeling like she'd only slept a couple hours. The softness of the mattress would take some getting used to; she'd spent most of the night tossing and turning. Her door remained closed, but a frost seeped through the cracks. Rather than face the ice, she stayed in her room, working through old exercises her mother had taught her. She played with her favorite spells of summoning fire and sending lightning between her hands. She tested the limits of her control, seeing how long she could sustain the flow, and all the while conscious of the chill creeping into her bones. Eventually, deep cracks boomed within her and she hurried out for fresh air.

She rushed through the tunnel, blindness giving way to the blessed sight of the mountains in daylight. She expelled stale breath and inhaled a crisp freshness that sparked up and down her body. It resembled nothing like Carcassonne's oppressive stench. She sat on the edge of the cliff with her feet dangling over the precipice. Before her towered white-haired guardians. Below lay grass-covered valleys and an azure lake. She spied not a soul, neither human nor animal, on this clear day.

If only her mind were so clear.

At least here she could breathe and try to order her thoughts. If Elaine didn't speak to her, how could she be expected to help? Guilt scalded her throat. She thought she was being strong and looking after herself, but there she was, sitting alone and avoiding her mother.

Elaine had been the goal all along, a promise whispered. But she'd misunderstood. Her mother hadn't just wanted a daughter; she'd needed an ally. And that meant compromise. But it didn't mean there couldn't be love.

Aurelia.

Her body tensed at the sound of her name. She turned her head, thinking Elaine had come for her, but she wasn't there. She frowned, then slowly swiveled back to the open air.

"Must have been the wind," she said aloud to reassure herself, but her body didn't unwind. She searched the sky.

Aurelia!

A man's voice rocked her. She couldn't deny hearing it that time. Needles pierced her veins. *Xadrak!* She scurried back from the edge.

AURELIA!

It came again and her head rattled with his desperation, but it wasn't Xadrak's. The voice was younger than Henri's and lacked the hate and evil she'd felt from the demon.

Fighting her panic, she closed her eyes and took deep breaths. She tensed, waiting for another call, but when one didn't come, she forced herself to calm. Laying down a ring of protection she hoped would repel malevolent spirits, she opened her mind.

Words and images flooded into her, but she held firm

against the torrent. The more she panicked, the less she received, so against her common sense, she relaxed and let it flow through her.

Bare seconds passed before the voice faded, dissipating in mid-thought, but she'd seen enough. Opening her eyes, she ran inside, shouting for her mother.

Her calls brought Elaine flying into the chamber. "What's the matter?"

"Your oracle. We need to go to him." She pulled her mother towards the tunnel, but she resisted.

"Wait. Wait!" Elaine forced her to halt. "What are you talking about?"

She repeated the message, but she hadn't finished before her mother was running, dragging her along. Barely a step into the light, Elaine propelled them through the ether with a force strong enough to tear Aurelia apart. Only her mother's grip kept her whole.

They materialized in a forest, and she caught a glimpse of an old wooden hut before she swayed. Sick gurgled up her throat and she bent over, focusing on the ground to alleviate her nausea. When she was sure she wasn't going to heave, she stood upright, and went inside after Elaine.

"…getting worse. There was something in his eyes I've never seen before." She heard his voice before she saw him, the accent matching the one that had sought her help.

"You think he's possessed?"

"What else can it be?" The man ran his hand through his red hair, the light catching it and turning it to flame. The crinkled locks bunched up then cascaded down as his hand freed and rested on the back of his neck. She watched every muscle shift in this simple action, forgetting to breathe. It was only when Elaine turned to look down on the cot and he noticed her that she inhaled.

Jade eyes held her as he walked over. He stopped bare

47

inches from her, his body radiating heat, carrying with it the scent of the forest, a rich earth that made her belly growl.

She squeaked as he took hold of her right hand in both his large ones.

"Thank you." He raised her hand to his lips and kissed her palm. His lips branded her flesh.

"I…I…" she stammered; warm molasses coated her mind. Swallowing hard, she found her voice. "I didn't do anything."

His head whipped up. "You heard me. No one has ever heard me." He said it with such earnest and gratitude her heart burned with greater intensity. Her cheeks flushed.

"Aurelia!" Elaine shouted, her voice like a bucket of water thrown over her head. "Get over here."

She slipped her hand from his grip, raced to her mother's side and cried out when she saw the tormented oracle. Frail and sunken, his skin glistened with sweat, and his face twisted. His muscles clenched and unclenched, making his body writhe like a sack of yowling cats. Every now and then he buckled, his back arching to raise him off the cot, only to slam down again.

"What's wrong with him?" she asked.

"Something has infected his mind."

"Xadrak?"

"Likely."

"The demon?" the redheaded man said. "But how?" He stood behind her, his warmth against her back.

"He got free yesterday," Elaine said.

"Xadrak is meant to be locked up. *You* were meant to keep him from getting out."

Aurelia cringed as he laid the blame on her mother. "It's not—"

Elaine spoke over her. "What's done is done. Now we have to save Loic."

"But is that even possible?" he asked.

"I don't know."

"You have to help him. This is all because of you."

"Do not lecture me, Hame. I know my responsibilities."

And Aurelia knew hers. "What can I do to help?"

"We need to get inside Loic's mind. I don't suppose you've tried, have you?" she said to Hame with a slash in her voice.

He folded his arms across his chest and glared.

"I'll go," Aurelia said.

"No!" Elaine barked. "Xadrak might be waiting in there for whoever comes to flush him out. You're not strong enough to confront him."

"Better me than you. Let me try."

Loic let out a long howl, lifting off the cot so high Aurelia thought his spine would snap in two. Hame dove between her and Elaine, pushing them aside so he could hold onto Loic and lessen some of his strain.

"Please come back. Please come back." He said it so softly, but she heard it and the plaintive call punctured her heart. Loic eventually lowered, and Hame sat back on his knees, holding the oracle's hand.

"I'm going in," Aurelia said, reaching out to touch Loic's temple.

But Elaine slapped her hand away and pressed her fingers against the oracle's head. Her eyes closed and her body settled into a relaxed pose. Aurelia's chest seized at seeing her mother disappear so quickly.

What if she never comes out?

Hame's free hand grabbed hold of hers and he squeezed it. "Thank you for trying."

She meant to say more, to tell him it was because of her Xadrak had been free to do this, but Hame's attention had returned to the cot. Loic no longer thrashed or howled. He lay still on his back; his grey eyes stared at nothing.

Elaine's hand trembled.

IX

THE ORACLE HADN'T WITNESSED HIM ESCAPE FROM HIS flesh-and-bone prison. Instead he had been focused on the past and the life of the two Ikiri-rai in their true home. Xadrak lashed out when seeing the battles again—his rise and fall, his descent into the portal and death—and sank his claws further into Loic's mind. He attempted to twist the oracle's meagre abilities to divine his and Sinara's futures, but it was futile under such pressure.

And then *she* came burrowing in.

Only iron restraint kept him from grabbing hold of her the instant he felt her presence. He wanted to make sure as much of her was inside as possible before he snared her. He prowled around her awareness, keeping low and in the shadows of this feeble mind. Sinara searched, but for what?

Ah, she searches for me.

She crept, picking her way through a dying and inhospitable land. She delved further, feeling for any traps he might have laid, being careful not to draw his eye. He expected her to be protected, as if she carried a bow and arrow or had fashioned a shield.

Getting closer and probing her boundaries, he stopped. There was no protection. She was open and traipsing down a dark path, ready for the taking. But only a fool would believe such a thing of Sinara.

And he was no fool.

What could she possibly have done that would be undetectable to him? She was here as an invader. This was his territory and he should have been in control.

Trickery. Sinara was always good at tricks.

That was how she'd broken his wing and lost him his army. He growled at the remembered failures, and anger rippled out before he could wrestle it under control. She sensed it and spun towards his presence. Power surged from her and white light blinded him. He broke his cover and rushed forward to where she'd been, but she had fled.

Half-blind from the attack and his fury, he shredded Loic's mind. Howling and bellowing, for one moment he merged on a deeper level with Loic, his screams becoming the oracle's as he was torn to pieces. One thought couldn't follow another, couldn't connect with another ever again. With a final slash, he quit the diseased and dying mind and erupted into the astral, in search of a way to repay Sinara for her treachery.

X

LOIC GAVE ONE FINAL SHUDDERING BREATH AND HIS HAND
went slack. Tears dripped off Hame's cheeks, and cries
clogged his throat. He tilted his head and wailed, releasing
the stark horror he'd barely been able to block from his
thoughts.

If he'd been a real oracle, Loic would not be dead. He
could have predicted this. He could have helped keep Loic
safe. He could have dislodged the demon sooner.

The demon…

This was Elaine's fault. She was meant to keep that evil
locked up. Anger pushed him to his feet. He grabbed her
and slammed her against the wall.

"You could have saved him," he growled, uncaring that
her eyes were red and wet. "He's dead because of you."

She kept still but her muscles tensed beneath his hands.
"There was nothing I could do. Xadrak had already
destroyed him."

"Liar!" He wanted to crush her. "If there's anyone who
could have helped him, it was you. But you didn't want to
risk your precious hide."

Her nostrils flared. "And what of you? If you showed any skill at prophecy, you could have seen this." Her words winded him, loosening his grip, and she forced her way out of his hold. "You weren't the only one to lose a friend, Hame."

"You used him," he whispered.

Elaine drew back to slap him.

"Stop!" Aurelia shouted. "Loic is dead, and all you two can do is bicker."

Elaine dropped her hand. An apology formed in her eyes, but he sneered at her sympathy. He returned to Loic's bedside. Aurelia touched his arm. Instinctively he hugged her, and she nestled against his chest. He inhaled the orange scent from her hair, each breath sweeping aside his hostility for Elaine and letting his grief spread as he sobbed.

Loic was all he'd had. He'd left his family, travelling down from Scotland through the hostile lands of the English, before stowing away on a boat crossing the Channel. Frightened and alone, he'd poured his faith into the vision that Normandy was where he was meant to be. And there on the dock, the oracle had waited for him, a big grin stretched wide across his face, a smile he'd loved from the start. Loic had greeted him in an unfamiliar language, but the words weren't important. He knew Loic wouldn't cause him harm. After so long without kindness, he'd collapsed into the stranger's embrace and wept. Loic had lifted him into his arms and carried him away to a new home. There was nowhere else he'd wanted to be.

The memory plunged back into the deep. If Aurelia hadn't shifted in his arms, he would have followed it and dragged back to the surface all the other happy and painful recollections of all too short a time spent with Loic.

He released her and sagged without her support. He

sniffed, then wiped the snot from his nose, slumping onto the edge of Loic's cot to stare at his dead friend. Loic's eyes, which had sought to see so much in life, were fixed and glassy. He was gone and there was nothing Hame could do about it. That powerlessness scrubbed him raw. He pressed the base of his palms against his eyes and ground them until they hurt. Aurelia pulled his hands away, encasing them in her tenderness.

"Will you sit with me a while?" he whispered.

"Of course." She pulled up a stool to sit beside him and didn't let him go. "I'll stay as long as you want me."

Elaine left, her departure confirming what he'd suspected all along. No matter how she tried to convince him otherwise, for her Loic had only ever been a tool.

Hame stayed beside his friend until twilight fell and Loic's body grew cold. When he became aware of the dying light, he didn't understand how so much time could have passed. Aurelia spoke his name, but it took seconds to seep through the fog clouding his mind.

"We should prepare a grave," she said.

He winced. A grave meant burial, meant separation.

"I'll help you."

"No! I have to do it. He has to know I did one thing right."

"I'm sure you did many things right. I'm sure he was proud of you."

His chest hollowed. "I wanted him to be, but I could never match his ability. And now I never will."

"Of course you will. It just takes time."

"No, I won't. And I don't want to. Look at what it did to him."

He braced himself, expecting her to try to persuade him otherwise. Elaine would have if he'd said it to her, even if she believed him broken.

"Very well. Where should we lay him to rest?"

That was it? No argument? He stared at her until she repeated the question, and he gave her an answer. Really, there was only one place suitable.

They walked to the ring of oaks, Hame carrying a shovel over his shoulder, then he stabbed it into the ground in front of the dolmen and dug the soil.

The effort felt good, his muscles working hard to carve out a suitable resting place. The night was old by the time it was finished. He returned to the hut and carried the oracle out. He was so light and small, his body empty of its formidable will. Loic had taught him that even though the body dies, the soul lives on and returns in another life. Death was never the end.

But right now, his tutor's lessons were as heartening as a bowl of cold lard on a winter's morning. He would do anything to have Loic back.

His tears dripped onto Loic's body as he walked back to the grove. Aurelia waited for him. She'd summoned orbs of soft white light that floated above and around them. He climbed into the hole, careful not to lose his footing, and gently lay him on the earth. He stood a while, fighting the urge to lie next to him until Aurelia spoke and he scrambled out of the grave.

People said things at funerals, but he had no words to utter. The ache in his heart was beyond speech, a force that expanded and contracted in his chest, at once massive, the next so small and dense he thought he'd crack from the pressure. His pain served as a prayer for his master, his father, and his friend.

When he couldn't bear to look at the mask that was nothing like the vibrant man he'd loved, he took up the shovel again and filled the hole. It was finished quickly. He turned to the dolmen standing guard behind him and made a silent plea for it to watch over the great oracle.

Aurelia slipped her arm around his back and hugged him close, and his vision blurred.

ELAINE WAITED UNTIL AURELIA AND HAME HAD LEFT before she approached Loic's grave. She hesitated, as she always did when faced with the dolmen, before reminding herself that it held no real power. No demon could come through it.

And no demon could be banished through it either.

She sank to her knees and placed her hand on the disturbed earth. She had cried all her tears, but still a question hounded her to the point of exhaustion. What was she going to do now that Loic was gone?

He'd found her as she'd wandered in search of answers. He hadn't been able to help her with the magic, but he'd given her peace and assured her she wasn't mad. Even so, it had taken her a long time to accept that a demon lived within her.

"You saved me, Loic," she murmured. "I wish I could have done the same for you."

Hame was right. She had a duty to protect those who aided her, and she'd failed. It didn't matter that it had been Aurelia who'd freed Xadrak, or that Xadrak had been too strong for Loic. She was Sinara, and every horror Xadrak committed fell to her.

Hame would not go the same way.

She stood and dusted her dress, kissing the tips of her fingers and waving them over the grave, blessing the earth with good health and abundance.

"Thank you, my friend. May we meet again in happier times."

The grass had already started growing by the time she turned for the hut.

She arrived as Aurelia pulled the door closed. Seeing her, she held up her hands to bar entry.

"I need to talk to him."

"Now is not the time."

"But he has to—"

"All he has to do now is sleep. He's exhausted, and if you go in there and shout at him, he's going to push you away again."

Elaine sagged, some of the fight hissing out of her. There was so much to be done—not least of all regaining Aurelia's trust—that just once she wanted to get through something without an argument. She almost let Aurelia lead her away.

Almost.

She brushed her daughter aside and opened the door. "Hame, I—"

"Leave me alone!" he roared, loud enough to halt her. He glowered at her from his seat at the table, his hair wild, teeth bared and the muscles in his neck straining. A half-empty plate of food and a cup sat in front of him.

Such a meagre meal.

"I can't leave you here by yourself." She approached, wary that he might lunge at her.

"I'd be a fool to go anywhere with you. Now Loic's dead I'm nothing to Xadrak so long as I stay away from you, something I fully intend to do."

The hate in his eyes made her heart heave. She needed Hame to be the oracle Loic foretold he would one day be, but now she was in danger of losing him.

"Please, Hame, I did what I could. You have to believe that."

He slammed his palm down on the table, shooting up from the stool so fast that it toppled and clattered on the floor.

"I don't have to do anything, least of all believe you."

He stalked over to her, and she resisted every urge to back away. Though he wasn't as big as Henri, he was nevertheless an imposing and powerful man, made all the more fearful because of his grief. She clasped her hands in front of her to stop their jittering and forced herself to hold his glare.

He stopped inches from her. "I never want to see you again," he said, each word clear and grotesque on his mouth.

But she would not be bullied, not when there was so much at stake. She raised her hand, her index finger wielded like a pike. "Listen to me, Hame—"

Aurelia gripped her wrist. "Mother, we need to go. Please, you're making this worse."

Her vice-like hold and the shock of being manhandled by her daughter gave her a moment to think. Aurelia was right. Grief clouded Hame's judgment. It had been a long night, and they had both lost so much. She opened her mouth to apologize, but the look he gave her withered her words on her tongue.

She nodded to Aurelia, and the two of them left the hut. The door slammed shut behind them.

"Mother?"

Elaine stopped, so weary that she swayed. "What is it?"

"He will be fine, won't he?"

"As long as he takes the proper precautions. But I'm afraid if he thinks he's done with this, he's mistaken."

"You can't force him to do your bidding."

She spun as if Aurelia had struck her. "*My* bidding? You make it sound like I do this for my own amusement. This is duty too, Aurelia, real and ugly. No one escapes it. Not you, not me, and certainly not him." Her voice cracked.

"But——"

"Enough! I haven't the strength to argue with you anymore. Give me your hand. I want to get out of here."

Aurelia quickly smoothed away the worry that had molded itself to her mouth and brow and took Elaine's offered hand.

They flew through the ether, and though she didn't feel the slimy gaze of Xadrak slide over her, she knew he was out there somewhere.

Waiting.

———

"Good night," Elaine said firmly before shutting herself in her room.

Aurelia rubbed her arm, trying to warm a chill that had nothing to do with the air. She raised a fist to knock on her mother's door but froze. She sighed, let it drop, and retreated to her room. With a wave of her hand, the candles ignited. She sat on the edge of the bed, slipped off her shoes, and lay down.

Tangled knots writhed in her belly. She hugged herself, hoping to alleviate some of the feelings that were going to keep her awake, but the act only reminded her of Hame's arms.

Pressed against his chest, she'd inhaled his scent of sun-warmed earth. Recalling the aroma unlaced the ties that kept her weighted. She hummed as she floated free into the memory of him.

For all his strength and size, he'd held her like a butterfly cupped in his hand and protected from a gale. Thierry had been easy with his affection for her, but this was different.

During the course of the night, there had been many moments when she'd felt Hame near, as if he were drawn to seek comfort, little realizing how his presence soothed her. He had put his arm around her and hadn't shied away from her touch. If anything, he'd leaned into it.

And when he'd kissed her palm…

Her breath hitched in her throat. She had never experienced anything more beautiful. His soft, full lips pressed against her skin sent shivers up her arms.

Then she remembered the broken look in his eyes, and guilt chased the phantom away. How could she think of him in such a way while he grieved?

But still she craved him.

"Oh, Hame."

She curled on to her side. She wouldn't sully his innocent need with her selfish lust. Pushing it aside, she searched beyond the way her body responded to his and realized he touched a vulnerability in her. One she also saw in him. They could help each other. He would not find peace while Elaine hounded him, and if he were left alone, he would never attain his full power as an oracle.

She spun her legs off the bed, ready to run to him, but stopped. He had pushed them both away. He'd asked her to leave once she'd settled him. He'd done it gently, saying he wanted to be alone. She had to wait. Her hands closed, gripping the quilt beneath her.

Not tonight. Wait.

With a harsh breath out, she undressed and slid underneath the covers. Extinguishing the light, she lay there, peering into the darkness. When sleep finally came, desire followed, and Hame appeared in vivid color.

———————

ELAINE JOLTED AWAKE. THE ACCUSING FACES OF HER children and a horde of others chased her out of a hard-fought but restless sleep. She wiped the sweat off her brow, glad to leave the dream behind, but a feeling like melted wax continued to ooze throughout her body. She wasn't going back to sleep anytime soon.

She threw off the covers, climbed out of bed and pulled on a prized robe of cream silk, printed with cranes and willows. With feet bare, she hurried into the corridor, across the entry chamber and down into the spiraling tunnel.

At the bottom, she entered her sanctuary. Torches burst alight, illuminating the white marble room. In the center sat a low altar made of obsidian, which raised and lowered as she required. Tonight, she needed to sit. She closed the door behind her and sat cross-legged behind the altar.

On the gold pentacle carved into the black altar-top lay the objects she used to focus her will: an athame—or cere-monial knife—a wand, and a chalice. She didn't rely on them anymore—her skill having exceeded far beyond such things—but they provided steadiness while her mind was in turmoil.

And with Sinara inside her head, it was a wonder she didn't need them all the time.

At times she hoped she were two people stuck in one body and could find a way to separate herself. Because right now she wanted to weep and howl for the loss of Loic and the pain she'd caused him and Hame; meanwhile,

Sinara was near frantic wondering where Xadrak was, what he was doing, and whom he'd hurt next.

Restlessness made her leg twitch, Sinara wanting out, wanting to hunt.

She closed her eyes and inhaled deeply, seeking some calm. Her mind tore this way and that, wanting to dwell on her grief one instant, and plan her revenge on Xadrak the next. Loic's face flashed in front of her, the gentle one she'd known for so many years, before it contorted into the tortured mask she'd seen at the end.

Another deep breath and she was through, leaving it behind temporarily.

That was what she'd told herself when she'd left her children. She'd come back for them; she'd protect them. But once gone, it was easier to stay gone. The twins didn't mind, and they wouldn't have understood anyway. They didn't have Aurelia's skill, but they did have power of a kind.

Thierry's invisibility—he had Sinara to thank for that —and Olivier's charisma—bestowed upon him from Xadrak—weren't to be ignored. And then there was the fact of their existence, their *purpose*, that was more essential than Aurelia's magic, or even her own. Without them, this would be for naught.

Had she made the right choice in hiding from them? Would they have been more amenable had she told them sooner? Knowing what she'd seen of Olivier, she doubted it. He wouldn't go willingly to anything. Perhaps if Thierry asked him...

She shook her head. What was done was done and the future beckoned. She had to seek Xadrak on her own. Though she couldn't divine the future any more than Loic could send his body between one place and another, she could send her mind out onto the astral. A slick of fear coursed through her mind, an aversion to venturing onto that plane where Xadrak held great power. Being of pure spirit now, he had the advantage. She was strong, but she was still human and earthbound. She almost allowed herself to think this was foolish, but her mind rebuffed the concern. A need—whether hers or Sinara's, it didn't matter—drove her. Loic had done this for her. She couldn't shrink from it.

She breathed with her whole body, her chest inflating, shoulders rising and falling. Darkness filled her mind, silence reigned, and concerns scattered like spores on the wind. She projected her mind out of her body and into a copy of her sanctuary. With a jet of power, she pushed out of this representation into a void that contained everything and nothing.

Here flew the minds of those skilled enough to handle such things, navigating a great ocean of knowledge, impressions, visions and emotions. Here witches and oracles discovered hidden truths. Here the spirits of the dead waited before being sucked back into the whirlpool of an earthly existence. And here flowed the foul and putrid contamination of Xadrak's evil.

She took care to contain her thoughts and keep her presence small. She cloaked herself with shields, studded with pentagrams. But the astral's fluidity meant that nothing remained truly hidden. It touched all, saw all, felt all. And someone with enough talent and power could find anything.

If she thought too *loudly* about Xadrak he could detect it, so she drifted, bending her mind to track him without focusing *on* him. Sensing strong, powerful anger, she flowed in that direction, much like she'd paddle down a dark channel.

Dipping into the emotion, she caught his essence, that

slickness coating her mind with grease. Now she was in it, she had to be extremely careful not to alert him to her presence.

The more she traveled, the harder it became. His fury beat against her shields and threatened to shatter them. Panic flapped inside her breast. At any moment she could be sucked down into the mire. She had to focus on the way forward. She dragged and before long she may as well have been wading through mud. It rose up to claim her, covering her in an ever stickier, even more malignant hold. And still she was no closer to finding him.

"No, but I've found you."

The voice shook with malevolent laughter. Her shields erupted with light, an instinct that saved her life, but alerted him absolutely to her presence. She lashed out at him. He drew back, a snarl cutting through her, but she took advantage of his distraction and fled.

Out of the astral, out of the darkness, she escaped as fast as she could and left him behind, hoping he hadn't tracked her, hadn't latched onto her like a poisonous barnacle. Back inside the relative safety of her chamber her eyelids fired open, and she collapsed to the floor, her breathing harsh and choked. Blood pounded in her veins so loudly that she thought Xadrak had her.

What if she'd been caught in his net?

She lay for a while, thankful for the press of the hard stone beneath her check. As the cold seeped through her body, she came to realize her two halves—Sinara and Elaine—were in absolute agreement.

They were both completely and utterly terrified.

XI

THE NEXT MORNING AURELIA WALKED INTO THE KITCHEN to find her mother seated at the table and staring into a cup.

"Mother?" she asked gently.

Elaine lifted her head. There was no recognition in her eyes, just a faraway stare that looked as if it belonged to someone else.

"Sinara?" she asked as she came closer. Her mother blinked rapidly, and her gaze returned to normal. "Are you all right?"

"Fine." Elaine lifted the cup to her lips and took a sip.

Aurelia sat opposite her. She wanted to ask more questions to make sure Elaine was as fine as she said, but she knew such inquiry would be unwelcome. She moved on.

"I want to help Hame, but I can't do that without answers."

Elaine placed the cup on the table. "What do you want to know?"

"If you already know everything about your past, why do you still need Hame?"

"He needs to find the key. Without it, I can't send Xadrak back to his realm."

"Can't another oracle locate it? There must be others."

"Loic said Hame would be our best chance to find what we need to defeat Xadrak. Not all oracles get all visions, but Loic and Hame, perhaps having worked with me, are specially attuned to visions about Xadrak."

"And what does the key unlock?"

Elaine didn't speak and Aurelia knew that whatever it was, she wasn't going to approve. But she'd made a promise to help and that meant knowing everything.

"Tell me."

"The key unlocks the portal to Xadrak's realm."

She got the impression Elaine hadn't told the whole truth. "You've already located the portal, haven't you? Where is it?"

"Right now, they're in Seville."

"They? You don't mean…" Her mind stuttered over the memory of the twins the night they'd been turned. "But they're not human anymore."

"Even better. They're practically indestructible and they're immortal."

She tasted copper. The matter-of-fact way Elaine said it, as if she had been talking about the weather or the latest harvest… "We don't mean anything to you, do we?"

Elaine's nostrils flared. "You cannot possibly under-stand how it makes me feel to know I've given birth to chil-dren who I have to *use*. Think of me as an uncaring monster if it makes it easier, but you put yourself in my place and see how you'd handle it."

Elaine shot out of her chair towards the door.

"Surely there's an alternative."

Elaine stopped at the doorway and gripped the wall, her head hanging down. "There isn't. Thierry and Olivier

67

form the doorway through which Xadrak must be banished."

"What happens to them once it's done?"

Elaine sighed and returned into the room, but the more she said, the more Aurelia shrank into her chair.

"There has to be another way," she whispered to herself.

"I pray we find one, but I fear it's unlikely."

"Does Hame know?"

Elaine nodded. "Loic kept him informed. He was there during many of my visits."

"So he knows what he has to do?"

"Now more than ever. You say you want to help him? Then we need to find a way he can access his visions with the same control Loic had. Right now, it's too haphazard."

"But if Loic couldn't teach him, how can we?"

Elaine shrugged. "I have to try."

"He won't listen to you. Not after what's happened to Loic."

"He has to."

"Send me instead."

"But I know your abilities. I haven't taught you to scry yet, and that's probably our best hope."

Aurelia sat up. "What's scrying?"

"The ability to see people and places you already know from a distance. You use a smooth surface as your point of focus, and then, with luck or skill, you'll see whatever it is as if it's in front of you."

Her heart fluttered inside her chest. *I can see Hame whenever I want.*

"Teach me now."

"We haven't the time."

"We do. Hame needs to be alone to grieve. Give me

two days and if I haven't learned by then, we'll try something else."

Elaine regarded her. She worried her mother could see into her heart. She wanted to help their higher cause, of course, but the mere thought of Hame made her blood hot. The heat rose rapidly and the edges of it burned beneath her skin. Elaine looked away as it burst onto her cheeks.

"Come with me."

She followed her mother into the workshop in the next room. Shelves ran along the back wall, heavy with vellum tomes. Scattered here and there were rocks and feathers, bits of bone and antlers, knives and goblets and wands. Elaine lifted a large bowl off a shelf and placed it on the long wooden table in the center of the room. She went around to the far side while Aurelia stood opposite.

"This is safe, isn't it?" she asked.

"Yes. Xadrak won't be able to interfere. It'll be like looking through a window at a storm without being in it yourself."

"But how will this help Hame? I'm not able to see the future."

"If we can get him to scry, he should be able to use what Loic taught him to project and divine."

Even if Hame accepted her tutelage, she worried he'd scoff at what she had to say. Hame had lived with Loic for years and no doubt had learned everything he could. Hame probably knew things she had never even thought of. She'd feel silly going to him with this, like a child offering its toy sword to a blooded knight.

But she bent her head and listened to the instructions. The scrying bowl was three-quarters filled with water and lined with silver. The goal was to unfocus her eyes, and to let her mind see *through* the shimmering silver as it filled her vision. She waited for the world beyond the window to shift.

Nothing happened.

She continued to stare, waiting for her mother's disapproval to pierce her wavering concentration. Eventually it came, and though she'd been expecting it the sharp sound made her jump.

"Well?"

"Nothing." She straightened her back.

Elaine tutted. "You're not concentrating."

Aurelia ground her teeth and bent over the bowl once more. She wouldn't argue. Instead, she poured her already stretched concentration into seeing something in the bowl, but the harder she tried, the more aware she became of Elaine's eyes boring into her. She flicked up her head.

"It'd be a lot easier if you weren't standing there."

Elaine huffed, but left the room. Aurelia didn't dwell on the thought that Elaine might have left because she knew it was hopeless. Instead, she was grateful she'd taken heed.

The pressure in the room shifted with Elaine's departure, and Aurelia now felt more at ease. She brought over a chair and began again.

Hame. I'm doing this for Hame.

With her goal in mind, she let her vision blur.

Hame.

The silver stayed silver, but she didn't let that bother her. She let her mind drift with thoughts of Hame. His face appeared as it had the night before, those blood-red lips downturned and his green eyes so heavy and sad.

Because of me.

The thought struck her; a sting so sudden she cried out. She tried to get herself under control, sniffing hard and wiping away tears as even more came.

Because of her, Loic had died and Hame suffered. The guilt clawed her insides. She couldn't have known this would happen, but that didn't lessen her pain. The only thing she could do was to make it up to Hame as best she could.

Perhaps by being more than just a guiding hand.

The resolution drained her sorrow and the mist cleared from her eyes. She peered into the scrying bowl, seeking Hame and vowing she wouldn't move until she'd found him.

HOOKS SUNK EVER DEEPER INTO ELAINE'S HEART WHEN SHE heard Aurelia cry, and they hauled her to within steps of her daughter. She ached to put her arms around her and hold her close, but she resisted. Aurelia was proud and wouldn't want to be seen in so wretched a state. Though her daughter bled, she dragged herself out of earshot.

Her concern for Aurelia didn't ease. She fidgeted, anxious for the day to pass and to hear a triumphant hollering. She paced up and down the tunnel, from the vaulted chamber to her sanctuary and back again. Her home became a dungeon, the rooms too small, the walls too thick. The mountain crushed her.

The thoughts of what she should be doing with her time stole the oxygen out of the air. She could have searched for another oracle, or strengthened her mind, or meditated on ways to confront Xadrak on the astral plane without fear of being torn to shreds. But she was in too much turmoil.

She had to get outside. She ran through the tunnel and emerged into the fresh air of the Pyrenees. Her troubles dispersed like flies shooed from a rotting carcass.

Soon twilight would descend, that calm part of the day she loved so much up here. She hadn't appreciated it when she'd lived in Carcassonne, the narrow streets and the confines of the town yoking her head down. But back then she'd been interested in other things, having fallen for Henri.

She shook her head. They'd both been so different when they'd first met. They had always rubbed against each other, but at first it had been flirtation. Like so many of the women, she'd been made for work. There was no time to be demure and coquettish. Men wanted women who had a bit of fire, and she had that in abundance. Thrown together with Henri's heat, there wasn't an inferno quite like theirs. For all that he was combustible, he wasn't then the brute he later became. There had been love; she had to believe that. It seemed too cruel to think she'd never had any.

But it seemed a lifetime ago now, and up here with the blushing sky now it was unimportant.

"Mother!"

Aurelia's call shot down the tunnel, and Elaine turned her head. Her daughter soon appeared with a victorious smile on her face.

My daughter. Elaine's heart swelled.

"You did it?" She couldn't help but match Aurelia's grin.

Aurelia nodded enthusiastically, appearing like the child Elaine had once abandoned. How many moments like this had she missed?

Elaine's smile faltered. She tried to save it, but the wound gouged too deep and it crashed. Her daughter saw and shut her pride away suddenly.

"I may have taken a while, but at least it's done." She shifted on her heel and disappeared back inside.

Elaine wanted to run after her. There was still much to teach her tonight: how to travel through the ether by herself, for instance, a skill she'd kept out of her daughter's reach in case she came looking for her. But she held back. Nothing she said could make up for what she'd put her daughter through. Making her strong, independent, and powerful had once seemed like good consolation, but it fell short.

Sighing with her whole body, she stayed to watch night fall and the comfort of twilight fade.

XII

"Hame," Aurelia called through the door. "Please let me in."

He knew she'd be coming for him. Another damn vision had plummeted into his head the day before. Like a meteor falling from the sky, his world reverberated with the power of it, knowing what he'd seen was the future and how it would decimate him.

He struggled to hold onto Loic's memory. He wanted to disappear into the grief that had sucked on his bones, but the vision of Aurelia had dislodged its lips.

And now she was here.

She knocked again, a timid sound, but it echoed inside the empty hut. He hadn't tidied away Loic's cot. In fact, he'd slept on it since the night Loic died, inhaling what remained of his bark-like scent. When he woke the next morning in a fog, he believed Loic was there, a heavy arm wrapped around him. But his mind cleared, reality returned, and he grieved again. He still didn't clear away Loic's things, but their—*his*—home felt empty.

Aurelia stopped knocking, and he thought she might

leave. He didn't know whether he wanted that or not. She'd brought him solace the night Loic died. He couldn't deny how good it felt to have her in his arms, how it completed him. He'd felt her grief, through whatever connection they had, and he'd wondered how deep it ran. But the visions of her frightened him. After all, she was Elaine's daughter.

He swung out of bed and gripped the edge of the cot. Looking around the room, he sighed at how lifeless the place had become in a short space of time. The hearth had gone cold. Food had started to rot, dispersing a sickly-sweet smell into the air. He lifted an arm and sniffed his pit, the musk making his nose wrinkle. Loic would have chided him for getting like this.

But that would mean Loic would be here.

Aurelia banged again. He wasn't going to get any peace if he didn't tell her to go. He stamped over to the door and wrenched it open.

She paused mid-knock, and her eyes swept down his body. She blushed and looked away. He looked at himself, realizing he was wearing only a pair of underdrawers, and even then, they didn't cover much. With a curse, he slammed the door and hurriedly dressed. When he returned, he was sure he caught a glimpse of disappoint-ment in her eyes, but it was gone too fast for him to be certain.

"I thought you might like some food." She offered a basket filled to the brim with bread, meat, fruit and a bottle of mead.

His body turned to stone as the vision and reality slid perfectly over one another. The moment he invited her over the threshold, he would never be rid of her.

"I'm sorry, Aurelia. I don't want you here."

Her body jerked; the basket dipped. She composed

herself quickly, and a painted smile brushed across her face. His hand squeezed the doorframe.

"I know it's a bit soon after Loic's passing, but it's not good to be alone."

"I don't mean any offence, but what do you know about it?"

"I've lost people too, Hame. I might not know exactly how you felt about Loic, but I know what it is to lose people you love."

"Then you should accept that I want to be left alone."

"But you're never alone, are you? He haunts you. I can see it in the shadows in your eyes. You're stuck, but I can help you."

"No, you can't. You'll make it worse."

"You think I'm going to hurt you?" Her eyes narrowed.

Jagged rocks tumbled down his throat. "No, I didn't mean...look, I—"

She thrust the basket at him. "Take it, I'm leaving. I should just let you starve."

He held up his hands, refusing to accept the basket. "Let me explain."

When he wouldn't take the basket, she let it drop to the ground. It tipped and the food spilled onto the dirt.

She turned and walked away.

His heart mashed with each step she took.

This was what he wanted, wasn't it? If she left him alone, he wouldn't get sucked into the hurricane she and her family whipped up. He wouldn't get these cursed visions any longer.

You know that's a lie.

He cringed at the disappointed voice inside his head. How many times had Loic told him he was meant for great things, only to be rejected by his pupil every time? He hated Loic's persistence, and prayed he'd give up on him because the shame weakened him. And here he was, *knowing* that Aurelia brought with her the steps to achieving what Loic—no, what *he*—had always wanted, and he was sending her away.

I'm a coward and a disgrace.

"Aurelia, wait!"

He ran to catch her, hooking her arm and slowing her to a halt. She fixed him with a glare that he knew to be one of Elaine's finest.

"You wanted to be left alone, then let me go."

"I…I had a vision."

She frowned. "A bad one? About me?"

He shook his head. "Not as such, but I wasn't sure I wanted it to come to pass."

"And now?"

He sighed. "If you come inside, I'll tell you about it."

She bit her bottom lip and looked back over her shoulder at the hut. "It would be a shame to waste the food."

He snorted. She turned around and his arm slid low down to the small of her back, guiding her into the hut. They collected the basket and he invited her inside, knowing that once there, he wasn't ever going to be separated from her again.

He didn't give her a quick explanation. He didn't give her anything at first, just made her wait while he gorged on the food she'd brought. She thought the men in her family had been big eaters, but Hame put them to shame. The amount he stuffed down and the speed with which he shoveled it into his mouth made her wonder how long he'd gone without eating. From the first bite of bread and draught of mead, he became absorbed in the feast.

Eventually he slowed, his body changing from the hunched frame of a hound wolfing down its food, to a person remembering that he was in the company of another. His eyes flicked upwards frequently, checking she was still there. She encouraged him with her smiles, lessening the intensity of her gaze, even though she could have stared at him for hours.

His hair held her fascination the most, the colors running from a crimson so deep it was almost black, to streaks of bright orange that set the whole thing aflame. Her fingers longed to stroke it.

"Do you want anything?" he asked.

If she'd been lost any further in her daydreams, she'd have given an answer that would have turned her cheeks as red as his hair.

There wasn't much left on the table, but she'd eaten not long ago. She told him not to worry, but now he'd spoken she wanted to know about his vision.

As soon as she asked, he rolled his shoulders. He stretched his jaw to dislodge something caught in his teeth, then drained his cup.

"I saw you."

A bony hand gripped her spine. Had he seen her the way she had seen him? In her heated, secret dreams? Maybe that was why he hadn't wanted her in the house. He knew how she desired him, and he didn't reciprocate. All those furtive looks across the table made sense now.

But she wouldn't cringe from this. She tilted her chin up. "And what was I doing?"

"That scene we just had at the door. I saw that."

She relaxed a little. "But what was so bad about that?"

He didn't give her an answer straight away. Instead he stared at her until she grew restless.

"Why are you here, Aurelia?"

"I thought you could use the company."

He laughed, a sharp bark that chipped something in her. "You're a terrible liar."

"I'm not lying!"

"Then you're not telling the whole truth. Remember, I'm an oracle." He winked at her.

But from the way he spoke, he didn't even know half of it. He didn't know how much she wanted to slide her hand down his cheek and brush his lips, to feel them against her own. He didn't know how she'd thought of him nuzzling the sensitive skin where her neck met her shoulder. All that and more, she'd lock inside herself until she could make it a reality. She rubbed the back of her neck, and her hand came away damp.

"I'm here to help you unlock your visions."

He leaned back, folded his arms across his chest and flicked up his chin. "Elaine sent you?" The cocky way he said it spoke more about his own prejudices than any prophecy.

"No, actually, I came because I thought I could help you."

"And she doesn't stand to gain from this?"

"We all gain from you fulfilling your potential, Hame. Even you."

She expected him to scoff and slide away from her gaze, but instead he deflated. The bravado had been an act —perhaps a last attempt to evade that which he already knew was going to come to pass.

"Your vision told you I was going to help you, didn't it?"

"In a way. I saw you at the door with the food and with

it came a knowing that if you came inside, I'd never be rid of you."

"You make me sound like a nuisance."

"How would you feel if someone showed up to give you everything you thought you would never have?"

"I know all too well."

"Really? Then tell me. I'm interested to hear what you have to say about it."

He thought she was a child, too young to run with the older boys. Olivier had condescended the same and the tone had rankled her then, as it did now.

"You don't trust it because it's something you've been denied so long. You think it's going to be taken away at the last moment, and you couldn't bear the pain if that happened." She looked down at her lap. "And then, when you do get it, it's not what you thought you wanted at all. It's worse, much, much worse. Because nothing is given freely. It all comes with a terrible weight that you're not sure you can hold." She looked at him and cocked her head to the right. "Does that sound familiar?"

She couldn't help the razor-cut in her voice. His arrogance had drawn blood and she had to defend herself.

"I'm sorry. I didn't think…"

"It doesn't matter. The fact remains that you have a gift, and you are being pushed towards it. I'm already in the door so you can either mope about it for another day or two and then begin, or you can forget the self-pity and get started now." She hadn't meant to speak so harshly, but she was glad she had been able to use that emotion to encourage him, rather than go for the jugular. If it had been anyone but Hame…

"You don't hold back, do you?"

"You've met my mother."

He laughed and the sound resonated in her breast,

dislodging the last defensive shards. Happiness looked good on him, and that strengthened her resolve. There was hard work ahead, but for the first time in a long while she had hope.

———

AFTER THEY'D EATEN, SHE CLEARED A SPACE AND SET UP A wooden bowl for him to scry with. He told her it would be no use, but she rode over his objections and gave him the instructions anyway, then left the hut. Though she wanted to watch him, she knew from experience how distracting it could be. But it made little difference to his abilities. Hours passed, and she began to doubt the vision he'd had of her. When she stuck her head in to check on him, he'd sunk low into his chair and pulled his hair forward to hide his face.

All of a sudden, he swept the bowl off the table and water sprayed across the room. He slammed his fists down, making the table jump, and then stormed past her, growling and muttering as he went. He marched over to the woodpile, picked up the axe and his grumbling gave way to the sound of wood splintering. She twitched with each blow. She went inside, picked up the bowl, dipped it into the bucket and put it, half-full, back on the table.

Maybe scrying wasn't how he was meant to tap into his abilities. Perhaps they'd been wrong about it, but it had seemed a good place to start. However, instead of easing him into his greater skill, it agitated like a sandstorm. It whipped her too. Even with him out of the cottage, it still whirled within her, its center humming a sorrow charged with his failure.

Her heart skipped.

He's projecting.

This wasn't some imagined empathy. She really was

holding herself—her mind—against the brunt of this tempest.

"Of course!" she said.

He'd contacted her before when Loic was dying, so why not again? It might not help him see the future, but it would remind him that his mind could achieve the unexpected.

She opened her mouth to call out to him but stopped. There was no time to waste on discussion. She had to show him. She needed to get his attention, but she had to go gently, like knocking when asking to enter someone's home. She used that idea to build a picture inside her mind. Then, with a shift of perspective, projected it out.

She imagined she walked down a path that led to a cottage, much like his own. With each step she got closer to him. A grey mist leaked beneath the door and limped along the path. Soon she stood in it, her toes lost beneath the sticky fog. She hesitated, conscious that whatever emotions broiled within him would likely flow out and engulf her. She steeled herself, reached up and knocked gently three times.

The fog sucked back in, gone, as if it had never been. He'd felt her and sought to protect himself. She knocked again, this time calling his name. The handle turned and the door opened a crack. He peered out of darkness so thick she could barely make out his form.

"Can I come in?" she asked.

He blinked. "How are you doing this?"

"*We're* doing it, Hame. Together. And if you can do this, then you can scry, and you can bring forth the prophecies."

She told him what she'd done, how she'd imagined a path, and he took it in.

"Let me try," he said, and shut her out.

She pulled back, let the imagery fade and opened her eyes. She waited, but after a while nothing came, and she began to fear he'd not managed to master this either.

If you don't have faith, then how do you expect me to have any?

The sudden appearance of his chuckling voice inside her head shook her like a quake splitting the ground. Great fissures appeared at having him so close without her knowing. She clutched her head in her hands, squeezing against her temples as the pressure within her head expanded to expel him from her mind.

Real arms locked around her and she lashed out with her magic. She couldn't be touched, not after being so open and defenseless. Once Elaine had trained her, she had never wanted to be so vulnerable again. She heaved a great breath, her chest expanding and contracting, and all she could feel was a sinister tongue in her ear, a rough hand between her legs, and a violation so deep she'd thought it buried long ago.

When nothing else came for her and she could finally separate her memories from the present, her breathing eased, her heart slowed its frenetic pace, and she opened her eyes. Hame slumped unconscious against the wall.

"Oh God, what have I done?" She ran to him, placing one hand on his chest, the other against his cheek. He breathed. Thank Christ, he breathed. "Hame, wake up!"

She shook him harder, his bulk almost too heavy to move. She summoned an acrid breeze to waft under his nose. His head twitched and shot back. He blinked rapidly, looking at her as if she were going to strike him again then slowly raised his hand, the back of it an inch from her face. She didn't pull back, and his hand slid down her cheek. She eased into it, hoping his touch would wipe away the filthy smear that Henri had left behind.

XIII

Elaine shot into the astral, the tension she'd gathered during her preparation enough to send her flying into its higher levels. She didn't seek the demon. She didn't even think his name. She jettisoned the negative emotions weighing her down. Guilt, revenge, hate, all cut away.

She held on to happy memories, proud moments when Aurelia had shown great aptitude, or even simply smiled and hugged her. They added extra lift. While it would be harder for the demon to ascend to such heights, she nevertheless surrounded herself with protective shields, weaving in defenses and alarms, and overlaying it all with a pentagram.

She searched for an oracle. She had only known of Loic, and he'd said that only a handful of oracles existed at any one time. While she hoped Hame would thrive under Aurelia's tutelage, she needed a contingency. If he couldn't divine the future, or if anything were to happen to him, she would be blind.

In her flight, she left the earth behind and soared into a grey world that held no solid form. Up this high, the light was composed of more white than black. The astral expanded and contracted at will, aiding those who knew how to control it. This place offered the best chance of finding an oracle, and to do that she needed a beacon. She created a clearing in a forest, and in its center, she built a temple with a domed roof. Around the outside she carved into the stone the three Delphic phrases and imbued them with the power to attract a soothsayer.

She stood at the edge of this unreal place, looking out at the mist, and waited. Time passed without any discernible rhythm. The only thing telling her that she had been here a while was the weariness chewing on her concentration.

She tried to remain light but the longer she waited, the harder it became to do so. Her will wavered, tiredness letting in the doubts that stole like a virus through her body. She would soon have to abandon this search.

The oracle's place faded a little, and she was about to disperse it when a purple light appeared in the distance. Strengthened by the appearance of such a mystical shade, she tapped a reserve of strength. The temple hardened as if made of real marble. She even heard the leaves rustling.

The light approached, oblong in shape, about as tall as a person, but as yet it lacked features. She stepped back, checked her shields. It was unlikely to be anything sinister this far up, but too many near misses had finally taught her not to take anything for granted.

The violet light floated nearer, and then gradually, deep within it, a person emerged. A man strode across the mist and each step revealed more of who he was. Familiarity sliced her open, and her hands shot to her mouth.

It couldn't be.

Not here. Not now.

But there was no denying it.

And even as the tears flowed—tears that shouldn't have existed here on the astral—she knew who he was. He stopped two feet away from her and smiled that warm and happy smile that had always been such a part of him.

"Loic!"

She sobbed, and he embraced her. His body was real, his scent filling her head.

But how?

He sighed. "My Elaine."

She pulled away from him.

"How is it that you're here? I…I saw you die."

"And I am dead. I waited for you to come, but I don't have long. My soul needs rest."

He slipped his hand into hers. For all the urgency in his words, they could have been strolling through a field on a warm afternoon discussing the flight of sparrows. At first, she itched to hear what he had to say, but the feel of his hand enclosing hers and the peace he exuded blanketed her, and she wished they'd never part. They walked to the temple, and he peered in.

"Impressive," he said, "though I always preferred something more natural." He turned and sat on the steps, patting the marble.

She joined him, and the need to atone for her failure broke free. "I'm sorry I couldn't save you."

"Rest easy, dear heart. There was nothing you could have done."

He didn't understand what it meant to her to lose him. "But your death was—"

"I know you blame yourself, but it was not your fault. I lived a good life and died in service to a cause I believed in."

His words didn't wipe away her guilt, but they relieved

some of the sting. "I have tried to help Hame. I know how much he meant to you."

"I am not worried about him. It is you I am here for."

"What have you seen?"

"Xadrak can be beaten, but it will not be easy."

"Nothing ever is."

"He will create an army. The longer he stays in the astral realm, the more his power and his reach will grow. Witches will flock to him with his promises of stronger magic."

"An army? How do I kill him?" She was strong, but she couldn't defeat a battalion alone.

"You cannot kill him on the higher realm, or anywhere on Earth. Only back in Crion can he be truly slain."

"But without the key, that's not possible." Her breath caught. "Have you seen it?"

"I wish I had happier news for you, but it remains hidden."

"Then how do I stop his power?"

"While you live, you will never be strong enough. You may be the strongest of the witches on Earth, but up here he is akin to a god. You cannot command both."

Elaine understood, but she was almost too afraid to speak it, as if doing so would pull apart the threads of her being. She closed her eyes for a moment and took a breath to steady herself. "And if I were here with him?"

"The gateway to the world of the dead is easier to open in the astral realm. Push him through it, and he will be trapped in blood and bone."

"I can't send him back. It would put Aurelia in too much peril." Her daughter was an adept witch. Once she'd mastered scrying, it hadn't been long before she could travel too. But facing Xadrak would be too much for her.

"As a mortal, did you have full knowledge of your

power, or did it awaken within you? Did he know his true nature, even when it tried to break out of him?"

"No, but what if—"

"Aurelia shall guard the Earth while you harry him on this plane. There, his true nature will always be muted. He will be strong but not invincible."

Her belly plummeted. She had to leave her children behind again. Her control frayed and the remains lashed her.

"I am sorry, Elaine. I know how much you wanted to stay with Aurelia, but the truth is you and your family are sacrifices. They always were and always will be, but their purpose is pure, and the price matches the magnitude of the gift you will give this world."

"Why must it be me?" she demanded. "I fought him in one lifetime—why must I devote the rest of them to seeing him vanquished?"

"You could no more turn your back on this than you could have abandoned Aurelia forever. That is not who you are. Do not deny yourself the pride and the strength that comes from knowing your love and your duty are righteous. Death does not kill that which has existed between a mother and her children."

She sniffed and wiped her eyes. The mist beyond the glade darkened.

"I am sorry," he said again and stood.

She clutched his hand. "Do you have to go? Can't you wait for me?" She could accept this with more courage if she knew he'd be there to meet her.

"I wish I could, but now my purpose is done, I have not the strength to remain." He pulled her up and hugged her again. For all that he was a being of light, he felt so solid, so real.

He kissed each of her cheeks. "Be strong, Elaine. You shall be victorious."

He faded, and the body she'd known disintegrated as purple light burst forth. She held on as best she could but soon nothing remained. His smile was the last recognizable thing to disappear into the light. Then even that was gone, and she was alone.

A grey storm threatened. Her anger—at her unavoidable future, at Xadrak's ability to inflict such torment on her life—swelled until the rage thrashed in her chest, seeking something to sink its teeth into.

Clouds as black as tar approached, sending tendrils snaking forward to snare what she had created. Xadrak had come. A slick evil invaded the clearing. How dare he threaten her? How dare he lord his strength over her? But for all her fury, his power pressed, ready to crush her. She had to get out of there before it was too late.

She plunged out of the astral and into her body, the process taking a fraction of a moment, but his claws scratched her soul as she fled back to earth. Her eyes fired open and white purifying light erupted out of her, reaching deep inside and scouring the last trace of Xadrak's touch.

Satisfied she was safe, she stopped the light. She hunched forward, sweat pouring from her forehead, down her spine, from exertion and from terror. He had gained strength and confidence. How long would it be before the astral became his domain entirely?

Loic was right. She needed it for her stronghold.

She had to die.

XIV

"I wish I'd been there to stop him," Hame said, after hearing tales of Aurelia's family life. Rope twisted inside his gut, a tautness he couldn't shift. What Aurelia had been through—the little she'd confessed—made him want to strangle someone. Too bad Henri was already dead.

"Thank you, but it wasn't your place."

"No, it was Elaine's."

She placed her hand on his fist, the touch soothing him into relaxing it. "Don't let it poison you, Hame. Henri is the one who violated me."

"Is that why you're helping her? So you can see Xadrak brought to justice?"

"You'll scorn me, but I'm helping her because she's my mother and she did what she thought was right."

"You should try saying that without the murderous look in your eye."

She laughed, and he felt good hearing it. "Fine, I want vengeance, but I also don't want to see Xadrak's evil released onto this world."

Suddenly she looked away.

"What were you thinking?"

She shook her head but wouldn't meet his eye.

"Tell me." His mind brushed against hers, a gentle touch at the edges. When she'd recovered from her breakdown, he'd apologized, and they'd established the rules. She also went to work building shields around her mind to keep out unwanted attacks. The shields she used with him were thinner than gauze, but he respected them. The shame of his earlier lack of thought and care still lingered at the back of his mind like a kicked dog.

Her mind retreated and he withdrew, but she spoke in a rush of words.

"It's not Elaine's fault Xadrak slayed Loic. It's mine. I killed Henri, even after Elaine told me not to. I'm sorry, Hame."

He stilled, frozen and lifeless as a lake in the dead of winter. He should have been angry with her, and no doubt there was some of that buried below. He blamed Elaine enough for Loic's death, but after hearing how Aurelia had suffered because of Henri, he didn't have it in him to blame her too. If he were Aurelia, he would have gutted Henri long ago.

"Thank you for telling me," he said as the ice thawed.

Her eyes shot up, light glistening on their surface. He gave her a small smile and nuzzled his mind against hers. The conversation gradually began again, the silence too uncomfortable to maintain, and he found he liked hearing her talk just as much as he enjoyed having her listen. They traded stories as the night grew old and he told her of how he'd traveled from the Highlands to Normandy as a twelve-year-old boy in pursuit of a vision. It felt good to talk about Loic, remembering the life the man had given him, the love they'd shared. But when she asked him about his training, he rebuffed her.

"I'll tell you another time." He faked a yawn. "We should get some sleep."

"Oh, yes, you're right. Lots to do tomorrow." She stood and made her way to the door. "I'll see you in the morning."

He didn't want her to leave. He didn't want to be alone in the hut with memories of Loic. "Stay. You can take my bed."

"Are you sure?" She twisted strands of her hair.

"Of course. I'm sure it's not as pleasing as what Elaine has given you, but it's good enough."

"All right. Thank you." She gave him a shaky smile, and he realized what a dolt he was. She was nervous about getting undressed in front of him.

"I'll face this way while you get into bed, and you let me know when you're ready and I'll put out the light. I'm used to undressing in the dark."

He thought he saw her cheeks blush, but she turned her head and disappeared behind him. He heard the rustle of her dress, then the shake of the blanket and the creak of the cot. "I'm ready."

He turned and looked straight into her green eyes, the blanket pulled up to her neck, her arm exposed over the top of it revealing her smooth olive skin. Having her here felt right. He smiled and went over to the candles, extinguishing them one by one. He undressed and got into bed, and despite the trials of the day, or perhaps because of them, he soon drifted off to sleep and slept better than he had in a long time.

When Aurelia woke, the first thing she saw was Hame's empty bed. She'd eventually fallen asleep after staring into the darkness, hoping to make out some shape of him. She drifted off listening to the gentle sound of his breathing. Now the bed was bare, the blanket rumpled. He wasn't in the hut either. She got out of bed, dressed, and went to the table, where the scrying bowl sat half full.

She searched for him, wanting to catch a glimpse of him unawares, at ease, simply to stare at him a moment without him knowing. She knew she was spying. It was wrong and unfair, but she had to see him. The surface of the water revealed him bathing in the river.

Water ran from his soaked hair down his shoulders and his chest. He had a body made for adoration, but there was more to it than just his physique. It was everything that came along with it, the physical and the emotional. The ease with which they had communicated mentally only strengthened their bond, and the consolation they gave each other was deep, heartfelt, and pure.

Hame disappeared beneath the murky water and his form wavered as he swam. His streaming hair, back, ass, his legs, all maddeningly distorted. He breached, standing waist-deep in the river, and squeezed the water out of his hair, causing the droplets to cascade down his chest, his stomach. But as he stepped up the bank, revealing more of his skin and his fat cock nestled in the fiery bush of his crotch, she turned away.

This is wrong.

She wanted to see him but not like this. Not without his consent. She blinked and the vision ended. She waited a while to ensure her guilt was in check before approaching him telepathically. He responded, greeted her, and said he was on his way back from bathing.

When he entered, she had figured out what they were going to do next.

"We're going to go to the nearest village," she said after

he came through the door fully dressed. His damp hair still shimmered the color of blood.

"Why? I thought you wanted me to scry."

"I'm hoping that by meeting a few normal people, perhaps attuning to their essence, you might be able to scry for them."

"Can't I just look for you? For Elaine?"

"It hasn't worked so far. I think we're too much a part of the magical world. Maybe you need to interact with some everyday people for a while."

"I don't want to go to the village."

"Why not?"

"I haven't been there since before Loic died."

"And they knew him?"

He nodded. "Some of them came here. Not many, but enough. They know who I am, too. They'll ask about him; they always do."

"You'll have to tell them."

"And when they ask for prophecies, what then?"

"Do what the fortune tellers do. Make it up."

His eyebrows shot up. "I'm not going to lie."

"What difference does it make?"

"A big difference if I tell them one thing and something else happens instead. I'm likely to find them at my door with scythes and a noose."

She chuckled. "If they haven't come for you by now, they're not going to."

He screwed up his face, but she grabbed his hand and pulled him out the door. She took them in one direction, not knowing where she was going, until finally he broke his silence and, with a huff, pulled her another way.

Carrouges was a few miles away. She hadn't been there before so couldn't use her magic to jump them from the hut to the village. She was glad of it. What with still being new to this skill, she didn't want Hame to see her fumble. Instead, she cast a spell that made their strides devour the distance. The sun had barely reached its zenith by the time they arrived.

———

PERHAPS BECAUSE HE WAS THERE SO RARELY, HE DREW THE villagers' attention more readily. His size, the brilliance of his hair, and his unusual accent made him an object of interest. People gawped. He hated it. Over the years, he'd perfected an expression that warned most away without causing the men in the village to take issue with his unfriendliness. Not that many of the men he met were eager to start something with a barbarian like him. Thankfully, the forest provided plenty of what they needed, and the seekers brought some additional items—food and clothes mainly—so venturing into the village was an infrequent chore.

Stepping into the village with Aurelia by his side was sure to be something they talked about for the next decade. She was not exactly dressed like a peasant, her green embroidered dress likely to rival anything worn by the nobility. When he whispered as such, she looked at herself and groaned. He laughed and put his arm around her shoulders. It felt good to know she'd be as uneasy as he was.

"Where would you like to go first?" he asked.

"Somewhere dark. The sooner I hide this dress the better. Is there a tavern?"

"Probably, but we've already been spotted." He nodded up the street where the baker's wife was hurrying over to talk to him. He'd caught the wide-eyed surprise on her face before she controlled herself and replaced it with the sour expression he was more used to.

"It is good to see you, Rosemarie," he said.

"Mmm. You too, 'Ame," she replied, dropping the unfamiliar *H* sound. Her eyes roved up and down Aurelia. Her nose wrinkled. "And how is Loic?"

He'd known this would be something he'd have to answer, but he couldn't have prepared for how it kicked him in the balls. "I'm afraid Loic passed away the other day."

Rosemarie crossed herself. "Such sad news. How did it happen?"

"It was quite sudden," Aurelia interjected. "He died peacefully in his sleep."

"The Lord takes us when he sees fit, I suppose." Rosemarie ignored Aurelia completely. "And do you follow in his…trade?"

He would have loved to tell this woman that he didn't, especially with how quickly she'd moved on from hearing the sad news. Having to scry into her future had been dull for Loic, and it was likely to be the same for him, too. But Loic had done it anyway. Now it was Hame's duty to provide guidance and support, whether the future was discernible or not.

And like Aurelia had suggested, he could always make it up.

"Yes. Though I need a little time."

"Of course." Her bony hand squeezed his arm before she nodded goodbye to him and went on her way.

"I should have set her hair on fire," Aurelia said once she was out of earshot.

He laughed. "Rosemarie isn't the nicest of people. But we'll get one good thing out of seeing her."

"And what's that?"

"She'll have told the whole village that Loic is dead within the hour."

They entered the tavern, which was less than half full. He hadn't been in there before, never having wanted to tarry any longer than he needed to in the village. The place was dark enough that Aurelia found a corner to hide in where she altered her dress to reduce its brilliance.

"You can't sit with your back to the room," she said as he took the bench opposite her.

"I'm shielding you from the other patrons. A beautiful woman needs to be protected."

She shook her head. "Stop trying to get out of it and sit next to me. There are plenty of people here for you to see and with any luck they'll help you learn to scry."

He groaned but did as she said and rose off the bench.

"What can I get you?" a man said behind him.

Hame turned to look into hazel eyes and a boyish grin. His short hair was the color of acorns and for all the gloom in the place, he could see this man as brightly as a meadow on a clear day.

"Uhhh," he replied.

The taverner's brow twitched in the middle, reminding him of a rabbit scrunching its nose.

Hame gave a short breathy grunt that was almost a laugh. "Yes, sorry. An ale and a mead and whatever is good to eat, please."

"Sure," the man said, giving him a wink that delighted and confused him in a way Hame couldn't understand.

Remembering what he'd been doing before the man came along, he turned back to Aurelia and moved around to her side of the table. She studied the other people in the tavern, while he searched for the man who unsettled him in such a sublime way.

Eventually, the taverner returned carrying two cups

and two plates of food. He barely looked at Aurelia, a quick glance as he placed the meal in front of her, but he gave *him* the full force of his attention.

"I haven't seen you two before," he said. "What brings you to Carrouges?"

Aurelia watched him like an owl tracking a mouse.

"We're here for supplies. I live in the forest," he said, not sure why he didn't say they both lived there, but certain it was important to make that distinction.

"Ahhh, very nice," the taverner said, his cheeks becoming even fuller.

Aurelia cleared her throat, and he began to retreat after giving her an uneasy glance.

"Well, I hope you visit again."

Hame didn't want him to leave, but Aurelia's mood pricked him, and he decided it would be safer to let the taverner go. He needed time to think what this meant, and he couldn't do that with the stranger standing so close.

What he did know, however, was how much he liked it.

XV

Despite Aurelia's prompting, Hame struggled to pay much attention to anyone in the tavern except for that man. All too soon, she bid them rise and depart. He dragged his feet, which turned to anvils when the taverner gave him a honeyed smile. He swallowed, trying to wet his parched mouth.

Aurelia pulled him away and out of the village, then flung them through the ether to the hut. Unprepared for the crossing's jarring, when they landed, he doubled over and retched.

"You could have warned me," he said after he stopped heaving.

"I'm sorry," she said softly and went inside.

He couldn't figure out what was wrong with her. He followed her in, but when he spoke her name, she fixed him with a stare that jammed the rest of the words in his throat. He decided to wait until she was in a better mood.

"It's time to get back to work," she said flatly.

The scrying bowl was set, and she looked down at it. He didn't fancy further disappointment, but she insisted.

"You've been to the village; you now have plenty of people to scry for. Do your best. I'm sure you could—" She'd been about to say more, her tone suddenly off-kilter. After a pause, she continued. "You should start." She hurried from the hut before he could argue.

He raked his fingers through his hair. He was on the verge of discovering so much about himself, something that had the ring of the forbidden about it, but Aurelia's demeanor had him all twisted. His mind reached out to hers, but she closed herself tight. She'd come around, and when she did, he'd ask what had upset her.

He stared into the bowl, remembering how spectacularly he'd failed yesterday.

But yesterday he hadn't been to the tavern.

He punched breath out of his lungs. He yearned to see the taverner; that face, that chest, that labor-hardened body stripped bare. His cock twitched at the mere thought of it, and he cupped himself until his shaft hardened. He'd pleasured himself plenty of times before, but the memory of acorn hair and hazel eyes added something. He chewed his bottom lip and massaged himself.

No.

Aurelia was just outside, and he had to scry. He'd deal with himself later.

But when he looked into the bowl, nothing changed. All he saw was the wood grain at the bottom. Like many of the objects in the hut, he'd carved it himself. He remembered the fire in his back as he swung the axe and felled the tree, then the careful carving of the wood. He loved working with his hands and the bounty of the forest.

An idea sparked in his head and tingled up and down his spine.

Perhaps…

He closed his eyes and imagined he was a tree. His

roots plunged into the earth to drink its nutrients. His trunk stood thick and strong, pushing him into the soil while supporting a great crown of branches and leaves that waved at the sun. He connected the earth with the sky, and the powers of each coursed through him. He strengthened the visualization until his mind clicked, the sound so loud it shook him. He grinned.

He'd found it.

He leaned forward with eyes open, grappling with the rising joy within. He was a proud and grand oak that had stood for a thousand years. Lightning ricocheted down his body from tip to toe, awakening that which had long lain dormant. He nearly crowed from the ecstasy of it, but not wanting to lose this feeling—even though he was now certain he could reach it again—he turned to scrying.

And to the taverner.

No sooner had he looked through the water did the man appear, as real as if he stood here in front of him.

Hame fell back on the chair, his belly jumping with laughter. Aurelia came running, and he leapt from his chair and hugged her.

"I did it!"

She struggled against his chest. "I can't breathe!"

He released her, giving her his best I'm-sorry-but-please-forgive-me smile. She scowled at him, which only made his cheeks strain more.

"Fool." She rolled her eyes, then gave into the happiness that had been muscling its way onto her face. She fell into his arms, and he nuzzled his chin against her head, happy she'd been there for that moment. She'd known what he was going through and she'd kept pushing him until he'd achieved it. The next step was to divine, but he was confident it would only be a matter of time before that came too.

H<small>AME</small> <small>SPENT</small> <small>MOST</small> <small>OF</small> <small>THE</small> <small>EVENING</small> <small>SCRYING</small>, <small>THE</small> <small>SKILL</small> becoming easier as time went on. The visualization of the oak became less necessary but stood at the back of his mind. Aurelia summoned a feast to celebrate and they gorged. They talked of happier times and it felt good to laugh, even better to do so with her.

Eventually they sought their beds, but while Aurelia's breathing soon slowed, sleep evaded him. Having learned to scry, he wanted to push on to experience things he had never considered or that had always been out of reach. Once he unlocked his ability to divine, the future would unfold for him to see—death and pain, a hunt for a demonic spirit and the possibility of madness. Loic's twisted and tortured face rose in his mind, but it quickly morphed into his own.

He didn't want to dwell; he wanted to feel good for a while longer.

He slipped out of bed, picked up his clothes, and crept from the hut. Outside, he dressed quickly then ran through the forest. He slowed to a jog when his lungs burned, but once the ache dissipated, he exerted himself again. Dripping with sweat and huffing like a well-ridden horse, he ran for what felt like hours. His legs started to tire, but just when he thought they'd buckle beneath him, he reached the edge of the forest and sighted his goal.

Carrouges looked different at night. A few lanterns dotted the street, but it was a gloomy place when the people were in their beds. He walked towards the tavern, hoping no one would come out and recognize him until he got to its door.

Light eked out through the murky window, and murmuring voices wormed out from behind the closed door. He reached for the handle but hesitated as fear pricked in his blood.

This is a mistake.

He wasn't meant for villages; wasn't meant for people. He belonged in the forest, alone, safe—or as safe as he could be. The handle rattled and he turned to run. A slurred voice limped after him then he was struck from behind and pitched forward into the dirt. The dead weight of an unconscious man flattened him.

"By the hairy ass of Christ, are you all right?"

He tensed as a strong hand gripped his upper arm and pulled him upright, the comatose man tumbling off him with all the grace of a cow falling down a hill. Hame grunted, and quickly dusted himself off.

"It's you." Hazel eyes widened. "I didn't expect you to still be around."

Hame stammered over some words that were meant as an excuse to leave, but before he could remove himself from the taverner's hold, he was shepherded inside with promises of a drink.

The taverner seated him at a bench, brought him some ale, then went off to attend to the other patrons. Left alone, Hame thought he could slip away, but the man caught—and held—his eye. Hame's cheeks blushed, and he stopped looking for an escape.

The taverner laughed with the other men, a deep throaty sound that made his Adam's apple jounce. His arms swelled, no doubt from weeks and months of rolling barrels and carrying three tankards in each of his big hands, and his shoulders flexed as he bent to deliver one such load to a table.

Gods, what would it be like to be held in those arms?

Warmth spread from his belly—and it had nothing to do with the ale.

One by one the men left, and finally he was alone. The taverner cleared away the empty cups and wiped the tables before returning to Hame and nodding at the tankard in his hand.

"Do you want another?"

Hame drained it, then dried his mouth with the back of his hand. He shook his head as he set the cup on the table. Ale often made men courageous, but he must have been drinking from a dud batch. His gaze flicked to the taverner's crotch.

Somewhere a barrel dripped into its own puddle.

"Or is there something else you want?"

He froze—caught out—but then thick fingers brushed underneath his chin and tilted it up. Eyes bent level with his, searching…for something. His smile broadened.

Then the taverner kissed him.

Skilled lips kneaded against his. The soft-yet-hard touch encouraged his timid desire to unfurl in a hot breath through his body. He moaned and pressed harder against that delicious mouth and growled when it retreated. The taverner sniggered and pulled him up from his bench before kissing him again.

Big hands slid up Hame's torso and massaged his chest, greedy and grinding. A savage ache spread from the friction against his nipples, but Hame didn't care. He pulled off the taverner's shirt, quickly following with his own. Feral lust slammed them together like two sparring bulls—muscle crashing against muscle—and their pelvises ground together until his rigid cock throbbed.

Harsh teeth on Hame's neck extracted a gasp as pleasure racked through his body—such a simple thing, but God, how he wanted more. Teeth bit him again and he pushed forward with his hips. Weakened and dizzy, he lolled when the taverner—a man whose name he didn't even know—withdrew. He didn't fight when the rest of his clothes were torn from him and his cock sprang free. That gorgeous mouth grinned wide at seeing his hard shaft then gripped it in his rough, hot palm, jolting fire against his most sensitive flesh. He threw his head back as all sensation localized in his groin, then he pressed his brow against the taverner's shoulder, unable to support himself any longer, gasping as he pumped him.

"That feels so good," Hame grunted, gripping the strong arm milking him, wanting him to stop, wanting him to keep going. The taverner's thumb grazed his head and his vision shattered.

A rustle of clothes and the taverner stood naked and erect. Hame reached out to touch, wanting to feel the man's cock, but he was spun round and forced forward over the table. Determined hands gripped his ass and spread his cheeks, and spit landed on the cleft and slid down. The head of the taverner's fat cock rubbed against the puckered opening, making his hole clench and release.

Then he thrust forward.

Hame bucked against the pain, trying to pull away from the branding iron forcing its way through his innards, but a heavy chest pinned him in place. Lips touched the bare skin of his back, and the stranger shoved into him, inch by painful inch.

He sucked in his breath, clenched his eyes shut. "It hurts."

"It'll pass." Hot breath burned against his ear. "Then you'll really like it."

He doubted it. Not with this fire tunneling through him. He took hold of himself—not surprised to find he'd gone soft—but stroked until his erection returned to distract his mind from the pain. A tingling stirred in his groin, like a glow in the ashes of a dying hearth, and he started to move. The pain faded until finally the taverner slid in and out with ease.

Hame's body rocked with their motion, the pounding igniting him. Then the strongest, hardest charge struck something deep that forced his mouth open, only for nothing to emerge. What he felt was so intimate that it was beyond sound—and he wanted to feel it again. He pushed back against the taverner, who laughed, then penetrated him again, hitting that spot so hard his legs buckled. Only the iron arm around his waist kept him from falling.

He moaned with each plunge and withdrawal. His body hummed, starting in his toes and rising up his legs, a strong swirl in his groin—*oh God, yes, harder*—and then up his chest, higher and higher. The feeling was so vital it made him aware of what was happening at that very second, of the slap of masculine skin against his, of the rough fingers digging into his hips, the heat of a man's breath on his neck, and the way the taverner reached so far inside him—all of it brought together into one crystalline second. The knot tightened in his balls, threatening to unravel him until finally he could hold it no longer. His toes curled, his ass tensed, and he came with a prolonged grunt, shooting onto the floor as the taverner released into him.

But Hame was given no reprieve as his shuddering body shook his mind free and a vision grabbed him.

And violence and horror lay waste to his ecstasy.

XVI

THE DREAM'S LUST FORCED AURELIA AWAKE. SHE
summoned a light in the hut, confirming what she already
knew. Hame's bed lay empty, the blankets cold. Not
wanting to see the truth, but needing to, she rose and
crossed to the table. She looked into the scrying bowl and
searched for him.

She jerked back, casting aside the scene she'd
witnessed, but though she no longer scried for him he
didn't leave her thoughts. She turned for the door and sat
outside on the grass, gazing up at the stars. For all the
peace in the world that night, her hands shook, and her
eyes stung.

I will not cry!

She held back the tears, and fire roared inside her
head. She wanted to destroy the hut. She wanted to *kill* the
taverner, beat Hame, hurt any who came near her. How
dare he hold her close and make her believe she was loved?

The screams jostled inside her throat. If she let them
out, she'd likely set the whole forest ablaze, so she pushed
them down until her throat eased. A cold breeze blew

through the trees, and the uncaring stars glared down at her.

Pre-dawn light stirred her from wide-eyed slumber as she stared into a nothing that gradually took on shape. Eventually, one of those shapes became Hame, ambling through the undergrowth, his head down.

"Did you have fun?" The acid in her voice scoured her heart.

He jumped then must have seen the look on her face. He sighed. "I'm sorry, Aurelia. I didn't—"

She batted away his excuses. "Don't."

He sat next to her. Heat radiated from his body, and she remembered seeing the sweat coursing down his back as the taverner —

She wriggled away from him, putting distance between her and the memory.

"Do I disgust you that much?"

"What?" She thought she'd already been given all of the night's surprises, but it seemed there were still a few more to leap out at her.

"Do I disgust you?"

"You think I have a problem because it was a *man* you fucked?" Her voice raised an octave.

He didn't say anything, but his glare was enough of an accusation.

"You really are blind, aren't you?" she spat and pushed to her feet. She hastened inside for no other reason than she wanted to get away from him. Any minute now she'd travel back to Elaine and then her mother could deal with him from now on.

But she didn't go.

She couldn't.

He entered after her.

"Do you love him?" she asked, her voice timid and low.

"I don't know. This is all new to me."

She scoffed. "New? Don't lie." She turned to see his face darken.

"I swear to you, I had no idea. I've never thought about it, never had the chance."

"Then all my blessings on you both," she growled, sweeping past him.

He grabbed her arm. "Don't leave, Aurelia. I need you. There's work we have to do. Together."

"You're wrong. You don't need me. You don't want me." Her voice cracked.

"I need you more than I need some man."

She laughed. Memories of how Thierry and Etienne used to look at each other splashed across her mind. "I've seen all this before. I've seen what love does to people, and how it destroys them. I'm just glad I realized before it was too late."

His grip loosened; his mournful eyes desperate for some solace she couldn't give. She hurried to the door.

"I had a vision."

She stopped. It was one of only two things he could have said to make her stay. She wished it were the other.

She sighed. "You've had them before."

"Not like this. It was powerful, and it came to me when—"

She winced.

"I think I can control them," he said quickly, "but that's not what's important. It was about your mother."

"What about her?"

He paused. "She's going to die."

And with those four small words, her world stopped. Everything turned to stone. Elaine's dying was not a possibility.

"You're wrong."

"I'm not," he said, coming to her.

With her hands pulled back to her chest, ready to push him away, she exited the hut. She stumbled as she turned but righted herself. He called for her to stop, but she kept going. He couldn't be right. He'd said it to hurt her.

But why would he want to do that?

Because he wants me gone.

Then he'd be free to fuck whomever he wanted and not have to see the pain on her face.

To hell with him.

She'd leave him behind. She prepared herself to travel, hovering on the edge, when he took hold of her arm. The shock released her power, and they both shuttled through the ether. His grasp was the only thing that kept him from being thrown off, and if he'd fallen during the journey, she didn't know what would have become of him. When they landed outside Elaine's lair, her arm throbbed. He swayed on his feet, her body the only thing stopping him from pitching forward. She threw him off, and he hit the dirt.

He coughed and rolled onto his back, scrunching his eyes shut. His face paled. She ground her teeth, but it didn't stop her guilt.

She bent and put her arm underneath his shoulder, helping him to sit. She wasn't forgiving him but seeing him so poorly and not doing anything to ease his suffering left a bitter taste in her mouth. As she steadied him, her mother's voice shot out of the tunnel.

"Why are you here?" Lines ran deep across Elaine's brow.

"Mother, I—"

"I had to speak with you," Hame said. "Can we go inside? I need something to drink."

Elaine shot Aurelia a look, but it wasn't the one she expected. She'd been prepared for an interrogation and a thorough dissection of her failure. Instead, she saw...apprehension.

Hame put his weight on her hand, distracting her, and the moment passed. They entered the tunnel and the sense of gloom infected her. What if Hame had told her the truth?

XVII

Aurelia guided Hame to a chair in the kitchen, then rested her hand on his shoulder. Though she hadn't forgotten about the taverner, there were now more important things to worry about than her heart's sick desperation. He placed his hand over hers, and his touch hushed her jittering nerves.

Elaine brought a cup of water, which he downed in one gulp. "You're here because you've seen my future."

Aurelia's stomach shriveled and copper crystallized across her tongue.

"You know this already?" he replied.

Elaine chewed her cheek before speaking. "I had some idea."

How could her mother be so calm? "That's all you have to say? We have to fight this."

"No, it's necessary," Elaine said flatly.

"How could your death be of any use to us?" Aurelia's nails gouged into her palms.

"This has to happen," her mother said.

"Why show us the future if we can't change it?"

"I know this is hard——"

"What do you know about it? You've already left me behind once before; I expect this will be easy for you." Her words were unfair, but she wanted more of a reaction than this resignation.

Elaine's shoulders tensed. "Nothing is harder than leaving you. But it is a sacrifice that I—that *we*—must make. I'm not strong enough to defeat Xadrak here. He grows more powerful and will draw others to his cause. I need to battle him where we are evenly matched."

"If you die, you will become just like him. I don't want some demon. I want my mother here on this plane, not floating around like some ghost in the great beyond."

Elaine's eyes leaked pity, and Hame's hand pressed against hers. But neither fought. Two people she loved— lost in one day. How could they accept this?

She allowed Elaine to embrace her, and gradually she unwound enough to hold her as well, relishing and memorizing the feeling of her mother's body—real, human and here—before she pulled away.

"Come, I have something to give you both."

Elaine tired of being strong, but she persevered for Aurelia's sake. What good was weeping when she could not change what had to happen? Hame's stiff confirmation of Loic's prophecy chilled her. The boy's concern for her death stopped at the damage it would cause Aurelia. She wanted to sneer at him but couldn't deny her gratitude that he would be there to care for her daughter.

She'd have to give him the gift as well.

She instructed Hame to wait while she led Aurelia down the tunnel and into her sanctuary. Candles burst alight when they entered. She positioned Aurelia on one side of the raised altar while she stood on the other.

"What are we doing here?" Aurelia's eyes took in the objects on top of the altar.

"I am giving you that which I cannot have for myself. I am giving you an eternity."

"I don't want it."

"You must. I don't know how long our mission is going to take."

"I refuse. You'll just have to stay here and do it yourself."

Aurelia wouldn't have any success in bargaining out of this. With time, she hoped her daughter would understand why.

"Aurelia, please. I don't want to die. I have had this same magic cast upon me, but I know, and the oracle knows, I am not meant to remain here forever. Please help me."

Sadly, immortality meant only longevity, not immunity. A dagger through the heart would still end her life. Only her sons enjoyed that kind of resistance.

"If I don't, then what?"

"Then my death will be for nothing."

"But—"

"There are no 'buts' in this. I will die. You will remain. This is your path, and I have mine."

"You don't know what you ask of me."

Pieces of her heart peeled away, a tearing that balled her hands. "I do, and I'm sorry for it. I know this is not what you want. This is not what I want either. But Xadrak is poisoning the astral. He will corrupt witches in this world, and he will eventually conquer it unless we stop him."

His power could be channeled through others. Her

daughter would have to bloody herself slaying whomever Xadrak drew to him.

Aurelia didn't speak, but the righteous sorrow in her eyes spoke volumes.

Hugs won't fix that, Sinara's voice sighed inside her head.

"Please give me your hand." Elaine picked up the dagger from the altar and positioned the chalice in the center.

At first Aurelia didn't move, and Elaine's temples burned. She could only be patient for so long and deny her own rage in the face of this inevitability. None of this was fair, but that was the way of the world. She tightened her hold on the dagger's hilt.

Eventually, a trembling hand raised and lay wrist-up in hers.

Looking into Aurelia's eyes, she gazed into a mirror. The same determination lurked behind the fear. Aurelia was hers, through and through.

She touched the blade's tip to her daughter's wrist and took a deep breath.

"Blood is the key to everything."

———

AURELIA FLINCHED WHEN HER SKIN SPLIT BENEATH THE blade and hissed at the cut's sting. Elaine turned her wrist and a few drops of blood dripped into the chalice before she was released.

Her mother spoke an incantation containing simple words Aurelia hurriedly committed to memory. Elaine pointed the wand skywards and raised her power. The room buzzed and the air became laden with orange blossom. Aurelia breathed shallowly as the power intensified.

Elaine aimed the wand at the chalice, and with a

shouted word, green light fired from the tip of the wand and ignited the blood. Aurelia jumped back, raising an arm to protect herself as purple, blue and red light rose from the mouth of the cup. Coalescing around themselves, they reached higher and higher until their tips brushed the ceiling.

"*Vita aeterna!*" Elaine roared.

The three tongues of flame tightened into one beam, then lashed out and shot towards Aurelia, attacking so fast that she screamed. It delved into her open mouth and filled her, permeating throughout her body until it was all in her, like a snake that had slithered into its burrow. She reached out to steady herself and looked at her mother, expecting her to be pleased the working was done.

But Elaine's eyes were screwed shut.

It's not over.

A great tearing ripped through her and brought torment without end. A high-pitched cry erupted from the bottom of her gut and echoed around the stone room. Her whole being shredded like cheap muslin into thousands of pieces. She wrenched her eyelids open to check she remained whole. Flipping her hands over, she saw that whatever was happening only writhed inside her.

Knowing that didn't help. She couldn't ease this agony. She clutched her stomach, collapsed to the floor and curled in on herself. If she could make herself as small as possible, perhaps the pain would abate. Pulling her knees close to her body, she quivered as the torture swept up and down her until finally and suddenly it stopped.

She couldn't move. So quickly had it gone it felt as if her stomach had been ripped from her. Silent, she laid there, her eyes closed, afraid it might come back.

She jerked as a hand touched her shoulder.

"It's over, Aurelia. It's over."

Elaine pulled her up to lean against her and stroked her hair.

She was too spent to resist. She'd been hacked out of the spiral of life and death and paid the price for doing so. She prayed for sleep, and thankfully, as her mother's warmth soothed her, unconsciousness came.

AURELIA WOKE IN HER BED, NOT KNOWING HOW LONG SHE'D been out. The aches and pains were gone, and she felt no different than she had before entering her mother's sanctuary. Still wretched. Still fighting against the inevitability of what was yet to come.

She stayed in bed, not wanting to see either her mother or Hame, her heart battered by both of them. Her body demanded rest and she dozed, waking again when the door opened.

She saw his silhouette. He didn't speak as he crept in, closed the door and climbed onto the bed to lie beside her.

Did he think he could crawl into her bed and everything would be as it was before? They may only have each other now, but she wasn't about to let him off that easily. She pretended to sleep. Regulating her breath was harder than she'd expected.

"I know you're awake." His words tickled her ear. "You're trembling like a little earthquake."

She forced herself to remain stoic. She wouldn't let him back into her heart.

"Do you hurt as badly as I do?"

Yes.

"Who knew becoming immortal was such hard work?"

In spite of everything that had happened the night before, her hand sought his. For better or worse, they were now joined by something that went far deeper than love.

He didn't say anything else, and soon she slept. The weight that had crushed her lifted slightly, and she breathed easy for a while.

XVIII

"First, you give me eternal life, and now you want me to take away the lives of others?"

Aurelia was shrieking, she knew that, but her mother had just told her what she expected her to do with her immortality.

"You don't have to wring their necks, if you don't want." Elaine's unwavering tone had returned. "Burn their power out for all I care, but the fewer there are who can wield the magic, the better."

"Why can't you do it? Xadrak was able to kill Loic, why can't you do the same?"

"I will do what I can, but I will need you to help me."

"You're turning me into a killer."

"You became one when you incinerated Henri."

She had done a good job of suppressing the reality of what she'd done to Henri, but Elaine was right. She'd burned the bastard to ash.

"He deserved it," Aurelia snapped back. "I don't even know these witches."

"Fine. Get to know them. *Then* kill them."

Hame laughed from his chair by the wall. Aurelia glared at him, but he just smiled sweetly.

"I can't believe you're laughing at a time like this."

His face smoothed into one of serious introspection. He held his hands up as a way of offering his apology—or surrender. She sneered at him.

"I won't do it," she said.

Her mother glared. "We'll see."

"No, I will," Hame said.

Aurelia snorted.

"Fine," Elaine said. "Don't kill them. Then see what happens when Xadrak sends them to hunt you and Hame down."

"Let them come. I'll deal with them then." Her mother opened her mouth to object, but she snuck in first. "I said, I'll deal with them then."

The certainty on Elaine's face wavered. "No, this is important. I won't simply be there to fight Xadrak, I'll be working to send him back to earth."

Aurelia's eyes bulged, thinking she'd misheard. "You can't be serious!"

"I have to force him back into a mortal form."

"And I'm supposed to let him wander freely?" Bile cloyed at the back of her throat. Xadrak couldn't become human again. She couldn't allow his evil to infect other innocent lives.

"When he's human, he's manageable," Elaine stormed over her objections. "If he becomes a threat, burn him out. If that doesn't work, kill him, and I will fight him on the astral and send him back again. He has to be on Earth to return through the portal."

"You want me to be his minder?"

"In a sense. Hame will help you too. He'll use his abilities to keep an eye on Xadrak."

"Absolutely not," Aurelia said. *Not after what happened to Loic.*

"He will be safe while Xadrak is on Earth, and I'll protect him when in the astral. You don't have to worry for his safety."

Hame didn't say anything, just sat there with his face smooth and shoulders relaxed. She wondered if he and Elaine had already had this conversation.

"And what will you do while you're up there and Xadrak is down here? Surely you can come back to Earth."

"I can't risk it. I need to search for the key."

"Hame will find it."

"He might and he might not."

Their arguments volleyed back and forth, neither willing to give ground. No matter what she said, Elaine remained adamant her death was the only option available to them.

"You don't need to die to do any of this," Aurelia pleaded. "You can stay here with me. We'll find these witches together, convert them to our cause, instead of his, and find another way of wrestling him back into a mortal body."

"I wish we could, but it's impossible."

She tried hard to keep her hurt from tipping over, but her mother's weak declaration of surrender nudged it over the edge.

"You don't want to try." Her words jabbed. "You'd rather leave me than fight to stay."

Elaine's face flushed and her eyes flared, but Aurelia ran. She hurried into the tunnel, the pain propelling her through the ether back to Hame's hut. She needed space to think.

Hame bridled at being stuck with Elaine, but at least he was able to send his mind away. Hunched over the scrying bowl, he located Aurelia. He wished he could go to her and give her some of the comfort she'd given him. Then Elaine spoke and the vision of faded.

"What did you say?" he asked.

"You will look after Aurelia, won't you?"

"That's what I'm trying to do." One day he'd be able to scry without the bowl, but for now it was the easiest method. He peered into it again.

"Do you know how I'm going to die?"

The woman rubbed him raw. He still hadn't forgiven her for putting Loic in harm's way, but he wasn't totally uncaring. And the plaintive tone in her voice made his anger so petty. She was going to die. She knew it and she was forcing herself to not fight it. Realizing what she was going to lose, he saw her for what she was—a mother terrified of losing her child.

"I'm sorry, but it will be by Xadrak's hand," he said as gently as he could.

She gave a few quick small nods and closed her eyes, seeming to become as cold and hard as diamond. "I will not let him," she whispered.

He didn't have the cruelty in him to tell her it was going to happen whether she willed it or not.

Her eyes opened, lit with a fire that made a black-smith's furnace seem dim. "My death will be my own and unsullied by his foulness. I will choose the time and the method. He shall not win."

"You would commit suicide?" He stood and faced her.

"Better by my means than his." She held his gaze.

"Aurelia will not let you."

"No, but you will."

He tensed. "I will not help you end your life."

"Why not? You are fine with giving me my execution orders, yet giving me peace and a death I choose, you baulk at?" Her spine straightened. "If it cannot be changed, then I will embrace it, but in the way I see fit."

He felt her pain, could see she was doing her best to make a bad situation better. What would Aurelia think of him if he allowed Elaine to do this? Yet how would she feel if Xadrak tortured and killed her mother? He sighed, wished he'd never had that damn vision.

"I will not help you end it, but I will grant you peace. I will distract Aurelia so she will not stop you."

"How I wish——"

The vision hit hard. Aurelia's terror slammed into him, blocking out all else.

All the saliva in his mouth dried and his lips opened and closed without emitting any sound until he wrenched himself back and forced out a few words.

"He has her."

———

WITHOUT HER MOTHER THERE TO GUIDE HER, AURELIA relied on the little she knew about projecting onto the astral so she could hunt Xadrak. Her stomach hopped about, but necessity drove her. After a few attempts, with desperation providing some missing skill and dumb luck doing the rest, she appeared on the astral. She stood in an otherworldly copy of Hame's hut and then, once she'd fashioned a shield, she ventured into the forest. Familiar yet not, her concentration faltered, threatening to slam her back into her body with spine-snapping force. She quickly corralled her focus.

Once outside the hut, the world shifted beneath her as she sped towards her old home in Carcassonne. The grey and empty streets looked like the ones she'd walked along for most of her life, but there was a difference. It took her a while to realize what it was, and then it came to her. There were no shadows. There was no sun, yet everything was lit and flat.

She walked down the unreal streets, past the illusory houses until she reached the one where she'd killed Henri. If she was going to find the demon, this was the best place to start.

She risked much. She trembled if she stood still too long and she kept looking over her shoulder, spooked by shadows that weren't there. But she had to do something to protect her mother, and right now that meant forcing Xadrak back to Earth, however that could be achieved.

She imbued her shields with more power and entered the hovel she'd once called home. The first room was empty, as was the second, but instead of a bed, Henri's ashes lay heaped in the center. It seemed that even on the astral her deeds were writ large.

"You get your temper from me." His voice hissed behind her.

Cockroaches scuttled inside her as she spun to protect herself. Her shields brightened, but they only illuminated Xadrak more. He towered above her in all his terrible glory—his horns of oily black, his eyes of brimstone red, and his wings the shade of charcoal. He shredded her shield with one swipe and grabbed her.

Squeezed in his fist, her bones creaked. She wasn't here in body, but the effect was the same. Panic stuttered her power, and what should have been a blast of light that could burn through anything was nothing more than a flicker that could barely singe a hair. Pulled nearer to his vile maw, his sharp teeth lathered with saliva, she screamed, the sound pulling up from her toes and erupting out of her mouth.

And with it came the thought that Hame was wrong.

Elaine wouldn't be the one to die.

AURELIA'S SCREAMS GUIDED ELAINE AND SHE SWOOPED IN behind Xadrak, wielding a burning sword. With a vengeful roar, she plunged it into the foul demon's back. Though he was only spirit, the blade slowed as if it speared through flesh. Sinara craved it, remembering when she'd done this to him in Crion.

Xadrak dropped Aurelia and reared around to face Elaine. The sword disappeared as his contortions ripped it from her grasp. It had wrought damage, but not enough to kill him. He was a hideous thing, made of black tar from the pits of Hell. He advanced on her, but a flash burst against his back.

"Get out of here!" she screamed at Aurelia as Xadrak spun back towards their daughter.

"I'm not leaving you!" Aurelia shouted.

She had to goad Xadrak into killing her and not her daughter. Aurelia wasn't strong enough to withstand another attack.

"You are a coward, Xadrak," she roared. "You know you cannot beat me, so you go for the weakest and easiest kill."

He looked over his shoulder at Elaine. "Destroying your bitch daughter will bring its own rewards." He marched towards Aurelia, and she blasted him with a jet of power. He staggered but did not go down.

"Liar," she cried. "You were always afraid of facing the

strongest of the Ikiri-rai, and now you quake in fear before two lowly humans. You will never win." She released her own magic and it burned into his back.

He snarled and couldn't ignore her assault. She summoned another sword as he spun.

"You were always the weak one, Sinara. The moment I fucked you, you became nothing but a whore for my pleasure. And now, I'm going to shove my claws in you."

He charged, and Elaine rushed forward to meet him. She had no hope of defeating him like this, but she would die in battle and take as much of him with her as she could. Her blade barely pierced his chest before he grabbed her. Her sword failed, and his putrid contamination poisoned her spirit. She grunted as his fists squeezed her.

There came another explosion from Aurelia, but Xadrak paid it no heed. His eyes locked onto Elaine's face and soul-deep hatred burned within him. She wrestled to break loose. He was going to crush her and then Aurelia would seek to avenge her. She couldn't let that happen.

I'm sorry, my darling.

She summoned her power and slammed it into Aurelia. The force knocked her unconscious and sent her hurtling back to her earthly body. She whispered a farewell, laced with a wish that when they met again Aurelia would have forgiven her.

Xadrak's hands ripped into her, shredding her apart. She held to her hope like a raft in a flooded river, keeping the agony from drowning her mind, from feeling that pain. She would not give him that.

She would not give him her terror or her suffering.

Her connection to the Earth severed and she gained a small amount of power, enough to jettison her tattered soul from his grasp and fly along the astral breezes, far away from his sight and his power.

Hope carried her and hope kept her from fading.

AURELIA WOKE WITH HER MOTHER'S NAME ON HER LIPS. She tried to sit up, but her body screamed in protest. The hut was dark. Night had fallen. Yet none of it had been a dream.

Only a nightmare.

She had killed her mother.

She touched her sides and winced at the pain that lanced through her. Bruises covered her, erupting from the trauma of having been slammed back into her body. But she didn't linger. She had to get home.

Gritting her teeth, she forced herself off the bed. Her power had rejuvenated enough during her unconsciousness to enable her to travel to her mother's cave. Once inside she called Hame's name as she staggered from room to room. No one answered.

She entered the corridor to the bedrooms, and her mother's door stood open. Inside, Hame slept in the chair. She let him be.

Elaine lay in the bed, beneath the covers, not breathing. She seemed so small; if life had made her large and strong, now there remained this empty husk. Aurelia crawled over the bed, pulling Elaine's body close to her, trying to hug her, trying to stir her. But she would not wake. She knew this but she had to try, the terrible sadness thundering inside her. Grief ate her strength, so she let her mother's body rest and held onto her cold hand.

She didn't know how long she stayed there, but eventually her tears stopped and she was left with the realization that had she not defied her mother repeatedly, none of this would have happened.

She shouldn't have killed Henri.

She shouldn't have gone into the astral to face him.

While she knew the past could not be changed, she kept throwing herself against its sharp indictments and cutting herself until she bled. Lost opportunities, harsh words, and regret were all she had left.

That and a mission.

And for her penance, she would see it done.

Or die trying.

❧ II ❧
ONE PEBBLE AT A TIME

1792

I

THE WOOD BLOCK SPLIT BENEATH THE BLOW OF HAME'S axe. He'd chopped more than he needed, but there was little else to occupy him. He'd tidied the cottage, made the bed, even cleaned out and relit the hearth. And still the bats flapped in his stomach.

The afternoon sun beat down, the forest air stifling and oppressive. He wiped the sweat from his forehead, lined up another piece of wood, raised the axe and brought it down with a satisfying grunt. The two halves fell either side.

A cough came from behind him.

So. He's arrived.

His hand slid up to grip below the axe head. He squeezed the handle and the pressure quelled his anticipation only to have it come fluttering back when he turned.

"Do you know the oracle?" the man asked in a rough approximation of French.

He looked exactly as he had in the visions. Short blond hair the color of wheat, eyes the color of bluebells, and a body Hame wanted to lick. He had a bag strapped to his back and wielded a long, thick walking stick—the sort handy in a fight. Considering the size of him, though, Hame doubted anyone would give him trouble.

Hame brushed his hair back over his scalp, his muscles flexing. The man watched every movement, his mouth opening a fraction to let his tongue peek out.

"I've been waiting for you for a long time," Hame replied in English, wishing he could use the seeker's mother tongue.

The man shook his head as if he'd been startled awake. "You…you knew I was coming?"

"Of course. I am the oracle, after all." He hefted the axe from his right hand to his left as he strode over to shake the man's hand. "My name is Hame. What's yours?"

The man's hand stopped short, then closed into a fist. "If you're an oracle, shouldn't you already know that?"

He laughed. "I don't know everything, but I do know you've come from Wales. The village of Ewenni, to be exact. I know you're the fourth of six sons."

The man pulled back slightly. Hame enjoyed seeing him so unsettled. It made up for how he'd been made to feel for the past five years, ever since he'd had the first vision.

"And I know you're a witch." He straightened his hand again. "But I do not know your name."

Numbly, the man slipped his hand into his grasp. "My name is Carn Gwyn."

Hame held Carn's grip longer than it was polite to, but the feel of the man's skin against his calmed the bats and brought them to roost. Whatever misgivings he might have about Carn's future, he wanted to get to know the Welsh witch better.

He must have stared too hard because Carn's cheeks flushed and he looked away, pulling his hand free. He'd seen that uncertainty in many lovers over the centuries. He himself had no such concerns anymore. He wouldn't force Carn into anything he didn't want to do but, from the open looks Carn had lavished on his body, there wouldn't be much he didn't want to indulge in.

"Would you like to come inside?" Hame picked up some wood. "You must be tired after your journey."

"Yes, thank you." Carn helped with the load. "It's a long way from Wales to Ambert."

Hame chuckled to himself. *Not as far as Scotland to Normandy.*

On the walk back to the cottage, they chatted about Carn's journey. He kept up a steady stream of questions to head off the one Carn no doubt wanted to ask about his future.

They dumped the wood beside the cottage and went inside. Hame slipped on a shirt, then gestured for Carn to sit while he poured two cups of ale. He got Carn some food, which he fell on. He filled himself as much watching Carn's strong hands tear into bread and meat, or the muscles in his neck working while he swallowed. Having Carn here—finally—felt like the beginning of something momentous, and not just because of the vision.

Every time it had been the same. Carn walked down a dirt path. On one side the forest burgeoned with lush, vibrant trees, heaving with green leaves and fruit. Deer, rabbits, and birds traveled unafraid. A river ran through it of fresh, clear water, brimming with plump fish. On the other side of the path, the forest stood desolate. Burned and broken tree trunks speared the sky. Snakes, ravens, and wolves hunted, and the river was nothing but mud. And all the while, Carn walked between them.

Towards him.

And Aurelia.

Even in the vision Carn's beauty had struck him, and

he saw not a man to be feared, but one to be guided. Eventually the path would fork, and he'd be taken one way or the other.

Carn gave a hearty sigh and leaned back in the chair, looking like a man with a contented belly. His other urges wouldn't be so easily sated.

"So, why do you seek the oracle?" Hame asked, finally ready to give Carn what he'd come for.

"A friend sent me to you. He said you'd be able to help me find Aurelia."

Her name on another's lips was like hearing the forbidden name of God. Such a rarity electrified him.

"Who's your friend?"

"Blythe."

He knew of the witch. He'd sent Aurelia to him when he'd found Blythe screaming on the ether for a little guidance to stop the madness. Aurelia had arrived in time to aid him, and he'd proved a useful ally. If Blythe had sent Carn, Hame was reasonably confident he could be trusted. Still, it wouldn't do to come across as too eager to please.

"What makes you think I know this Aurelia?"

Carn laughed. "Blythe said you wouldn't make this easy. Look, you've already told me you knew I was coming so there must be a reason for it. And I'd hazard a guess I'm going to get what I want, so it would be quicker if you'd just introduce us."

Cocky bastard. Even so, he loved the Welshman's confidence.

"You're making a lot of assumptions. How do you know the vision wasn't of something else entirely? Something more to my liking than yours." His voice lowered, and his eyes widened just enough to hold Carn's attention. Heat slithered through his veins when Carn bit his lower lip.

"I'm sure you and I like a lot of the same things."

Now it was his turn to look away. He hadn't tumbled with a witch before. In his opinion, being with someone who not only took the magical side of the world seriously, but could also manipulate it, created an unstable balance. He had always been the one who was in control with his lovers, his knowledge giving him greater insight and power. But with Carn?

He needed time to unravel his tangled feelings before he took that leap. When he looked back at Carn into a lusty stare, he didn't think he'd need long.

"Aurelia will be here soon. She might help you, she might not."

And considering what else he had to tell her, she was not going to be happy. Still, there was nothing that could be done about it. She had to know, and some things were better said in person.

"Will you talk to her for me? I've heard she listens to your advice."

"If you prove useful to her, I won't need to say anything."

"But you will, won't you?" Carn's grin turned knowing, and the sight of it was like fingers strumming up and down his back. But as much as he wanted to be played with, he needed to maintain a clear head. The vision hadn't changed in five years; it still contained a warning. However, he did think the longer he kept Carn around, the better chance he had of steering him down the right path.

All for the good of the world, of course.

II

ANOTHER WITCH LAY DEAD AT AURELIA'S FEET. THE grizzled old male had taken her a while to track down. She'd eventually unearthed him in St Petersburg, burrowed in among the aristocracy, and attempting to convert more to Xadrak's cause.

Meanwhile, Xadrak himself was silent. This witch hadn't had contact with the demon's spirit for more than thirty years—she'd tortured the information out of him with a simple illusion, showing him his worst fears and letting them torment him. He'd squealed quickly enough, terrified of having his toes bitten off by turtles. She didn't know if that fear was the result of Xadrak's corruption of the man's mind, or something he'd always had. Not that it mattered now.

His admission confirmed what Hame had been saying for some time.

Xadrak was back on Earth. But where?

The burned carcass was beyond recognition, blackened skin so dark he looked like an overcooked piece of meat. She had let her temper get away from her. He'd used an effective cutting spell, resulting in a deep gash on her left arm, a cut across her forehead, and a wound to her right thigh. She'd deflected the greatest brunt of them, so the injuries weren't life-threatening, but they stung.

For that, she left the burned witch where he'd fallen for the dogs to ravage.

She vanished and reappeared outside the house Hame had built in the woods, west of Ambert. Though she'd tried to convince him otherwise, Hame preferred to live by himself. He'd lived with her briefly after Elaine died, but he'd eventually returned to the forest. Not that the distance really mattered.

And she couldn't begrudge him his work. Like Loic before him, Hame provided his services to those who sought him out. He did what he could, though most of the time he provided solace more than prophecy. Her tongue clucked when he told her that. She could imagine the kind of solace he gave some of them. Those green eyes. That red hair. The well-built body. He was as much an entice-ment as his divination. While most of the seekers were women, a string of lovers with broken hearts littered the centuries, hers the still beating one among them. She burned when she thought about them and how she'd never know him that way, but she cooled her head as she walked up the path to his sanctuary.

Her hard-won coolness evaporated in a jet of steam as she saw the blond man exit the house. Tall and strong, he lingered at the door once he'd closed it. He was beautiful, and the sort that Hame swooned over. And from the goofy look in the man's eye, Hame had already speared this one.

I will not be jealous.

She repeated the mantra while approaching the house. The man looked up as she neared, the new-love sheen wiping from his eyes as he spied her injuries and darted his gaze from one bloody wound to another. He shuffled out of her way.

"Aurelia?" He spoke her name with a foreign tongue's unease.

She charged her power, held it invisible in case she needed to kill him. "How do you know who I am?"

"Hame—I mean, the oracle—told me you were returning."

She held her tongue. She'd deal with Hame later. When she didn't respond, he continued on.

"My name is Carn, and he said you might be able to help me."

"I don't—"

"He also said I could probably help you, too."

What was Hame playing at? Until she knew, she wasn't about to give this pretty boy anything. She'd lived long enough to know that trusting someone's word was the quickest way to get burned.

"And what could you possibly help me with?"

He shrugged. "I'm a witch, too. But I don't have anywhere near your power. I was hoping you'd teach me."

"There are already too many power-hungry in this world, and I won't feed you." She turned away from him, opened the door and entered, slamming it in his face. With a wave of her hand, she barred the door so not even a herd of rhinoceros could knock it down.

Hame sat on a pile of cushions on the floor. He preferred to entertain the seekers there, thinking it lent some mystique to the whole thing. Never mind he could have visions wherever he wanted. The rest of the cottage was as expected. A kitchen bench, a table and chairs, and hearth on one side; his meeting place at the other. A doorway led to two bedrooms, one unused, but the other fitted with his large bed. There weren't many things in his home, but it was filled with warmth of heart. She loved coming here. Except when she had just been ambushed by one of Hame's beaus.

"I know you're not in a trance," she snapped. "You're smiling."

"That's because I'm looking at a very happy future."

"Wouldn't have anything to do with that blond thing drooling outside your door?"

"I hope you were nice to him."

"I kicked him a few times, but he didn't seem to mind."

"Oh, Aurelia, you are wicked."

She rolled her eyes, but the effect was lost as he kept his closed. The wound in her leg pulled as she knelt down and kissed his cheek. He inhaled deeply and his smile broadened.

"You smell like a roast. I take it our Russian friend won't be troubling us anymore?"

"Left for the dogs." She sat back, sucking her breath in sharply as she did so.

Hame's eyes shot open. "You're wounded."

He bound to his feet and grabbed a bucket of water and a cloth. Some of the water sloshed out in his haste. She batted him away, told him not to worry, but he wouldn't retreat. Instead he cleaned her wounds, and she melted beneath his touch.

"I'll heal them in a minute," she said, but he didn't stop administering to her.

"You got complacent, didn't you?"

"Who? Me?"

"Perhaps you should leave the scars, especially this big ugly one across your pretty head, as a reminder that you're not invincible."

"I need no reminder." With a surge of power, the wounds closed as if they'd never been. Once the skin had knitted together, she sagged. Healing drained her more than anything else she did, but it was a necessary skill. Thierry's back had been saved because of her, not that he'd known what she did. Hame threw the cloth into the bucket and positioned himself so she could lie against him.

"That wasn't smart," he said, with gentle admonishment.

"What else do you suggest?"

"Reiner?"

She scoffed, then rolled her eyes. "I'm sure he'd have no questions at all."

Reiner—an accomplished healer if only he could accept his gift—was nephew to one of the few friends she had in this world. But it wasn't his power that had initially brought him to her attention. His soul was that of her old friend from Carcassonne, Etienne—her brother's deepest love.

Long ago Hame's visions revealed Etienne, too, had a part to play in all of this, and ever since, she'd watched for his soul. When it showed up in Reiner, she'd befriended his aunt, the Baroness Liesel, to get close to him, but over the years the necessity had become pleasure as she had warmed to the aging aristocrat's maternal nature.

"It's probably just as well. Your brothers are on their way to Liesel's."

"I must stop them." She rushed to stand, but Hame held her back.

"You can't."

"Don't tell me that, please. I can't let anything happen to her, or to Reiner."

"Reiner and Thierry are drawn to each other; that is inevitable, that is written."

"Then they will finally be together?"

He shrugged, but it was the kind he gave when he knew the answer wouldn't please her.

"What evil will Olivier bring?"

"Whatever is necessary. Liesel will be fine, I can see that at least, but you must not divert them from their path. What happens next will lead to the discovery of the key."

Her spine prickled. If there were any words to give her pause, then he'd just spoken them.

"Are you sure?"

They'd been searching for the key to the portal for centuries. Meanwhile Xadrak appeared and reappeared, switching from one plane to another. He had been reincarnated seven times since she'd killed Henri, and she'd had to slay him in four lives because his power had grown to corrupt the world.

And each time he'd died, he'd slipped back into the astral realm and committed more crimes there. Aurelia believed Elaine's hand was in the whole thing, floating there beyond Aurelia's begging for contact. At first she was hurt by it. Then she thought Elaine did it to punish her for causing her death. Then she stopped worrying.

Perhaps Sinara had come to the fore completely and obliterated Elaine's memories and cares. By then, Aurelia was committed to the path, and she honored her mother's memories by sticking to it, whether Sinara cared or not.

"Your brothers' actions at the Baroness's castle will lead to the discovery of the key. That is not in doubt."

"But for that to happen, I must allow them to rampage through Liesel's life?"

"How is that any different to letting them wreak havoc on the rest of the world?"

"My dear friend isn't involved."

He pursed his lips. "I know you have more compassion in you than that."

"Then you'd be wrong."

She stood and brushed down her dress, mending the rips as her hand smoothed over them.

"I'm going to her anyway."

"You do what you think is best. After all, I'm just the oracle." He lay back on the cushions, all smug nonchalance. The beauty of him at that moment struck her heart, but she huffed at him all the same.

"And what am I supposed to do about that thing outside? He said *you* told him I'd have need of him."

He laughed. "Maybe not need, but he will be useful, that I can tell you."

"You're not a very good oracle at times. I hope you know that."

"I see what I need to see. Seeing much more would spoil the fun."

She held her fingers to her temple, in mockery of his ability. She closed her eyes and intoned in her spookiest voice: "I see much rumbling and tumbling, a white hare and red fox will twist and turn—" She opened her eyes and looked down at him, "— and fuck each other senseless."

"Oh, Aurelia, you do have the best prophecies."

Aurelia stayed a little while longer, trying to tease out more of Hame's visions for the Baroness's future, and snapping at him when he could give no more. Eventually, she left, looking forward to slipping into a scalding-hot bath.

But Carn stood against a nearby tree, straightening when he saw her exit.

"You shouldn't have waited," she said. "I cannot help you."

"I know you can."

"Know this: power corrupts."

"You seem to have avoided that curse."

"You have no idea what I've had to do in this long life."

"Then show me. Because I'm not going away."

The drive was there, the deep desire that had ruined so many witches in their quest for deeper knowledge and greater power. She liked to think she hadn't been like that, but she couldn't make the lie stick. She still wanted more, even after four centuries, and above all she wanted the power to obliterate Xadrak once and for all.

She sighed. She was going to regret this; she felt it deep in her bones. If she let Carn in now, he'd never go away. But Hame had told her the witch was necessary, like so many other things he'd insisted were necessary and turned out to be so, and she couldn't spurn this boy just to spite him. The look of lust she'd seen on Carn's face earlier had beamed on Hame's too.

"Show me what you can do."

He flinched, the burning ambition in his eyes sputtering. "Really?"

"If I ask you to do something, I expect you to do it. If you can't follow simple instructions, then there's no point in proceeding."

She flowed around him.

"Okay, wait, stop, I'm sorry," he called, but she kept walking. If he let her walk away, then there was nothing to him. No grit. And to survive in this, that's what he'd need. He didn't call out again, but she detected a subtle waft of violets.

Unusual.

Witch magic usually carried the scent of oranges, or—in the case of the fallen ones—sulfur. This was something else, and it intrigued her. But she didn't stop. Readying her own power, she wanted to see what he'd do to keep her here. She couldn't yet be certain Carn wasn't in league with Xadrak, but would discover that truth later, even if it meant cracking open his soul.

An invisible wall erupted in front of her, strong enough to stop her, but with enough give that she didn't hurt herself. The wall crumbled from a small burst of her power, then for good measure and sport, she spun and released a larger stream of her magic at Carn. He levitated off the ground and she surrounded him with a prison that rendered his magic useless.

He struggled—she'd be worried if he didn't—and he scrambled to summon his own retaliation only to discover his meagre strength contained. But despite his defeat, she appreciated what he had achieved.

"Who taught you?" she asked.

"Blythe. He said he knew you."

Blythe had been one of the more powerful mortals she'd encountered, and he'd agreed to aid her quest. He kept an eye on those with power, to see whether they would turn to Xadrak.

"And did he say I'd teach you?"

"He said you'd probably do anything but."

A good answer. The *right* answer.

She lowered Carn to the ground and removed the forcefield. "If you know Blythe, then you know he is a good man and serves my cause. If I teach you, will you do the same?"

"He told me only a few details, but I offer my services to you and will be a loyal disciple."

The proviso was left unsaid, but she heard it anyway: *If you give me the power I seek.*

A shiver ran up her spine, but she shook away the chill it left behind. She longed for that hot bath.

"Fine. We start tomorrow. I will come to you." She didn't want him in her home, wary of revealing its location. She'd taken many precautions over the years to ensure it remained hidden.

"Thank you," he said, almost breathless, and bowed low.

She nodded to him and vanished.

Tomorrow would be a trial, but right now she needed soothing, scalding water.

III

While Carn talked with Aurelia, Hame slipped into a trance. He formed an image of the witch in his head, and quickly the vision's memory surfaced. This time he faded out the scenery and focused only on Carn. Once his image stabilized, he sought a new prophecy.

It didn't take long.

Carn's hands locked onto his arms. On one side he went cold; on the other he boiled. Warring sensations butted hard inside his body, fighting for dominance over his heart. The heat scorched him but brought deep satisfaction; the cold chilled his heart but enlivened him. He struggled within Carn's grip, and all the while the witch kept his stare neutral, pinning his arms to his sides, so he couldn't break free. He fought and he didn't, wanting to stay but wanting to go.

Carn shook him violently and the vision shredded.

He woke to the witch leaning over him, with a hand clutching his shoulder. Hame threw him off and backed away until his back hit the wall. It took a moment for him to realize he'd escaped and returned to his body. He leant his head back and breathed heavily.

"Are you all right?"

Snakes writhed down his back and constricted around the base of his spine. If Carn hadn't shaken him, how long would he have been trapped? The feel of warm, strong hands remained, so he rubbed where they'd been. Carn took a step closer, but he held up a hand to keep the witch back.

"I'm fine. Just a tough vision."

"Does that happen often?" Carn crouched.

"Not as bad as that." In fact, he struggled to remember having one like it before. Prophecies were tricky things. They often came as a simple knowing and other times a viewing like he watched actors on a stage. Very rarely did he get involved.

"What was it about?"

"Nothing to concern yourself with."

But if Hame wasn't mistaken, that *was* concern on Carn's face and he *hmm*ed but didn't press further. Nor did he go away, and Hame's body remembered the fight that had raged inside him. He had no doubt Carn brought trouble, but he also brought love. And that would be worth having.

"Do you have a place to stay?" Hame asked, hopeful Carn didn't.

"I thought I'd head back to the village and rent a room."

"You could stay here. It would make it easier for Aurelia to train you."

Carn paused for a moment, his gaze filling Hame with warmth. "I'd be very grateful."

The witch's intent flicked his lust. He would have

launched himself at Carn right then if not for the heavy weight in his stomach. Maybe with a little time it would lift.

IV

THE LONG BATH AURELIA HAD WHEN SHE RETURNED HOME
didn't soothe her. Even as the hot water numbed her
nerves, her thoughts jumped to Carn and Hame and whatever they may be doing. She didn't scry for them or
attempt to enter Hame's mind, having learned that lesson
long ago, and after enough time wasted, she turned to
something more productive—a search for her brothers.

Olivier tore into the neck of his victim. Blood spurted,
and she flinched as an icy fist gripped her heart. She
scrambled to find Liesel and only when the vision shifted to
show the Baroness many miles away, safe in her castle, did
that crushing hold relax.

Returning to her brother, she examined the scene
better, saw it was just some hapless woman who'd fallen
into Olivier's orbit. She sought Thierry, and found him
sitting in a room, alone, a book open in his left hand, his
right clawed and gouging into the wood of the table. His
jaw clamped tight enough to make the muscles throb.

One gorged, while the other starved. At least they
weren't with Liesel and Reiner.

Yet.

When she woke in the morning, her mood had not changed. She dreaded having to spend time with the blond witch, especially after what had no doubt been a fun night for him and Hame. The only thing that stopped her reneging on her agreement was Hame's insistence. She reasoned there had been many men before Carn, and there would be many men after. This was a fling, and it would end in due time.

That didn't stop her from hesitating to knock on Hame's door the next morning.

Carn opened it. "Good morning," he said brightly, blocking her entry. At least he was dressed.

She pursed her lips. "Answering Hame's door already, are you?"

He frowned. "He's still asleep."

"I thought you would be, too."

"I grew up on a farm. Up with the sun."

"Well," she said, her voice clipped, "if you're ready, we should start."

"I'm at your command." And he shepherded her outside, closing the door behind him, despite her straining to see within.

She marched away from Hame's home and led Carn through the forest. She didn't really want to do this with him, especially when he would no doubt prefer to tangle with Hame.

She marched into the middle of a clearing: a flat space of grass surrounded by a ring of trees. There were many such places around, pinpoints of higher magic that kept them from being overrun. She erected a shield that sent out waves of unease for anyone who wandered too close.

"Oranges," Carn whispered. "You smell of them, like Blythe did. My magic smells of—"

"Violets," she interjected. "You smell of violets."

"Is that normal?"

"I'm not sure what it means. I've never encountered it before."

While Carn mulled over the question of scent, she took advantage of his engaged concentration and pressed her hand against his chest. Her power surged into him, and he arched back and opened. She rummaged for any taint from Xadrak, delving into his core. She brushed aside his infatuation with Hame, his hunger for power, latching on to anything that might indicate he had been corrupted. Disappointed, she retreated with as much abruptness as she had used going in.

He fell forward gasping for breath. "What was that?"

"I had to check something."

"What? My spleen? Do you have any idea how that feels?"

"Some."

"Damn." He righted himself and massaged the center of his chest. "A little warning would have been helpful."

"You might not have let me in."

"Could you blame me?"

"I might have thought you had something to hide."

"And now you know all my secrets, is that it? I'd call that a violation."

He had no idea what violation really was.

"Your innermost thoughts do not hold my interest. I found strong emotions—none of which are hidden from your face and your eyes—and you lack the taint of evil. You do not have to stand there so indignant."

"You have no right—"

She reared up to him, levitating off the ground so she could peer down at him.

"I have every right. You want me to teach you? Then

you are mine to do with as I wish. This is not playtime for little girls. Magic is power, and in this world that is the only thing that matters. I teach you so you will aid *my* cause. I care not what you want from this. I care not whether you think I am unfair or a raging bitch who needs to be brought to heel. I am four hundred years old, and my authority in this world will not be questioned. If you seek to do so, I will turn you away. Is that clear?"

A drum beat inside her chest, threatening to break through and crush the witch beneath its force. She held his stare, seeing his pride stand up to her, but if he wanted what she had to give, he would concede. She didn't have time for a pissing contest.

He bowed his head and stepped back. "I hope you found what you were looking for."

She wished she hadn't felt his desire for Hame, but she admired his humility at this moment. The boy was smart, and he sounded convincing. That would have to do.

She returned to the ground. "You are clean of corruption. That stands you in good stead. Now, show me what you have learned."

He didn't smile, his cheeks drawn in and jaw set. She could see Hame's attraction—the sharp lines, the strong brow and jaw. Even now, as he sulked, something about him tickled her desire. She squashed it, would not entertain it, because being in love with Hame was enough torture. She bit back a sigh and called herself a fool.

Carn summoned a ball of energy, a purple glow to match the violet scent. His brow creased as he enlarged it from the size of an apple to cover his entire hand and then some. Once it grew as large as his head, tendrils snaked out, becoming longer and wider, until they wrapped around him and locked together. A purple shield concealed him, and once fashioned in place, turned invisible. She came forward, brushed her hand over its surface, and felt its energy tingle beneath her touch. If she'd come at him with ill intent, she would have had quite a shock. He had built his defenses well

Carn's face beamed red.

"Breathe."

Air burst out of his mouth. The shield wavered and shattered, and the energy dissipated. His brow glistened. He had skill but not enough power. If he remained this weak, he'd never travel the way she did. If attacked, he'd have enough to protect himself from one strike but not a second, and weakness would eventually sour him. She had been lucky to be born of two demon spirits, their powers so great that they imbued her with a sizeable amount of their magic. She knew not where other witches gained their power, or why so little of it. Perhaps if they had more, Xadrak would not have so many willing to join his faction.

"You did well. Tell me what else you're able to do. Another demonstration of power might well knock you unconscious."

I sound like my mother.

She'd meant it as a compliment, but his eyes narrowed briefly. She disregarded his affronted honor. The sooner he came to terms with her methods and way of speaking, the happier he'd be.

She created a chair out of air for her to sit on, and in a moment of compassion, she did the same for him, coloring it a little so he knew where to sit. Did she see envy in his eyes? They were such simple tricks to her now, requiring a small charge, that she'd forgotten that in the beginning she had sweated and strained as much as he had. Guilt tugged at her.

Carn sat and told her what he could do—summoning energy, as she had seen, and manipulating it in various ways. He had an affinity for shields, though his lack of strength meant he couldn't sustain them for long. The one she'd seen yesterday had shattered at her touch, but she hadn't yet encountered a shield she couldn't break. He didn't talk much about offensive magic, but once she prompted him, he admitted to being able to control the lightning fire but only in short bursts. Though he meditated, he could not scry, nor could he travel or reach into the astral.

She wasn't prepared to give him access to additional power yet, but she could help him make full use of what he already possessed. He had good concentration, but he needed more than that. He needed effortless focus. He didn't need to *push* his mind, merely direct it. And from there she could teach him other mind tricks, and maybe unlock his ability to scry and send his consciousness out on the astral. His shields were good but, with an added mental acuity, he'd make them stronger, maintain them, and still keep breathing. For all her misgivings about teaching—especially teaching him—she nurtured a small piece of joy inside her at the prospect.

She was about to start their first lesson when Hame's mind knocked at hers. She let him in.

I've found Xadrak.

V

"Stay!" Aurelia slammed the door in Carn's face, and he barely avoided running into it.

Their lesson had been cut short, but when Aurelia said Hame needed her, Carn couldn't stay cross.

What riled him was being locked outside.

On the surface, Hame didn't look as if he needed comforting or protection. His size and wild red hair made him appear more warrior than seer, and yet vulnerability shimmered in his kind eyes and welcoming smile.

Carn had been prepared to do whatever it took to get Aurelia to teach him—including seducing her—but he hadn't expected to fall for the oracle.

Before they'd spoken, he had spied on Hame chopping wood, thinking he'd stumbled upon the oracle's helper. The way he swung his axe, making the muscles along his sweat-slick back ripple, stoked his desire, and he'd ached for a quick fuck.

But learning who Hame was brought on a seismic shift within him, and his plans collapsed. He could no more seduce Aurelia now than cut off his arm. One look from Hame bound him.

Which made last night so maddening.

His balls tightened thinking how much he wanted to feel Hame's body against his own. He knew Hame wanted him too, but he'd kept a wall between them. Last night they'd talked instead, and he couldn't deny the pleasure in its simplicity. They'd fallen into an easy companionship he hadn't even had with his brothers.

Being *different* in more ways than one had made him wary—not that he was a coward. His knuckles had turned purple more times than he cared to remember, but he'd always been closed off from others. Not even the willing baker's boy had been able to get near. He'd accepted he would always be apart and alone.

Until Hame.

The door burst open and Aurelia marched over to him. "I have to leave. While I'm gone, practice this."

She rattled off a quick description of the task, which wasn't a task in itself. It was an end result, and she didn't give him the tools to work it out. He fumbled over his words, trying to get more information, but she vanished before he made one complete, coherent sound. Her disappearance stunned him, and envy twisted in his gut.

One day...

Hame laughed at him from the doorway. "You've got the same look on your face I had when my master taught me."

The oracle leaned with his arms crossed over his chest.

"Are you all right? It sounded serious."

"I'm fine. Just a troubling message." Hame's smile faded. An expectant silence grew between them. What he wouldn't do to fill it with Hame's moans.

"I'd better—"

"You should—"

They talked over each other, then laughed at the silliness of it.

"I'd better get on with Aurelia's task."

Hame lifted his chin, then turned inside. He left the door open, a welcome sign.

Denying the need within him to follow the oracle and claim what he desired, Carn walked away to where he could avoid distraction. He'd come here for a purpose, and once he'd achieved it, perhaps then he'd consider himself worthy of sharing Hame's bed.

VI

Aurelia peered through the window at the clockmaker hunched over his workbench. There weren't many clockmakers in Salzburg, and Hame's description of the white-haired, spindly man in his late twenties was good enough that it hadn't been hard to find Georg, Xadrak's current human persona.

The clockmaker's shop stood out among its neighbors. Their storefronts were impeccable, their paint bright and shiny with the wealth they aimed to attract. Schwarz & Sohn did not bother with such finery. Smears and streaks on the window blurred much of Aurelia's view of the inside, while the faded paintwork on the outside belied the beautiful work within. A variety of clocks lined the shelves and while she had expected them to be poor things, they were anything but. The workmanship in each shone, from their housing to their faces, and no doubt their internal mechanics too shared in the same glory. Whatever else Georg may be, he was a master clockmaker.

At first that seemed unusual for one of Xadrak's incarnations, but when she considered who he'd been in previous lives, he'd always excelled in whatever he'd done. Henri had been a master butcher, William a master swordsman, and Rodrigo a master shipbuilder. Violent men, all of them, but they had been highly skilled. Yet, Georg's mousey appearance was so at odds with what she knew of Xadrak.

She left him to his work and decided to ask others about him. She didn't expect to hear much truth from the neighbors' gossip, yet his outward showing unsettled her enough that she wanted a broader understanding before venturing further.

The dressmaker laughed when Aurelia remarked how involved he was with his work. "Why, I'm sure he doesn't sleep most nights, just continues working on his clocks," she said. "He'll probably discover a way to make time stand still."

"He looks a little mad," Aurelia said.

"That's Georg's way. A more sweet and gentle fool you'll never meet." The dressmaker's dimples deepened.

The jeweler was less kind, but only because his clock hadn't yet been fixed. "He's always tinkering on something, but you try giving him a bit of paid work and he'll take years. Years!"

"Then why not use another clockmaker?"

"Because Georg is so *good*. He might take his time, but his clocks run perfectly."

Either they told the truth and Georg was nothing more than a harmless clockmaker, or he hid behind an elaborate mask. She had no choice but to talk to him directly.

When she entered the shop, he didn't look up from his work. His hands wielded the tools with precision as he tinkered in the back of a clock. Xadrak had never been adept at fine, detailed work, as it required too much patience. Yet watching Georg operate, she stared for a long time at the craftsmanship and his attention to small screws and gears. She fell into the beauty of his work, and for a second she wondered if Xadrak was capable of some good.

She jerked back from the thought, as if someone had yanked her hair. There was nothing good in Xadrak, and to think otherwise was abhorrent.

Her sudden movement didn't disturb Georg. Still he worked. The clocks drew her eye. They were in excellent condition, even more impressive now she didn't have to peer through the window's fog. Beautiful decorations embellished many of them: a golden stag on one, two delicately painted figurines, one of a boy and one of a girl, on another. Some seemed too rich to stay hidden away here and should have been in a palace. But gradually her attention turned from what she saw to what she heard.

The clocks ticked in unison.

With so many pendulums swinging and cogs turning, she had expected a cacophony of clicks to fill the room. But there was only one sound. Every clock kept the same time, and the sound of it passed in one loud *tick-tock*. The hairs on the back of her neck bristled.

Was this Xadrak's magic at work? It wasn't an important trick, but it could be a sign of leaking power. She needed to see his eyes, then she might have a better understanding.

With her will held taut and ready, she coughed. The noise brought his nose part way up, but his eyes remained downcast.

"Mmmmm?" His hands continued manipulating the tools.

"I would like to buy a clock, please," she said, for want of anything better to say.

"I have none for sale." His head lowered into the back of the clock once more.

"Then what about all these on the walls?"

But he didn't hear her.

She released a sliver of energy to slow the swing of one clock, speed it up on another, until the single sound of time syncopated. Georg's head flicked up and his gaze darted to the offending clocks. He jumped off his chair and carried them one by one to his workbench, deftly maneuvering around her.

"Excuse me!" she barked.

"Yes? What is it?"

His brown eyes met hers. She held him with the force of her will and searched.

"Nothing," she whispered.

When she had confronted Xadrak in the past, there was some sign of his presence, but in Georg there was none. Just a man obsessed with clocks. Had Hame gotten it wrong?

She released him.

"Then if you want nothing, I must get back to work."

He started to reset the clocks with his head cocked slightly to listen to the sound of the others. She'd been dismissed, but she'd seen all she was likely to. What she'd seen, however, she couldn't be sure. Either Hame was wrong, or Xadrak had also become a master of concealment.

VII

Two stones circled in the air around Carn. He called them stones, but they were barely more than rubble, as small a weight as he could find. The third *stone*, however, would not stay up. Aurelia wanted him to levitate three objects and have them fly around him. Initially he'd expected something trickier, so he'd begun with confidence.

He'd made one pebble spin around him with ease. He'd changed its trajectory, its speed, its direction, and it did what he commanded. He'd scoffed at the simplicity of the task ahead and wondered if he'd made a mistake seeking Aurelia as his teacher.

Then he'd started work on the second. He'd levitated it while still controlling the first, and it took flight. It had shaken at first, but eventually he'd smoothed out its journey, and he'd managed to keep track of the two pebbles in his mind. He'd cheated. He knew he'd cheated. He kept them close enough together that for the most part he saw them at the same time. When they went behind his head, he exerted more will to speed them back into his line of sight. This was not what Aurelia had in mind, but it was a start.

But when he'd tried to levitate the third, his mind floundered. He couldn't maintain focus on three objects at once. Attempt after attempt brought nothing but frustration, and his throat started to ache from holding back a stream of curses. He didn't want Hame to hear how badly he took his failure.

He fell back on the grass. The skin around his temples stretched as tight as a drum. He closed his eyes and massaged the sides of his brow.

"Giving up already?"

Aurelia's voice hooked him into sitting up as she stalked past him. Her tone wasn't as frigid as it had been earlier in the day, but still she mocked him. He started to argue, but she entered Hame's house and slammed the door. He couldn't understand why Hame tolerated her. Some mysteries defied explanation.

Fighting weariness, he returned to his practice.

One pebble at a time.

"How do you expect me to concentrate with you stomping around like an elephant with a sore head?"

Aurelia stopped. "I am not an elephant."

She released the ends of her hair with a flick and sat on the cushions in front of Hame while he investigated the latest Xadrak prophecy. She'd recounted her experiences with Georg, Hame bristling at her insinuation he'd gotten it wrong. She hadn't meant to sound accusatory but seeing Carn outside had the effect of turning her into a razor. At least she hadn't returned to find the two of them in bed. Or each other.

Now that she was still, Hame's breathing slowed. Having watched him work more times than she could count, she knew the moment his mind traveled elsewhere. His cheeks relaxed and lowered slightly, and a bump in his jaw smoothed out. They were subtle indications to others, but obvious to her who'd spent many years watching.

Minutes passed and the process reversed. He returned to his body, the few points of tension coming back, and his eyes opened.

"Nothing has changed. Xadrak is inside Georg."

"Then why couldn't I see anything?"

"Perhaps he's dormant."

"But why show you now?"

"Probably because he's going to wake soon."

That prospect thrilled her even less than learning Xadrak had returned. It meant a battle at worst, babysitting at best. At least she'd had nearly thirty years without having to watch him.

"Any idea when?"

"If I knew, I'd tell you."

She twirled the ends of her hair again, considering what she should do next. She could kill Georg now, return him to the astral where Sinara could deal with him. But if Xadrak didn't come to the fore for some time, then it would be safer to keep him here. Could she lock him up? She'd done it before and hired a jailer to keep him fed and watered.

"I do have some other news for you though, but you're not going to like it."

She tightened the hold on her hair, and her scalp sang.

"Your brothers will arrive at Neulehn in two days."

Her heart dipped.

Liesel.

"You don't have to go. You could leave them be."

But she couldn't. Whatever her brothers were yet to do, she at least wanted to give her friend some protection, however futile.

Chains lashed themselves to her wrists, dragging her down and weighting her to the Earth. She'd known becoming friends with Liesel would end in sorrow. Her friend aged while she remained, yet she couldn't stop herself, no more than she could stop loving Hame.

"I'll go tomorrow." She needed some light before the darkness descended.

"And what of Carn?"

"What of him?" Her response came quick and barbed. With Xadrak and Liesel on her mind, the last thing she needed to be reminded of was Hame's plaything.

"Don't be obtuse, Aurelia. The boy is out there, desperate to learn, and you've had him playing with rocks for the better part of the day."

"Rocks can be very educational, and they make great playmates. I have never seen a fiercer battle of wits."

"You're a bit old for jealousy, dearest."

"And you're a bit old for him, so spare me the affronted looks. Besides, I don't have time for this."

"He wants to learn, and he could be useful. Don't let your jealousy get in the way."

She wasn't jealous. He and Carn could do whatever the hell they pleased. She had more important things to do than tutor a fledgling witch, especially one who would rather fuck the oracle than master a simple trick.

"If anything will get in the way, it's you. The boy wants you more than he wants to study."

"He can have both, and that's why you're so upset."

"So, I'm supposed to wait until you've finished with him so I can give him his lessons, is that it?"

"He will follow wherever you lead. I will not stand in

his way, but I won't put up with obstacles to having him in my bed."

She opened her mouth to scold, but he spoke first. "Understand me, dear heart, I will not let this one go."

Hame saw through her, to that which even she tried to hide. The past four centuries had been bearable because of Hame's companionship and his love. Now Carn threatened that. If he took Hame from her, what would she have left? She knew she should retreat, that pushing Hame too far would push him away entirely. Hame could love who and how he wished, but her envy of his freedom to love another and have that love returned wanted to deny him that. She should have apologized. She should have taken a moment to collect her thoughts. But there were a lot of things she should have done in this long life.

"Do whatever you like with him, but he's not my concern."

She vanished, the anger propelling her home.

VIII

After a restless night's sleep, Aurelia awoke feeling drained and despondent. The mountain had never felt so empty—just her, the furniture and her mother's coffin. She made a move to enter Elaine's crypt, but shame kept her back. She should not have allowed Carn to get to her. What she and Hame had was special, as strong as it could be. A stronger bond than lovers.

Or so she had thought.

Now it seemed to crumble when she applied the slightest pressure. Didn't she deserve all his love, as he had hers?

Curse him.

She dressed in a pale green muslin gown, cinched at the waist with an emerald satin sash, suitable clothes for visiting Liesel. She brushed and fashioned her hair into a bouffant, its blackness entirely out of vogue, but she'd be damned if she'd wear a wig. Around her neck she hung a jewel-encrusted necklace. She powdered her face, rouged her cheeks, painted her eyes, and embellished her lips.

Once complete, she looked in the mirror and groaned at the need for all of this.

"But it'll be worth it," she said in an attempt to convince herself.

She packed her luggage, filling it with clothes and jewels. She couldn't deny that staying at Liesel's castle was a chore, requiring planning and a significant expenditure of energy. She couldn't simply appear in the hall; she needed to arrive by coach, and one befitting the Marquise de Villiers.

She'd adopted a French title some years before, when she'd first met the Baroness while circling her nephew, Reiner. His parents were altogether too dull, but thankfully he spent a lot of time with his aunt. Despite the rivalries between their two countries, the Baroness had not been put off by the Marquise's foreignness. And Aurelia had not expected to like her quite so much.

Liesel had a vivaciousness that attracted Aurelia like a bear to honey. The Baroness delighted in parties, for new things and discoveries, and for making friends. Liesel's infectious personality revitalized Aurelia. And when Hame could not provide her with what she wanted, she sought solace in Liesel's love.

Liesel knew about Hame, or rather the gist, and joked and consoled in equal measure about Aurelia's redheaded paramour and his denial of love. Liesel understood the reasons behind his evasiveness, which was perhaps why, despite all the preparation and the binding clothes and the subterfuge, when she was finally ready to depart, the weight on her shoulders lifted a little. She stood before the mirror in all her majesty. She had time before her brothers arrived, and she was going to enjoy herself.

Vanishing with her luggage, she reappeared in a carriage fashioned from magic on the road leading to the castle. Pulled by four black horses, a coach driver steered them from above. All were nothing but phantoms.

The road cut through a thick forest and wound into its center where the Baron and Baroness entertained during the summer. Aurelia had attended many of their parties over the years and the approach filled her with a heady excitement.

Her arrival set off a flurry of activity, servants bustling hither and thither to unload her luggage. She cast a spell over their minds to hide the sudden absence of the coach and its attendant once she left them, and a glamor that would make her appear as old as the person she spoke to expected her to be. She then ascended the few steps into the hall. The openness of it, with its grand staircase and richly decorated interior, lifted her mood, but when the Baroness entered with arms outstretched joy swelled in her soul.

"My dear, I'm so pleased you've come." The Baroness was in her fifties, slightly rotund with a great bosom that bounced when she laughed, but oh, the warmth that came from her. Aurelia craved it like a drug. She took the Baroness's arms, pulled her close, and kissed her lips.

"You have no idea how good it is to be here," she said, near breathless with the depth of meaning behind her words.

"No servants again, I see."

"You know how I prefer to travel without them. I hope it won't be too much of an imposition."

"Is it ever?" She laughed, hooked Aurelia's arm in hers, and led her towards the parlor. "Now, tell me, how goes the hunt for your red rabbit?"

IX

CARN DIDN'T SEE AURELIA LEAVE BUT HE ASSUMED HER departure was the cause of Hame's despondency. They made a fine pair that evening, what with his frustration at being unable to master Aurelia's lesson, and Hame's brooding. They slept apart again, which suited him fine. He didn't want to fuck angry, not the first time.

The next morning, he rose early and slipped outside to practice. The forest glowed with the light of the early sun. Having grown up on a farm, being surrounded by so many trees struck him as odd. He preferred to look across fields to hills far in the distance, whereas here trees fenced him in. But there was little to be done about it, so he settled against a trunk, facing away from the cottage.

Scooping up three stones, he rested them in the palm of his hand, attempting to levitate them one by one. The trials of yesterday and expectations of similar failure today knotted his shoulders and the muscles in his neck until they became as rigid as the bark rasping against his skin.

Soon he stopped trying to make the rocks circle, and

instead took to levitating whatever he could lay his mind on and fire it into the sky through breaks in the trees. Each object soared with the force of his anger. The upside of this little trick was that his strength grew. The weakness he'd suffered before had largely been pushed aside. It was still there, and he'd pay for it later, but he lost himself in this display of petty power.

Another pebble zoomed off into the sky.

"Anger is coming off you in waves, Carn."

He scrambled to his feet as Hame walked between the trees. "How long have you been watching?"

"Not long. Had some work of my own to do."

Carn bit his tongue. He wanted to ask whether he had seen him master Aurelia's test, but to do so would reveal his desperation and his shaken confidence.

"Sorry, I had no visions about you." Hame smiled.

"I wasn't—"

He waved his hand. "Don't be disheartened. We all have to start somewhere."

But before coming here he had believed he was already advanced, and that meeting Aurelia would bring him greater power. Instead she'd shown him how far beneath her he was. Blythe had been impressed with his abilities, particularly when it came to shields, but now he suspected he'd been indulged.

"Let's go for a walk," the oracle said. "We could both use a break."

They walked, the crunching of leaves and gravel beneath their feet the only sounds they made. Around them the forest kept up a hum of noise from the birds to the breeze and the faint rushing of a stream. After some distance, his frustrations at being unable to master the three stones eased and, in their place, settled frustrations of a different sort. His skin buzzed being this close to Hame, and suddenly he needed to fill the silence with talking or he'd fill it with something else.

"How long have you been an oracle?"

"A long time."

"You don't look old enough." In fact, everything about Hame seemed youthful—his smile, his body, even his demeanor. It couldn't be easy being an oracle and seeing the things he must see. "I'd say you have barely more than a score of years."

"I haven't been that young for a very long time."

"How old then?"

Hame halted. "I'm four hundred years old."

He choked. "Really?"

"Give or take a couple of decades."

"Magic?"

"What else?" Hame looked away, suddenly becoming more interested in the leaves than in their conversation.

"You and Aurelia are the same age."

Hame nodded, then started walking again. Carn followed after a few steps. He ground his teeth to wear away the jealousy crystallizing within him. No wonder Hame and Aurelia were so close; they'd had an eternity together. He couldn't compete with that.

He thought about what he would do with a life as long as theirs, of the abilities he could master, and the strength he could gain. One lifetime had always seemed insufficient, and now he knew he didn't have to settle for just one. What would it be like sharing those lives with Hame? The oracle walked with his head down. Knowing his true age did nothing to dampen Carn's desire for him. If anything, it burned stronger.

"You must have seen a lot."

"Sometimes I think I've seen enough to last me until the end of time."

The sad tone in Hame's voice made Carn itch to take the oracle's hand. "Have there been many horrors?"

"Too many to count. But that's humanity."

It seemed too cruel that this man should be forced to witness the worst of people. Carn wanted to protect him. "Can you ever not see?"

"If it must be seen, it finds a way in. Don't let it worry you, Carn. This is my purpose."

"It's unfair."

Hame laughed. They kept walking along a barely worn path. Carn didn't know where they were, but Hame seemed sure. He wondered how long the oracle had been here, and then thought it didn't matter. He probably knew much more than Carn would ever know. But that got him thinking.

"How much about me do you really know?"

He chuckled. "I get a lot of seekers concerned with how far into their lives I can see. Thankfully, I don't see it all."

"But with me? You know I have five brothers. You know the village I come from. What else?"

He thought Hame hesitated, a flick of his tongue over his bottom lip. "Apart from you being a witch, nothing really."

"And my future?"

"Unwritten, for the most part."

"And the part that is written?"

He stopped. Hame laughed again, only this time it sounded like stalling. "Do you really want to know?"

A fist squeezed his heart. "Yes."

Hame scrutinized him, while carving his fingers

through his hair. He spoke once his hand left his head. "You walk a path between good and evil, and one day you will have to make a choice."

"That's it? Hardly seems difficult."

Hame smiled and shook his head.

"Did I say something funny?"

The oracle looked at him from beneath hooded lids, a look that turned his rancor to hot desire. "How do you ever know that the choices you make are the right ones? They're just choices, often with unforeseen consequences."

He took a step closer. "But that's why you're here." His voice came out in a throaty whisper. "To see the unseen."

Hame's lips parted, like they were gates opening to welcome a returning conqueror. Carn surged forward, claiming his warm mouth. He moaned, desperate for more as his tongue darted in. His fingers coursed through fiery red hair and his palm cupped the back of his head. Hame pushed him against a tree, his body a crushing weight grinding against him. It had been so long since he'd tasted another man inside his mouth, feeling another's hungry need rub against his own.

To hell with waiting.

His cock stood firm between them, the friction bringing both pleasure and pain. He wanted the oracle, wanted to take him there on the ground. He wanted to fuck away the past, forget there were centuries between them, and that Hame was a powerful oracle while he was nothing more than a fledgling witch who'd likely never rival Aurelia in her strength.

But he had to stop.

His body screamed to feel naked flesh, but reason cut through the roar. His hands braced against strong shoulders, and he pushed him away, turning his mouth so Hame couldn't kiss him. It hurt, every inch of him wanting to keep going until he lay sweaty and spent in the dirt with the oracle resting in his arms.

Hame resisted at first, but then stepped back. He couldn't have felt further away if a wide and bottomless chasm ruptured the earth between them.

"I'm sorry," Hame said. "I thought…I misunderstood." He spun to leave.

Carn grabbed Hame's tensed bicep. "No, it's not that. I want to. *God*, do I want to. But I made a promise I wouldn't until I'd achieved what I set out to do."

Hame frowned at him, a disbelieving breath stuttering out of his mouth. "You know I don't care how powerful you are, don't you?"

He shrugged. "I'd like to believe it, but truly, what you think doesn't matter. This is something I have to do for myself."

"I see," Hame said, in a way that meant he didn't.

"I bet you were born with your abilities already in place." He couldn't possibly know the chest-sucking unworthiness.

Hame snorted and shook his head. "You sound like me back then. How Loic put up with me, I don't know. Come on, let's go home." He turned and walked back the way they came.

Resentment brewed within him, but he didn't want to be left behind. "Who was Loic?"

Eventually Hame told him the story of his master and how terrible a student he had been. He laughed throughout, but it was obvious the memories stung. That failure—knowing from the beginning you weren't good enough—never really went away. Loic died before Aurelia helped Hame unlock his abilities.

"What you should know," Hame said, "is that in the end it doesn't matter. Sharing a deep connection with someone, that's what's important. So even if you never master any of it, it wouldn't matter to me."

"I know. But it doesn't change the fact that it's something I want. You never gave up. Why should I?"

X

THE SUN HAD SET BY THE TIME AURELIA HAD LIESEL TO herself again. Their brief meeting when she arrived had quickly been swamped with others vying for their host's attention. The Baroness could not refuse, so she endured endless gossip about people whom she had never heard of. If Aurelia had been alone with her friend, it would have been a treat, but with these women…

Before long, her cheeks ached from holding a rigid smile. Only when Liesel caught her eye and encouraged her with a knowing wink did it ease into something real. Her friend knew how little she cared for these gatherings. Although she thought her a little strange for it, they nevertheless had a good chat when they later retired alone to Liesel's rooms.

"I do not understand how you can listen to that drivel." Aurelia collapsed into a chair.

Liesel laughed and sat with more decorum. "It's not as bad as all that."

"But it's all so trivial."

"What you see as trivial, I see as essential. Without

these small details of life, we would be swept away with terrible talk of a world gone mad. Hearing Christine talk tonight—please don't roll your eyes—I'm taken back to my younger days when life was fun and easy. You're still too young. Wait until you're my age."

Sorrow swamped her exasperation. She'd lived so long already and would continue to do so well after the Baroness had passed away, and yet Liesel had lived to the full, while she had hidden herself away. Her experiences were not those of a normal life, her journey wholly removed from her friend's, and yet the younger woman seemed wiser.

"Oh, my dear, I didn't mean to upset you. Are you thinking about your beloved again? There is little joy in loving one who does not return your favor."

She failed at a smile. While she hadn't been thinking about Hame, nevertheless he was always there, a part of everything she did.

"I know he cannot love me the way I would like, and I have accepted that."

Liesel hummed a laugh, which made Aurelia blush. "Whatever you say, my dear. But perhaps some other distractions might help."

"Being here is distraction enough."

"I am glad you feel that way, especially as I have two special guests arriving soon."

Her heart froze inside her throat. She had to cough to get her voice working again. "Oh yes? Who are they?"

"A most beautiful set of twins, young men I met in Dresden. Oh, they are young but such fun; well, one of them is. The other is more introspective, but their eyes. I don't mind telling you there is something totally *enthralling* about their eyes. I look into them and feel things I haven't felt for years. If ever." The Baroness giggled like a girl a quarter her age, but Aurelia couldn't muster the same levity.

"I see you don't approve."

"It's not—"

Liesel waved away her attempt at explanation. "I know it's not seemly, but you wait until you meet them and see how demure you can be."

The Baroness laughed, and the sound thawed Aurelia's fear enough to allow her to titter as well. At that moment the two of them could have been ordinary women talking about ordinary men. She tried to hold that feeling for as long as possible, but as the hours wore on and she eventually left Liesel to go to bed, her brothers' approach filled her soul with dread.

XI

Carn fired another pebble into the darkening sky. Though his skill at doing this had improved immensely, jettisoning the little missiles only made his frustration worse. He'd abandoned trying to complete the original task hours ago and grown weary of waiting for Her Holiness to return.

The vice that crushed his balls every time he looked in Hame's direction did nothing for his concentration either. As if the thought summoned him, the door to the house opened and out Hame stepped, watching him.

"I'd prefer it if you didn't look at me like I'm some helpless duckling," he growled. His belly twisted, but the words had already escaped. It wasn't Hame's fault he was useless.

Hame sighed, taking a seat on the grass opposite him. "She's going to flay me for telling you this, but the trick is to treat them as one. Levitate them, project out your power in one wave that affects *all* of them, and then set the power to the task, not the stones."

Iron sluiced through his veins, and his tongue thickened. He didn't want help. The tone in the oracle's voice made him feel every bit the dullard Hame obviously presumed him to be. He'd never want him now.

Hame tutted. "You're as stubborn as Aurelia. Instead of glaring at me like some teacher who's whipped you, why don't you humor me and give it a try?"

Carn didn't speak. Being compared to Aurelia was bad enough, but now he had shamed himself in front of Hame. It would be better if the oracle left.

"I'm waiting."

———

HAME COULD THROTTLE AURELIA. SHE SHOULD BE HERE doing this. Then he could berate her for running off the way she had. But she continued to ignore his summons. They had never gone more than a day without contact between them, but now she'd frozen him out, and his neck ached thinking about it.

Meanwhile Carn's black mood heated his blood. His tongue pressed hard against the roof of his mouth to curb his impatience. Children and their tantrums did not endear him in the slightest, especially considering the horrors he had to witness on a near-daily basis. But Heaven curse him, he wanted to help this one.

Just when he thought Carn was going to wait him out, he broke his stillness, shuffling his shoulders so he looked human again. He kept the scowl.

He levitated one stone, then the second, and finally the third. Grouped together, Carn kept them steady. He sent them out, slowly, one after the other to circle around him. But as soon as the third started to move, the other two dropped.

Carn snorted like a ram ready to butt heads.

"Don't get angry. Concentrate." He would be damned if he allowed Carn to give up on this. "Remember what I said. Set the power to the task."

Carn pierced him with a thorny glare, but he smoothed his face.

"Try again."

The stones levitated.

"The power affects them all as one, not as individuals. Feel it push out from you so that whatever it touches moves as the power wishes it to move."

One stone moved, then the second. The third began to shakily follow the others. The first two dipped a little, but Carn saved them. He ground his teeth together so hard he was in danger of cracking them.

"Close your eyes."

Carn refused.

Air rushed out of his nostrils. He repeated the order in a flat voice. "Don't see them; sense them."

Carn glowered at him, but Hame wasn't going anywhere. This was about more than Carn mastering some trick; this was about proving to Aurelia he was right.

And reaping the reward of Carn's gratitude.

Carn's eyelids closed and his body relaxed. The stones moved smoother than before, using awareness instead of force.

He's getting it.

And with his and Aurelia's guidance, he would be a staunch ally.

If Hame kept him on the right path.

"Carn, look."

XII

AURELIA EXPECTED STORM CLOUDS TO GATHER ON THE horizon, heralding the arrival of her brothers into this secluded enclave in the forest. Her jaw ached from clenching. She listened for any disturbance in the hall announcing their presence. She clung to Liesel, going wherever she went throughout the day, holding her hand whenever they sat. Yet for all her closeness, her mind darted elsewhere.

"You are distracted, my dear," Liesel said for the third time that day, patting her hand.

The gentle tapping brought her attention back into the parlor. "I'm sorry. I'm not sure where my head is at." She pressed Liesel's hand gently, just to feel her warmth. Too much of her life happened in the ephemeral, others passing away like wind dancing across a field, buffeting the grass but leaving it unharmed.

A servant appeared and informed Liesel of her new arrivals.

Liesel squeezed her hand. "Oh, they are here." She bounded up to meet the twins.

Aurelia remained seated, while the others in their little group filtered away, giving her polite but unfriendly nods. She didn't care. Olivier was about to invade her friend's home.

They've come sooner than I expected.

She forced herself to breathe as panic clawed her spine. Hame had said they would set in action a chain of events that led to the key's discovery, but she couldn't stand idle. She'd warn Olivier away from the Baroness and hope his own sense of self-preservation kept him from harming her, at least directly. It grated to know that so much depended on him, that for all his evil, for all his wickedness, he was their savior.

Well, him and Thierry.

She clung to the one consolation that the process assured Olivier's obliteration.

She rose from her seat, smoothed her dress and walked to the doorway, her sure and certain footsteps belying none of the tremor in her breast. Olivier and the Baroness, engaged in chatter, ascended the stairs.

Her nails sliced into her palms.

Calm yourself. He won't do anything so soon.

The Baroness was too low a target. She had no subterfuge, no airs. Olivier preferred a challenge. He went for the biggest, the meanest, the highest. Thankfully so far no one here fit that description.

With Olivier gone, she watched Thierry as he looked around the hall. Her beautiful brother with hair the same coal black as hers, and his hard, unsmiling eyes. He exuded a stone's geniality now, but she remembered the better times, the few there were. It had been many years since they'd been close, but this acquaintance from afar stirred up old gratitude of when she was a little girl and he'd protected her from Olivier.

184

If only she had protected Thierry from his twin, then he would have died long ago, perhaps in Etienne's arms. But then they'd have no hope of banishing Xadrak.

With a veneer of serenity in place, she emerged from the parlor and crossed the floor as Thierry turned to exit. She touched his shoulder.

Startled recognition danced across his eyes. "What are —?"

"Allow me to introduce myself. I am the Marquise de Villiers." She held out a gloved hand for him to kiss.

"Ahhh…my name is Tomas." His eyes narrowed.

They left the castle and stepped into the garden. Once alone, they dropped the facade but along with it went the civility, and they argued about what they usually argued about: Olivier.

Thierry couldn't give her the assurances she hoped for, and she knew she could not jeopardize the key's discovery. The best she could do was to preserve what she could. Before long, Olivier joined them, and his presence reminded her that she would follow fate and fulfil the promises made to her mother.

The key must be found, her brothers sacrificed, and Xadrak banished and slain.

As Olivier took her hand and gave her his jackal-smile, she easily saw the good that would come from his demise.

And now the players in their little drama had arrived, she could do little else but watch, wait, and mop up the blood.

XIII

IT WORKED. PRAISE THE GODS, IT WORKED.

Carn laughed and rocked on his ass as the three stones floated around him at perfect intervals without wavering. His happiness increased his energy and banished the heaviness in his limbs until he thought he'd levitate too.

Now that he had the hang of it, he added a fourth and a fifth, and sent all of them around Hame as well, tracing a figure eight. He watched them with wide eyes, but he didn't need to concentrate on them, just keep an output of power that pushed them where he wanted them to go. And then, with another release of energy cascading out of him, every stone within ten yards rose off the ground. They crossed over one another, each one intersecting without connecting. His heart buzzed, knowing he had achieved a great thing. And when he looked at Hame, he saw the same broad smile that had broken across his own face.

He leapt forward, knocking Hame back onto the grass, and kissed him deeply. He let go of his power, knowing he'd need all his strength and focus to make his redheaded oracle as happy as he now felt, and he didn't care if that meant the whole damn forest heard.

Hame's lips returned his hunger, his tongue sliding in and fighting his. The meaty wetness pressing, dominating had him moaning into the oracle's mouth. His whole body vibrated from the invasion until he thought he'd break apart. But he needed more, and his hand rushed down inside Hame's trousers and wrapped around the thickening cock inside.

Hame's body crunched forward. "Slowly." He pulled his hand away.

Carn drew back, his lips the last part of him to leave that divine body. He stood, ripped the shirt off over his head, and pulled down his trousers. His cock pulsed when he saw Hame lick his top lip.

"Get undressed," he ordered.

"There's no rush." Hame smiled. "I want to look at you a while."

Only deep breathing stopped him from diving onto the oracle. The beast raged within, but he managed to hold back, for a little while enjoying the appreciation of his naked form. He smoothed his hand over his chest, running over the light hair that covered his pectorals, and then rubbed his nipples. Eyes followed hands, and his skin prickled from the combination of the breeze cooling his sweat, the thrill of being ogled, and the hard pressure he used to explore his body.

As his hand slipped lower, Hame lifted off his shirt to reveal that beautiful body Carn had lusted after the first moment he saw it. But he was denied the full revelation.

Hame twirled his finger in the air. "Turn around."

His cock twitched at the command, but he didn't touch himself. He only wanted this man's hands on him now; anything else would be a poor consolation. He turned, tensing his ass as he did so. He heard the rustle of trousers being dropped, and soon heat blazed against his back. A rough hand touched his shoulder blade before it slid down.

"I like this." Hame's fingers circled around the three moles on his back in the shape of a pyramid.

He laughed. "I'm standing here naked and all you like is—"

Hame kissed the back of his neck, and bare flesh pressed against him. Carn moaned, a low sound that sent shivers rippling. He ground back, which earned him a quick and sharp bite to his nape. His heated blood powered his need. He'd had enough of games and waiting. He wanted the oracle now.

He spun round, preparing to take them both to the ground, but Hame's hand wrapped fast around his cock, causing him to shudder. The firm grip pumped up and down, each movement tensing his stomach and groin. He wasn't sure how long he could last. He grabbed Hame's wrist, halting him even though he wanted to keep going. He looked into green eyes and saw how much the oracle enjoyed having him this way.

But Carn wanted his reward for mastering the lesson. He forced Hame to the ground.

"I see you like to be in control." Hame chuckled.

Carn slid his hands over Hame's solid bare chest. Straddling the oracle, Hame's cock rubbed against the cleft between his cheeks. He reached behind, positioned him, and then pushed down, not caring how much it hurt. Hame's hips shifted away, trying to slow his descent, but he wanted the oracle inside him, and he'd take anything as long as he got what he craved.

He arched his back as Hame speared into him. It burned, but he wouldn't be deterred. Pain darted through his body, but pleasure spiraled after it. He moved in a rhythm that had his new lover bucking beneath him.

"Touch me. Please," Carn begged.

Hame's fist curled around his shaft, the coarseness of his hands like fire on his skin. He rose up then plunged down hard.

"Yes. Yes," he gasped as Hame's hand worked him.

He locked onto the oracle's eyes and lost himself in the knowledge shining within them that they were destined for each other, and all the joy and horror that would bring.

"I am yours," Carn whispered.

The words lit gunpowder. Neck straining, Hame thrust harder, punching into his ass. The pressure built and Carn was getting close. He breathed rapidly, the tension swirling within his balls and rising out of them, ready to shoot. He tried to hold it back, but it was futile. He moaned, and screwed his eyes shut as he erupted. Grunting, he shot over Hame's pumping hand, and his body caved, exhausted.

A second later Hame groaned, pounding into his ass with one final blow, but he was like a rag doll on him then, pulsing as the orgasm racked his body, the warm tingling rushing up and down his spine. His breath heaved out of him, and he wiped his dripping brow.

He managed to lift his drowsy head, the ecstatic haze shimmering over his vision making it hard to focus, but through it he noticed Hame lay silent. He breathed, but he stared into nothing, limp and unresponsive.

"Hame! Wake up!"

Hame jolted as if he'd been struck by lightning, and one word blew away Carn's after-glow in a puff of smoke.

"Aurelia!"

XIV

MOST OF THE MEN LEFT THE CASTLE THE NEXT MORNING to hunt. Olivier went with them, having already set his sights on the Duke and his son, Wolf, who'd arrived the night before. The Duke was like Henri; a lure Olivier could not resist. From her place on the steps overlooking a court-yard filled with servants and lords, horses and hounds, she wondered if all of them would return alive.

Thierry and Reiner vanished to follow other pursuits, something that brought a twinge of a smile. They had become acquainted over dinner the previous evening and it hadn't taken long for Thierry to recognize Etienne's soul. She hoped he'd find some happiness in the remaining days.

Her head pounded, and she rubbed her forehead to ease the ache a little. The worries of being here weren't the only cause; Hame had been trying to get through to her since the previous evening. She had no desire to let him in, not after his pleasure had flooded her, leaving her damp and sick with envy. He could do what he liked with Carn, but she refused to be an intimate part of it.

"Are you poorly, my dear?" Liesel massaged the back of Aurelia's neck.

Liesel's touch soothed her. The stabbing behind her eyes dulled enough to let her regain some composure. When she looked at Liesel, she thought for the barest of moments that it was Elaine who offered such tenderness. Her breath caught in her throat, then she coughed to cover her alarm.

"My head is a little sore. Perhaps I had too much wine last night." She laughed.

"Maybe you should retire for a while. The men won't return for hours, and I know how you weary of sitting with the women."

"No." She gripped Liesel's arm tightly. "I mean, thank you, but I would rather spend my time with you, alone if we may."

Liesel's brow furrowed; her eyes rimmed with concern. "Of course. Let's go up to my rooms."

Aurelia smiled easy, but she didn't let go of Liesel's arm until they'd settled inside her chambers. Liesel dismissed the servants, the door closed, and the hustle and bustle faded away. Hame sat in the back of her skull, tapping away, but she bricked him up. It was a reckless act. He may have had a vision that required her attention, but she forced herself not to care.

"Are you still thinking of your red rabbit?"

Aurelia waved her hand. "Ignore me. My mother always said brooding never did anyone any good."

"She was right." Liesel's warm smile, so unfettered and without falsity, hammered her heart. "I haven't heard you mention your mother before."

"She passed away many years ago."

"You must have been so young. I was lucky that my mother lived well into her dotage, but when she died, it was like I was a little girl again. What happened, if you don't mind my asking?"

Stone claws seized her intestines. She could have lied, but she had told Liesel so many lies. "She was murdered."

Liesel gasped. "Murdered? Oh, my dear, that is horrible. You poor thing. Your poor mother."

"It was so long ago now yet I wish for more time to know her, more time to be with her."

She kept her eyes downcast, tracing the gold inlay on the tabletop, but she looked up when Liesel sniffed. Tears shimmered in her friend's eyes. At first, she couldn't understand why. Liesel's mother had not been the one murdered, she had not lost, but then she understood.

Liesel's empathy cracked something inside Aurelia, and what leaked out yowled for comfort, and it needed Liesel's aged and wizened arms to enfold her. She ran to Liesel's side, fell to the ground and lay her head in Liesel's lap. She thought her tears had dried centuries ago, but she wept as Liesel stroked her hair, the way Elaine used to do. Each gentle brush of her hand scoured her heart, and she cried for what she'd lost and what she was about to lose.

And because she wasn't strong enough to find it again.

Sinara was out there, centuries had passed without a word, and now it was too late. It was all too late.

———

SHE COULD SEE IT ALL HAPPENING AROUND HER, BUT FATE forbade her to intervene. Thierry and Reiner became ever more entangled, and Olivier would soon uncover their secret. He already had Wolf in his thrall, and the Duke would eventually succumb to Olivier's plans. Liesel was drawn too, despite Aurelia's efforts otherwise, and before long she was alone. This world had moved on without her, its axle oiled with blood.

After arguing with Thierry and trying to get him to rein in Olivier, she chose to leave. She told him other events required her attention, and if Hame's persistent presence in her head was anything to go by, then it was likely true.

She locked herself in her room, forcing down the last bit of pride as she sat on the cushioned chair. Her focus turned inwards. She opened her mind.

Now are you ready to listen to me?

The headache eased immediately.

Hame, I'm sorry.

Silence.

Did you hear me?

Are you feeling well? I don't think I've heard an apology from you in the past hundred years.

Her displeasure snaked through like some toxic miasma.

Now that's the Aurelia I know and love.

Her pulse spiked. *I mean it.*

Yes, yes, apology accepted. I should scold you for keeping me waiting for so long.

You could try.

He laughed. *Have you checked on Georg lately?*

Aurelia's stomach sank.

Whatever trick he pulled before, it was a good one.

Is Xadrak back?

I can't see him, but I think so.

She let out a long string of curses, none of which made her feel any better.

It's not as dire as all that, Hame said. *Not yet.*

He told her what he'd seen, that Georg was no longer the quiet clockmaker but rapidly growing in his power.

Where he was, he didn't know but she'd have to locate him soon. She wished she had more help, the thought leaking out to Hame who eagerly snapped it up like a fox pouncing on a mouse.

Use Carn. He's mastered your test, exceeded it even.

She growled at the witch's name. *I'm sure you have more uses for him than I do.*

He laughed at her and sent an unwelcome flash of images, luckily too fast for her to see individually but she caught the gist. Her cheeks burned.

I think he's coming along nicely. But seriously, do not ignore this one.

I know, I know. He's important. They're all bloody important. Just once I'd like to meet someone who isn't.

He chuckled. *No, you wouldn't.*

And then he left, and her mind echoed with his warning. Spurred on, she scried for the clockmaker. She imagined his bespectacled face but as soon as she tried to search for the real thing his likeness shredded.

Could he be dead?

After attempting a few more times to find him, she swung her attention to his workshop. That came together without any difficulty, though it had changed.

Smoke blackened the front of the shop, the window-frame rimmed with glass teeth, the beams burned, and what clocks remained stood silent. Many of them were empty shells, their faces fallen off, their hands and cogs incinerated. For all the destruction, she saw no sign of Georg, corpse or otherwise.

She had to return to Salzburg.

XV

THROUGHOUT THE NIGHT, AURELIA ACHED TO SAY A PROPER goodbye to Liesel, but she held firm. She would wait until the moment of her departure, a cruel act far kinder in the long run. It was some hours after the sun rose before she prepared to leave. The servant girl dressed her, then she ordered for her luggage to be packed quickly and brought down to her coach, which Aurelia summoned.

She then left the room and stepped into the corridor. The quiet soothed her. Here she stood in between one action and the next, knowing that when she found Liesel, the emotions she'd rather not face would surface.

But it couldn't be helped. She had to relinquish her already weak grip on life at the castle and attend to matters that cared not for friendship and love. With no reason to delay further, she inhaled deeply, smoothed down the front of her dress, and went in search of Liesel.

She heard her before she saw her. Liesel's distinctive laugh, like that of a clucking hen, came as she reached the hall. Drawn into the parlor, she stopped abruptly, her heart stilling.

Olivier's grin sharpened as he spied her in the doorway. He sat beside Liesel, leaning forward a little as if he leered at her with his whole person. But Liesel didn't mind; in fact, she enjoyed it, putting on an unfamiliar coquettish air. Such was Olivier's power. No one else minded either; if anything, they looked like they wished to trade places with her. Wolf sat nearby with the same expression as the women. Her brother was the only one out of the ten other people in the room that noticed her. That realization stung.

He tracked her as she entered and sat beside Liesel. Her throat throbbed, refusing to swallow, and to show how much Olivier's predatory gaze unnerved her. Even though she could defend herself without any problem from whatever attack he might launch at her, she wasn't so foolish to believe he didn't pose a threat. He maintained a mirthless smile, his silence causing Liesel to finally wonder what had drawn his attention. When she turned and saw her there, a flash as cold as acid splashed across her eyes. Aurelia took hold of Liesel's hand, and soon her friend returned.

"Oh, my dear, I was wondering when you were going to join us," Liesel said. "We've been listening to the most wonderful stories."

"I am sure the good gentleman knows all sorts of tall tales." Her eyes flicked to his, but she may as well have been looking into the eyes of a statue for all the difference her words made.

"And I'm sure the lady does as well," he said.

"Sadly, we will not have the chance to exchange them." She returned to Liesel. "I am afraid I must return home."

Liesel's happiness tumbled from her face, and a small part of her rejoiced knowing that for all Olivier's charms, she was the one truly prized in Liesel's heart.

"Why?"

"I've received word about my estate, and sadly it must take me away."

Liesel's eyes narrowed. Aurelia rarely had cause to leave quickly and over the years she'd spent with Liesel, she'd never mentioned her estate. But what other reason could she give?

"I fear you are not being entirely truthful with me, but whatever it may be, I wish I could help ease your burden."

She tried not to squeeze Liesel's hand too tight, but she couldn't help but hold on. She was going to lose her.

"I wish so, too."

"The place won't seem the same without you." Olivier's voice slithered into her ear, and his hand reached forward and covered theirs. She looked up into eyes the color of fire and sneered at him.

But as quickly as he'd intruded, he retreated. He'd won, and they both knew it.

"I shall call your carriage." He stood and summoned over a servant.

"That won't be necessary." She rose from her seat. "It is already waiting."

"So soon?" cried Liesel.

She nodded, her hand still clasping her friend's, only this time the Baroness held tighter. She pumped her hand and bid her rise. The castle's ebb and flow threatened to drag her back down, and the weight crushing her chest made her legs quiver. It would be so easy to stay, to banish Olivier from the castle and to pretend—for a little while longer—that this life was real and possible.

She had to get away.

With Liesel by her side, she exited the castle, barely able to walk without stumbling. That dread hampering her even more until she thought she'd become rooted to the earth.

I don't want to go. I don't want to lose her.

Her carriage waited, and a crowd gathered. Thierry and Reiner emerged; her brother already aware of her plans to leave. On the steps, Liesel cried, and Aurelia embraced her. She held onto whatever strength she could so she would not shatter, but her eyes came away wet from that hug. She held the Baroness's hand until the last moment.

"I will see you again soon," she said softly. Her fingers shook as she pressed them against her lips, the pressure enough to hold her together and gather enough strength to face Olivier, who hovered nearby like a wasp. She spoke a few choice words to him, barely concealing her contempt, but he rebuffed her.

She gave Thierry a farewell look, then climbed into the coach, and it drove away. She leaned out the window and waved to Liesel as long as she could, until her vision clouded, and she collapsed against the leather seat.

MOST PEOPLE WALKED PAST GEORG'S WORKSHOP, already accustomed to the sight of a burned shop on their street. The place was as charred as Aurelia felt while standing opposite. The rooms above and the shops on either side stood largely untouched. For them, a new coat of paint and all would be well, but the clockmaker's shop?

"You were here the other week, asking about poor Georg, weren't you?"

She stirred to see the dressmaker. Her face was carved with the lines of a person who ached to tell the world its ills.

"Yes, what happened?" she asked, knowing full well

that whatever she heard from this woman would be anything but the truth she sought.

"He's dead. Gone up in smoke."

"How awful. Did anyone see it?"

"No, no." The dressmaker thought over her story. "Middle of the night; midnight. You see, I had woken up, being such a warm night and all, and my bedroom window was open to let in what meagre breeze we had. My lord, hasn't it been an awful summer? Quite honestly, the worst we've had in years."

The woman droned on. Listening to this fool natter made her long for the inanities at Liesel's. Charcoal, scratchy and caustic, coated her tongue, and she had to swallow hard to dispel the taste. She couldn't think of Liesel.

"So, you saw…?"

"Well, I opened the window a little wider, and began to hear the chiming of Georg's clocks. Surely you noticed how precise all those clocks of his were. At midnight they make quite the sound, let me tell you. All going off together."

"And then what?"

"Well, I listened to the chimes, counting them down. Despite the racket they make, sometimes it can be wonderful, especially Georg's clocks. I'm sure you'd agree. Just one look at those pieces and you can't help but feel all is right in the world. Oh, listen to me ramble, well, I counted eleven and then BOOM!"

Aurelia flinched.

The dressmaker cackled. "Oh, dear, I am sorry. I didn't mean to startle you."

"It burst into flames?"

"Him, his whole shop, all up in a blaze. The glass shattered and you could hear the wood crackle. My husband and I ran to see—we were the first people to arrive—but there was little we could do. Standing as close as we dared, we tried to see Georg, but there was nothing but an inferno."

"Did anyone find his remains?"

"Oh, what a horrid thought!" The woman gasped with anything but horror. "We searched but could not find anything of him to bury, not even a foot."

"Any idea what might have caused it?"

She shrugged. "A candle falling over perhaps? He was always falling asleep at that bench of his. I'm surprised something like this didn't happen sooner. Still, poor Georg. What a way to go."

The dressmaker waved at someone down the street, quickly made her goodbyes, and toddled away. It was still possible that Georg had combusted, even if Hame insisted Xadrak hadn't returned to the astral. It would make things far easier if he had. She sought more gossip and hopefully a lead.

The salons proved useless, the fops inside were either safely tucked into their beds at midnight, or else drinking in some parlor until the small hours. No one had seen anything, and more to the point, they couldn't have cared less about some old *shop*.

She tried the seedier establishments next, where there was a little less forced gaiety. She asked inside a tavern if anyone had seen the fire, and the owner jerked his head in the direction of a drunk in the corner.

Hunched over a cup, the man, with hair on the sides of his head but none in the middle, peered into nothing with a look in his eyes usually reserved for soldiers who came back broken from war.

"I'm told you saw the clockmaker's shop burn."

He started, and his eyes locked onto hers. He lifted the

cup to his mouth and drained it dry. When he put it down, he twitched.

"What did you see?" She sat on the bench opposite. She prayed he was just another drunk with a mind full of holes, but the scratching at the back of her neck told her otherwise.

He struggled to speak, first opening his mouth then closing it, coughing and caving in his chest as if to activate his vocal cords. She wanted to grab him by the ears and hold him still, but that approach would not work here.

In his own time, minutes during which he signaled for another drink and it came, and he drank again, he finally found the ability to speak, even if he slurred.

"The fire…I was. I was in the street. Late, I can't remember what time." He winced. "I'd been…I hadn't been here." A moment of clarity came as he looked at her, wanting to stress that this was not who he was.

She gave him a sympathetic smile, while drumming her fingers on the table.

"I'd been visiting friends and my home is down that street. I knew Georg, you see. Everyone knew him. Hiding in that shop all day." He took another slurp from his cup. "And I saw a glow and knew it would be him, sitting at his work. I was going to knock and speak to him, speak *at* him really, because Georg didn't speak to many people. But then the glow grew brighter and brighter until the window exploded."

He stared straight ahead; his eyelids wide like they couldn't open enough to see everything. His mouth shaped into a quivering *O*. A sudden chill had Aurelia rubbing her arms.

"I…I couldn't speak. I couldn't scream for help. Oh God, the horror of it, because I knew, I just *knew* he had been in there when it happened. I was about to run to him, but I stopped." He swallowed with his whole body. "Something emerged from the blaze."

"What was it?"

He looked at her and she saw the depths of his terror.

"A demon."

XVI

"It's not possible," Aurelia whispered.

"I'm not lying." He wept, grabbing at her hands and pleading with her. "Please, please, I'm not lying. I saw it. He had horns and a tail and these black wings, and eyes of fire."

"I believe you, shhh, calm yourself, please." She waved away the tavern owner. He scowled but left. "Then what happened?"

He sniffed and wiped his nose on his sleeve. "I hid around the corner but kept watch. He stepped out of the shop's ruins, opened his arms wide, and roared silently into the night. Then his horns, his tail, his wings all sucked into a *human* body. He examined himself, like he couldn't believe what had happened. Then he must have heard someone for he ran down the street, right past me."

"Where did he go?" Her heartbeat thundered in her ears.

The drunk sobbed, his head resting on his arm on the table. She shook him and repeated her question.

He shrugged at her. "He ran towards the river. I left as soon as I could."

"Can you tell me what he looks like?"

He mumbled a description that could have been anybody in Salzburg. Georg had changed into a young man with long brown hair, a muscular physique, a pointed chin and a bump in his nose. But it wasn't what he'd become that troubled her. His demonic form had broken through, though it seemed he couldn't maintain that body and had been wrestled back into a human shape.

But now that he'd changed, how aware was he of his past? How much did he remember of her and the plot to banish him? She had to slay him before he caused any lasting problems.

She left the drunk to his babbling and rushed back to the workshop. Without knowing exactly where he'd gone, she needed a way to locate him. She couldn't scry for him, not having seen him in person. Hame would have directed her if he could, but he had nothing new for her. She walked through the burned-out insides of the shop, the ash stirring into a low cloud around her feet as she kicked clock faces and kindling. The smell tanged at the back of her throat. There was nothing to show where Xadrak had gone, but perhaps she could find him another way.

She summoned a ball of energy only visible to her and tasked it with following the path of any who'd been in the building. Smaller orbs broke free and drifted out the shattered window. There were far more than she would have expected from Georg's little shop, but that was probably due to gawkers rather than customers. Most were dim, attuned to how much of that person's essence had been in the shop, the largest being that of Georg.

The orbs drifted, a faint one attaching itself to her dress. She wrapped her hand around it and reabsorbed the power. The largest and brightest orb floated down the street in the direction the drunk said Xadrak had fled. She drew the rest of the orbs into her and followed the one tracking the demon. She urged it on, far enough away that if it stopped, she could prepare for danger.

It flowed down through the streets towards the river. She crossed the bridge and followed it into another part of town, twisting and turning as Xadrak sought whatever it was he needed—a place to hide or someone to do his bidding. The orb rarely stayed in one spot for long. It darted down one street before shooting out the other end, lingering a moment outside a door or a window.

The orb steered her into the darkest part of town where the light struggled to touch the ground. She did not fit in here, her clothes too well made, too rich for the rags clothing the poor. She shrouded herself to avoid attention but couldn't shake the feeling of drawing nearer to Xadrak. It clung to her like oil and spread when the orb hovered outside a church and went no further.

She had found him, but she didn't hurry inside. What creature had Xadrak become? How much power did he have? Who had he already drawn to his cause?

She wrought a shield that hugged her skin, making her invisible and masking her magic. It took her ten minutes of focused concentration to weave the spell correctly, wrangling her fast deteriorating patience in line. Haste would only lead to mistakes. Finally, the shield locked in place with a click that resonated in her breast. She urged the orb forward and followed it into the church.

Being far from the wealthy part of town, the parish church was decorated more simply than the cathedrals patronized by the aristocracy. Whereas the Salzburger Dom was garish and bright, decorated to the full glory of God in His Kingdom, this church was barer and gloomier.

Empty of any worshippers or priests, she stuck to the sides, uneasy about walking down the aisle even though no one could see her.

The tracker continued up to the altar then floated to the left, stopping again, this time at a door. She ran her tongue over her parched lips. He couldn't be far now. She banished the orb, approached the door, and turned the handle.

Steps descended into darkness. Murmured voices came out of the deep. She stopped with her foot hesitating in mid-air, enough time for her to force down the fear bubbling inside her. She climbed down into the black, taking each stair carefully, her hand sliding along the cold, damp stone wall. The voices grew louder and, as they formed recognizable words, the darkness lightened. A dim glow permeated the black, and she reached the bottom to see five men standing at the back of the crypt.

She glided from the doorway and crouched behind a tomb. Of the five men, one stood in front of the altar, while the other four knelt in a semi-circle before him. This Xadrak wore a face she'd never seen before. This incarnation had a wide brow, a nose to rival Caesar, and an arrogance Olivier would be hard pressed to match. He flinched every now and then, his head jerking from side to side as if trying to catch whispers on the wind.

"You have given me your word," he intoned in a voice that expected trees to bend at its command, "and in turn I have granted you power beyond the reach of ordinary men."

Little differentiated one man from another; most had brown hair, one had black, none were well dressed or groomed. She realized that wherever the orb had stopped, Xadrak had recruited someone new, or attempted to.

"You have been charged with a task. Franz is already searching, and you shall enhance his efforts."

"We are honored to be chosen, Lord," one said.

She wanted to attack now. Yet five against one, no matter her power and skill, or how drained Xadrak might be, was unlikely to end well. And there was the missing acolyte, Franz. She'd have to kill them one by one. She'd wait until the chosen four departed, and then dispatch the demon as quickly as she could.

Awareness bloomed inside her mind, and she leaned into Hame's familiar touch.

I've found Xadrak.

He'll have to wait. You must return to your brothers tonight, or they'll kill each other.

A spike jammed itself into her stomach. *I'll go now.*

You can't. It's not time.

She held her thoughts back. She was in danger of losing control and the barest slip might alert Xadrak to her presence. She retreated from the crypt and out of the church. Only when she had walked far enough away from Xadrak's lair did she throw off her shield and connect again with Hame.

Who has to die? she asked.

Don't worry; it's not Liesel.

Small mercies.

Tell me about Xadrak.

He's working fast. He's got at least five acolytes already, and they've all been given his power. I think...I think there are too many of them for me to fight all at once.

Use Carn.

No! He's untested. We barely know him.

This is what he's here for, Aurelia. If you don't use him, you'll lose him, and there will be consequences.

What have you seen?

Nothing that can't be changed if you learn to be a little more giving.

I'm sure you've been giving him plenty. The boy could do with some denial for a change.

You know I'm right. Get back here, give him his dues, and USE HIM!

He left her mind abruptly. Hame was right. Carn could be put to use with the proper instruction. At the least he could watch what happened here.

She had to hurry. She'd gotten the impression from Hame's thoughts that the time of her intervention neared. Seeing Liesel again... She banished her worries. They would all come to fruition in time. Right now, her focus had to be on Carn.

IF AURELIA HAD EXPECTED CARN TO BE PLEASED AT THE added attention, she was wrong. He had a scowl on his face the moment she arrived outside Hame's cottage, displeasure so apparent she almost despaired of the whole thing. She bristled but Hame spoke first.

"He's mastered the task you set him. Show her, Carn."

Without removing his glaring eyes from hers, Carn raised three stones around himself and made them circle slowly. She was impressed. Many weren't able to grasp the concept, but he had. Of course, Hame's beaming face told her it hadn't been all Carn's doing.

She opened her mouth to chastise him on his inability to master the skill on his own, but he summoned another handful of rocks and arranged them in multiple lines, alternating their directions as they circled around him, forming a shield beautiful in its symmetry. And with each passing second, another stone rose and merged with his creation. He gave no sign of strain.

"Astounding." And she meant it. Whether he took it for sarcasm, she didn't care.

The stones lowered with minute control, and he dipped his head a little to show his gratitude, grudging or otherwise.

"I need your help," she began, "and I'm willing to unlock as much of your power as I can to get it. What say you?"

His voice sounded flatter than ever. "What do you require of me?"

"I need you to watch someone. You do not have to do anything—just sit and pay attention."

"Who am I watching?"

"One is a demon, and the others are fools who know not what they do but will pay the price for it."

He spluttered. "A demon? You're mad."

"I wish that were the case, but I assure you it's true."

"I can't face a demon. I'll be killed. How will I avoid detection?"

"A shield of invisibility. I can train you. But I must have your word on this, Carn. You are there to aid us in our mission. I need a scout, not a hero."

"And I'll be safe?"

"I promise."

He bit his lip and looked at Hame, who nodded gently. If Hame hadn't been there, Carn might have walked away.

"I accept," he said to Hame, not to her. She took his agreement anyway.

"This will probably sting." She stepped forward with an open palm, but he retreated.

"You're not putting your hands on me again, Aurelia. Last time was lesson enough."

"Fool. You think I do this for my own amusement?"

"I'm sure you derive a lot of pleasure from torturing those you consider your inferiors."

She ground her teeth, and the pressure chipped her jaw like a pickaxe. There were others in this world she could count on, and if she couldn't find them in time, then she'd work alone. She didn't need this insolence, and she didn't need Carn Gwyn.

But before she could let her displeasure really be known—she considered reducing whatever manhood Carn had between his legs to the size of an acorn—Hame interceded. Gradually he turned Carn's head. She noticed the way he caressed Carn's cheek, and how the Welshman leaned in like a cat being scratched behind the ears.

"She won't hurt you." Hame's eyes fixed on Carn's. She could see the intimacy between them, the curve of their bodies as they mirrored one another. They formed two halves of the one whole, and she didn't want to witness it.

"Will you, Aurelia?" Hame repeated.

"Not intentionally, but it will sting." Her nostrils widened, letting in the air she needed to calm her blood.

Carn's head swiveled. "I wouldn't expect anything else." He turned the rest of his body to face her and puffed up his chest.

She wanted to plunge her hand into his ribcage and rip out his heart. She knew what he thought, that coming into his full power would be enough to take Hame from her completely. But she had been playing games for a long time now.

She stepped forward, placed her hand over his heart, and plunged her power into him. She sought the pathetic trickle she'd identified in so many humans. When she approached it, Carn had more than usual, but it paled compared to what he could have.

She searched for the hole in the dam and immediately began to break away chunks around it. More power flowed through and rushed into her, catching in her breath. Carn screamed in the distance, but she couldn't let that deter her. She dug harder and his power surged. She prepared to tear it down completely but held back. She refused to call it envy so she called it mistrust. She didn't know Carn enough yet, and no amount of Hame's pleading would persuade her to set free a powerful witch. Carn had to earn it. He had more than enough for what she required him to do.

Pulling back, she resurfaced to see Carn lying in Hame's arms. The boy had fainted, his hair plastered to his skull with sweat and his lip bleeding.

"You did that on purpose," Hame snapped.

"I did nothing of the sort." She returned her hand to rest over Carn's heart. The energy tingled on her palm.

Yes, plenty of power.

"How long 'til he wakes?" Hame asked.

"We don't have time for this." She snapped her fingers and water showered Carn's face.

He sat up, spluttering and wiping his eyes.

"How do you feel?" She tried to hide her smile.

"Like I've been trampled by a horse." But then he looked at his hands, from one to the other, examining his open palms. Light sprung up from them and he laughed, shutting them off. He jumped to his feet, his hands smoothing down his body, sensing the power within him. She and Hame stood, and for all that she hadn't warmed to the boy, she smiled at Carn's happiness.

There were no thanks for her. Instead, he beamed at Hame. She caught the lust in his eyes.

"Don't even think about it. Right now, I need you to show me your shields."

They lost time to his inability to focus, the joy making him giddy and scatterbrained. She ordered Hame away because he was a major distraction to them both.

Once Carn concentrated, his affinity with shields served him well. He quickly became invisible, and from there it wasn't long before he masked the scent of violets and the resonance of his magic.

Then she made him do it over and over again, finally closing her eyes and telling him to move elsewhere so she wouldn't know where he was. When she opened her eyes, she was alone. She pushed out her senses, feeling for magic, sniffing for violets, but nothing.

He was ready.

Then she heard Hame laugh inside the cottage. She ran to see the oracle foolishly trying to catch empty air.

"Do you two mind?" The sides of her head burned.

Carn returned, appearing behind Hame's back, a proud grin on his face. He kissed the oracle's cheek and hugged him close.

Her heart crushed inside her breast. What had she done?

"It's late. We must go."

XVII

Carn sucked the shield closer to his body as sweat dribbled down his back. He and Aurelia had traveled into the crypt after she'd given him strict instructions to remain quiet the whole time. Invisible too, she'd kept her hand on his shoulder until he was in place, then slipped away.

It was easy to pick out the leader, a man—a demon—called Xadrak. Two unarmed guards dressed in black flanked him, and he stood facing twelve men arranged in a half-circle. At their feet lay human remains.

The group was divided into those with power and those without. A few trembled. All of a sudden, one broke and ran screaming towards the crypt exit. Xadrak raised his hand and gripped the air as if he held the man's neck, then squeezed. The man struggled, his legs dancing across the stones before his body went slack and he dropped to the floor, all too near Carn's feet. The dead man's eyes looked right at him and ice shot through Carn's blood.

He can't see me. He can't see me.

He wrapped his arms around himself to lessen his shivering. His shields were good, strong, but he doubted they'd be any match for Xadrak if he saw through them. He crept away from the corpse.

Xadrak beckoned and a supplicant stepped forward with a steady stride and an inflated chest. Carn wiped his clammy brow as Xadrak placed his hand on the man's head. He writhed beneath the awful benediction. Power filled the crypt, and the air turned sulfurous. The man's shrieks stabbed into Carn's marrow, straight into his soul, before they cut mid-howl and he collapsed. A couple of the brethren rushed forward to revive him.

The unblessed salivated, looking at each other with eager and awe-filled eyes—meanwhile the empowered smiled with sickening pride at their growing numbers. More than one appraised their newest member. Carn understood that distrust. Is this one stronger than I? Has this one been favored more than I? Will he still bleed if I stab him?

The latest convert awoke and, after marveling at his newly gained gift, prostrated himself at Xadrak's feet.

"All hail Xadrak, lord of the Earth and beyond," he intoned.

"All hail Xadrak, lord of the Earth and beyond," the others echoed.

Xadrak swelled with their adulation.

Then they repeated the whole thing.

Transfixed, Carn trembled at Xadrak's power. No other men fled. Their hearts and souls belonged to the demon, acolytes all.

XVIII

"Stop fidgeting. He'll be fine," Aurelia said.

Hame's leg jiggled as they sat staring into the scrying bowl on the table. Her concentration stuttered with what she'd witnessed, so maintaining the vision proved hard, even without Hame's distraction. Perhaps she should have given this task to Carn instead; then maybe Liesel wouldn't have to see her as she really was. But she knew he wasn't strong enough to handle her brothers, so it fell to her.

The bloody key better reveal itself after all this.

"Leave me be. I'm worried about him."

Carn's shield hid him from all things, even the scrying eyes of an oracle, but she understood Hame's near-panic. She'd felt the spreading evil in that room. Even now it cloyed in her throat. The sooner she destroyed Xadrak, the better, but right now she was watching the whole horrible scene at Liesel's castle unfold.

Olivier had slain Wolf and Reiner, and Thierry had returned to find Reiner's corpse. Her brothers now fought, a more vicious fight she'd never seen, and at any moment she thought one would kill the other. She itched to inter-cede, but Hame held her back.

The brothers tumbled into the hall, slamming on the cold stone floor where the Duke sat in a daze, holding his son's body.

Thierry and Olivier continued to fight, and villagers arrived to storm the castle and kill the monsters. The Duke stirred from his fugue and, seeing an army ready to attack, took charge. Olivier roared at them. His jaw stretched open, his fangs glistened with red-stained saliva and that look of pure hate turned his eyes black.

Hame tapped her hand. "Prepare yourself."

So much carnage. She wanted to search for Liesel but couldn't swing the vision.

Olivier wrenched himself free of Thierry's hold and the two broke apart. A powerful kick to Thierry's chest sent him flying. She readied herself for travel. The Duke launched himself at Olivier.

"Now!" Hame shouted.

Aurelia vanished and reappeared in the midst of the fight, a force-field rippling out of her. The Duke and Olivier shot apart. The Duke slammed against a pillar, his head lolling. Olivier was not so easily wounded. He crouched and circled around her. As he moved, she saw Liesel standing by the stairs. Her hand was held over her mouth, her eyes wide.

The knife in Aurelia's heart twisted.

Olivier taunted her. Thierry snarled.

"No more fighting." She spoke softly, unable to trust her voice to a shout, but the hall stilled at her words.

Thierry pleaded for Olivier's murder, and she'd be right to allow it. Wolf was slain by him, Reiner gutted by him. And her friend, Liesel, quivering so hard she looked about to shatter. She was her friend no longer—not after seeing her like this. But she had to fight her need for vengeance, all to keep this evil alive.

"Go ahead, Aurelia," Olivier sneered. "Finish me off, the way you always wanted."

"No."

"Because you can't. You don't have the power, you weak bitch." He spat blood at her.

Whether he taunted her because he wanted her to kill him and succumb to the same depravity beating in his veins, or whether he truly believed she was unable to control him, she couldn't let the slight go. He had to suffer for what he'd done here.

She raised her hand, and Olivier levitated off the floor.

He laughed. "Cheap tricks."

She gripped her hand tight and sent agony spiraling through his body. He squirmed and screamed, the sight and sound churning her blood. Her power surged. She wanted him to howl for mercy.

Because of him she'd lost Liesel, the one pure thing in her life. Because of him she was tied to this cursed existence, keeping him alive to slaughter as a sacrifice for another day. Her body quivered with the power thundering within her. She would destroy him.

No! Stop this. You can't.

How she wished she could, but she remembered her vow and she inched back, step by painful step, until her will pulled out of her brother and he plummeted to the floor. She turned to Thierry, but the shouts of the dissatisfied crowd stole her attention, and she released a blue shield that kept everyone at bay, protecting the children of Henri d'Arjou.

"Thierry, I know you're in pain, but I can't kill him." She squashed every bit of hate in her. "He is needed."

As are you.

He argued. She empathized, but Olivier must survive. He dashed for his brother, but she spirited Olivier far away, and Thierry shot through empty air.

"Why?" he roared.

She steeled herself to his cries, even as they rattled inside her heart.

"I told you why." She left him to weep, unable to console him, not when he wept for Reiner, for having lost again that which he thought he'd regained. Etienne would return, and with him might come the chance for them to love again.

She turned to the crowd. "Go back to your homes. We are leaving. Your village and this castle will be safe. You will not be troubled again."

"Witch! How can we trust you?" The Duke stood at the front; his sword poised ready to strike her down. Foam gathered in the corners of his mouth. She would have laughed at him, but Liesel's gaze burned into her.

"You will just have to take my word for it. I am truly sorry for your loss." She longed to push this fool aside and reach for Liesel's hand, to explain everything, to apologize, but mostly to tell her that her love was no lie.

"We demand justice for the havoc these demons have brought into our lives," the Duke shouted, and the crowd cheered.

She fixed her eyes on him. "There is nothing I can do. I am sorry."

"You lying witch!"

"Do not try my patience, Duke. Mourn for your son and your lost friends. You are not the only one to grieve tonight."

"We will have vengeance."

She turned away from him and away from dear, tender Liesel, and bent down to Thierry.

"It's time to leave," she said, a catch in her voice.

He looked up at her, his eyes blood-shot. "Why did he have to do it? Why couldn't he…?" He sobbed, and the sound pulled at her misery.

She stooped under the sodden weight of her grief and touched his shoulder. They vanished, but she couldn't escape Liesel's unspoken questions as they hounded her through the ether.

XIX

AURELIA LOCKED THIERRY IN THE ROOM NEXT TO THEIR mother's. Too absorbed with his grief, he didn't wonder where he was or what was happening to him. Later, he'd no doubt attempt to seek vengeance on Olivier. Bringing him to the mountain was the best way to stop him from running across Europe to tear apart his twin.

As for Olivier, she'd dumped him in the wastelands of Siberia. She hoped the bastard froze.

She couldn't rest, even though sorrow dogged her. She had to collect Carn. Travelling to Salzburg, her shield locked in place before she entered the church. Descending into the crypt, she searched for Carn while surveying the coven. They tested their powers on each other; another body had been added to the pile since she'd left.

Carn wasn't where she expected. Her hand swept in widening arcs, and she held her power ready to jump out of there the instant she touched him. Then, behind a tomb, her fingers brushed him. She lunged forward, locking her hand hard on his forearm, and ripped them out of the crypt before he shrieked.

She delivered him into Hame's arms.

"Tomorrow," was all she said, then returned to her home and crawled into bed. Alone, she finally had the time to dwell on what had happened, and the trials ahead. She had no tears to cry, not that they would have eased anything, yet her soul wept. Blessed sleep eventually took her, and she dreamed of nothing, thankful for this small respite.

She woke to Thierry's roars and hammering. She ran out and shouted at him to be still so she could open the door.

"As long as you promise not to run."

He battered and yowled again.

"Enough!"

He gave the door one more bang, then retreated. She released the lock, and he charged her. He slammed her against the wall, his body pressing against her. He'd stripped the bloodied shirt from his chest, but red smears ran down his face and across his neck and arms. His fangs unsheathed, his eyes blazed gold.

"Where is he?" he growled.

"Out of your reach."

"Give him to me!"

"No." She found the strength to shout him down, even as his hands squeezed her tighter. She would not let the pain through.

He snarled at her, but she held firm.

"You must not kill Olivier, do you understand?"

"He deserves nothing but death."

"I promise you, brother, one day he will be called to account, but today is not that day."

He held her for a long time, those eyes threatening to burn through her, but she resisted and eventually, slowly, he released her.

"And what am I do to now?"

"Be at ease. You are free of your charge."

"You mean my jailor."

"Then be happy for it."

"I was happy with Reiner."

He stalked back into his room and slammed the door. Would that she could do nothing but mourn in her room or go and ease her suffering by returning to Liesel and explaining what had happened. But there was work to do.

The clock inside her room chimed seven. She had to hear Carn's report. She needed to bathe first; the blood and sweat of the night before still clung to her. The bath filled quickly, and she slipped beneath the water, intending to be quick, but her mind drifted to Liesel.

She allowed herself to dwell, to feel the loss that tore strips from her. The hot water scalded her skin, but it paled in comparison to the acid burn inside her breast. She'd return to her friend in time to lay a protective shield over the castle. Olivier was unlikely to return, but she preferred to take precautions. If anything further happened to Liesel, then she would truly hate herself. Having a plan in place helped spur her to action, swapping her misery over Liesel for a need to destroy Xadrak.

She dressed and told Thierry she was going. He didn't respond.

Carn and Hame were awake and waiting for her when she arrived. Carn relayed what he'd seen—thirteen men ascended into Xadrak's ranks. His power flowed into theirs and made them stronger. As Carn talked, she noticed the way Hame maintained some level of contact, stroking his arm, rubbing his back, his head leaning on Carn's shoulder. The boy's voice sounded hollow, defeated, even with Hame's care.

"Did they say anything about what they were going to do next?"

"Encourage others to join them. They may have already picked some and taken them back. You should know he's given them your description and told them to kill you on sight."

"I'd rather kill Xadrak first, but we may be better off killing his minions while they're out recruiting. That way we can isolate Xadrak."

"There are at least two by his side at all times, acting as bodyguards, and he mentioned another—Franz—who I never saw."

"They shouldn't be a problem. Do you have the stomach for slaughter?"

Carn's face was already pallid but he nodded solemnly. "They are not worthy of my mercy or my tears."

She smiled. Carn was going to work out nicely.

XX

NOW WAS NOT THE TIME FOR DRAWN-OUT EXECUTIONS. Aurelia armed herself and Carn with enchanted daggers as a precaution in case they ended up in hand-to-hand combat. Also death-by-knife wouldn't sap their strength.

Using Carn's knowledge, they traveled to each of the acolytes under the cover of their shields. They arrived to find one having killed another. While the survivor stood gloating over his fallen brother, she drove the dagger into his back, the enchantment spreading rapidly through his body and dissolving his heart. She withdrew the blade and he died by the time he hit the floor. She grabbed Carn's wrist and they traveled to the next.

He was in bed alone, and from the state of him, he had been enjoying his newfound vitality with a prostitute. Thankfully, she wasn't there. Aurelia killed him in the same quick method as the one prior, a dagger plunging out of nowhere to steal his life.

"Do you want me to kill the next one?" Carn asked.

"Only if it can be done with a knife. I need your strength to stay in reserve."

"Why aren't I as strong as they are? I've seen what they can do without breaking a sweat, yet I try the same and I can feel part of me fade."

"We all have our strengths and weaknesses. Shields are no trouble for you, but offensive magic is more of a drain." A puddle of grease sloshed in the bottom of her stomach. "Xadrak's power lessens the imbalance but submitting to it corrupts the soul."

The next, a tall blond man, had attracted a crowd of six men and women. Despite his good looks and easy charm, his audience was of a rougher cut, without a smile between them.

"They're nothing but cheap tricks, Jakob," one of the men shouted, his thick arms crossed over his barrel-chest.

"They're not tricks, cheap or otherwise, Bren." The light in his hand grew and took on other forms.

Jakob's display suited Aurelia. There was nothing like a cautionary tale to scare people away from Xadrak's cult. A surge of her will and Jakob lit up like a bonfire. His screams chased after the others as they ran. She threw aside her shield and stalked forward as he dropped to his knees. Whether he saw her or not, it didn't matter.

"How many did you say there were?" she called to Carn.

"At least fourteen."

"Four down, ten to go."

They appeared in the house of the fifth, but he was ready for them. An orb of fire floated above his empty palm, and he watched the empty air. She threw her power at him, but a shield deflected it. He spun, unable to see her, but he lashed out with the fireball. It sailed past her, exploding against the wall and burning the wood to black.

She attacked again, bashing through his shield. It was built with strength but not much skill, and she knew Carn would not have made such a flimsy thing. The acolyte's eyes widened as the shield fell around him and he fumbled to repair it, even while wary of invisible foes. She readied her deathblow, but before she had the chance to use it, the acolyte fell over dead.

Carn gasped for breath. He became visible and bent forward over his knees.

She hurried to his side. "I told you I didn't want you getting involved like that unless I said so."

"I had to...do something," he managed to say in between deep breaths. "He was...going to protect himself."

"I could have handled it. Please, listen to me next time."

"Why doesn't it affect you the way it affects me?"

"I'm stronger. I always will be. With time you'll gain more strength, but right now it's too soon." Perhaps she had erred in not giving him his full potential. She tried to help him upright, but he pushed her away.

"I'll be fine."

"He had warning. Xadrak is going to move to stop us."

"I'm ready," he said, though his breathing labored.

The next two were walking fast down the street. They hadn't bothered with shields, so her magic snaked easily into their chests and exploded their hearts. They died in the road.

Number eight had almost reached the door to the crypt when they arrived inside the church. He spun as she attacked, rebuffing her magic. His shield was stronger than she'd expected but would not protect him forever.

Shoving Carn aside, she waited, drawing out the acolyte. He neared the altar, which made it easier for her to maneuver towards him. He gathered his power, summoning a massive amount of energy that burned her nose with the stench of rotten eggs. If he released it, he was likely to bring the whole church down around them. She closed in on her prey.

She slipped beneath his defenses and placed a hand on his chest. Shock widened his face but by then it was too late. With the slightest push, her magic tore through his heart. She drew in his built-up energy and transmuted it into her own source as he died. Buzzing with the power inside her, she turned, threw off her invisibility and called to Carn. He appeared.

"The remainders are in there?" She looked at the crypt door.

"As far as I can tell. Hopefully he didn't add any more while we were gone."

"Agreed."

Her heart hummed with the acolyte's power inside her. Heat bloomed and sweat slid over her skin. She wanted to make full use of this force, and blast as many inside as she could. She might even get lucky and kill Xadrak, too.

"Stay here."

"I'm coming with you."

"I can't worry about you while I'm in there. I have one chance at this, and I hope I can kill them all. Having to cover you will weaken me."

"I can protect myself."

"I don't want to take that risk. I'm ordering you to stay here. If any make it out alive, you have my permission to kill them."

He glared at her, and she resisted the urge to slap him. He was a child in this game, and in more danger of getting hurt than her. And she grudgingly admitted that if anything happened to Carn, she'd have to answer to Hame.

She fashioned the energy inside her to a peak and added her own considerable strength.

She became Death.

She vanished and reappeared in the crypt. The instant her feet touched the ground, the power ripped from her in all directions, blasting out in such force she thought she'd shatter. If there were defensive blows, she didn't feel them. Any shields were wiped out in a flash of light that blinded her. And when it was gone, her whole body tingled.

Her vision cleared and the light in the crypt returned to its ordinary gloom to reveal bodies strewn around her. She armed herself for a second attack, but none came. Cautious, she searched for Xadrak's body amidst the corpses.

Pain seared across her brain as Hame forced his way in. She gripped her head, trying to push him back, creating enough space to respond. His shouts flooded into her.

Slow down, what did you say?

He's got Carn!

XXI

A HAND CLAMPED OVER CARN'S MOUTH THE SECOND Aurelia vanished, and he was locked against a rigid body. He struggled to free himself, but he was bound. He reached for his power, but it had been smothered so he grabbed the knife. It flew from his hand and clattered on the church's stone floor. The tinny sound cut off as he was taken, ripped through the ether and away from Aurelia. His stomach plummeted. He was going to die.

But when they returned to Earth, he was thrown free. He spun to face his attacker.

Xadrak clasped his hands behind his back. If it had been one of the acolytes, perhaps he would have stood a chance. Facing the man sent a chill streaking beneath his skin. Carn couldn't bring himself to think of Xadrak as a demon; being here with his human form was horror enough. Especially seeing those eyes. Flames rolled around a center of purest black; and that grin was a little too fixed, a little too carved to be anything other than a mask for evil.

Carn had been brought to a large, round stone room. Columns supported the domed roof and formed an arched corridor around the edge. The lack of windows made him think they were underground—that and the damp chill in the air. The place made a fitting tomb.

"You and Aurelia have made quick work of my acolytes. I'd be lying if I said I wasn't a little upset."

Carn's tongue turned to lead in his mouth. He was going to be tortured. Xadrak would exact vengeance on him.

"Still, such are the games we play."

"I'm sure Aurelia grows tired of games."

"Oh, we all grow tired of games."

Xadrak stepped closer. A wave of nausea swept through Carn. His mouth watered, and he swallowed quickly to stop himself from being sick. Carn tensed as Xadrak placed his hand on his chest. Unable to defend himself, he prepared for death, regrets and longings tumbling over one another, wishes for one more night with Hame, and curses towards himself for getting involved with Aurelia. Xadrak burned through him like fire across a wheat field at the end of summer, and left ash in his wake.

"So much power," Xadrak sighed. "Pity she's left most of it locked up."

Carn blinked. "What?"

Xadrak retracted his hand abruptly, and with it his energy. The absence resounded inside his chest.

Such strength.

"You didn't realize? She has only unlocked a fraction of what you're capable of. A stream trickles through you when it should be a raging river."

"She—" He shut his mouth. His jaw creaked. She wouldn't do that. Not after what he'd done for her. Not after giving her his word.

"Ahhh, she told you that was all your potential would accommodate? Well, Aurelia has always been a bit controlling, wants everything *her* way. But if that works for you, then I see no reason to continue this discussion." Xadrak grinned at him. "See you in the next life."

———

AURELIA COULDN'T FIND CARN. XADRAK HAD BLOCKED THE witch's location and the longer she took to find him, the greater the likelihood he'd be killed. Already knowing it was futile, she sought Xadrak instead, but he was masked too. While still sweeping for Carn, she hurried out of the crypt to where she'd left him and summoned a tracking orb. But before she released it, she detected his presence. She caught the weak pulse, then it flared before fading to nothing. Though it was gone, she'd caught the trail.

But she didn't rush in. This incarnation of the demon was unlike any embodiment she'd encountered before. While some of the others had possessed great power, her dominance had always been assured. This time...

A trap waited for her. Perhaps Carn was dead already and what she'd locked onto was merely a fabrication. But rescuing him was not her goal, and she had to take this chance before it withered.

She gripped the dagger's hilt, thrilling a little at the prospect of plunging it into Xadrak's heart. Deep beneath that feeling simmered her fear, just out of reach in the bottom of her belly. Reforming her shields and with her blade ready, she entered the battlefield.

Carn lay on the floor beneath a domed roof in an underground room. Torches surrounded him but the room's outer rim remained in shadow. She'd materialized as far from him as she could. From her place nestled in the darkness, she watched his chest rise and fall, thankful at least that he lived. But as soon as Xadrak realized she'd arrived, Carn's usefulness would diminish. The boy dangled like a bit of flesh on the end of the line. For now, Xadrak didn't know she circled, but eventually he'd pull back the lure and hook her. She had to find the demon first.

She searched, passing closed doors that led off to any number of rooms. She trod slowly and carefully, struggling to keep her breathing soft and shallow. Xadrak had to be hiding here somewhere.

But she found nothing.

Heard nothing.

She stepped beneath an arch.

Flames rushed to engulf her as she passed through a trigger. Her shields held but they shuddered from the force of the blow. A jet of lightning streamed towards her, which she resisted, but another attack launched against her defenses and destabilized them.

Sweat sprung up on the back of her neck as blow after blow struck hard and her shield started to crumble. Her lungs burned with the need for air, and as she took in a great breath, she vanished out of the line of Xadrak's attacks and reappeared on the other side of the room. She fell to the ground, shoring up her invisibility. She muffled the sound of her staccato breathing, each inhalation sharpening the pain stabbing into her chest until gradually it dulled. Brushing her hair out of her eyes, she scanned the chamber for the demon. The assault stopped, and the room returned to normal. She didn't dare move.

Xadrak's voice came out of the silence. One moment it heckled beside her ear, making her jump, and the next it floated distant and barely audible. Yet she heard every taunt.

"You should really find something else to occupy your time instead of trying to beat me," he said smugly. "You never win. You think you do—sending me back into the astral—but I never go away. You and Sinara should realize that. And now I see you're trying to recruit." He tutted. "Come now, Aurelia, putting a child in harm's way? You must be getting desperate."

His voice wormed into her brain and slipped down her spine. This was the first time she'd actually heard from Xadrak while in human form. All the other lives there'd been a filter between him and her, the twisted ravings of whatever madman he'd become. This time, he seemed almost sane.

"You keep trying to bring me down, but I can do this forever, which is exactly what's going to happen. There is no key. If there were, you'd have it by now. And soon it won't matter because your brothers are going to die. Once I've killed you, I'm going to kill them. Your efforts over the past four hundred years have all been for naught."

He was goading her, waiting for her to speak so he could locate her and deal another bone-shattering blow. But she refused to reveal herself. She'd fought him before and won, and while he may be strong, he was not a god.

And he could be slain.

Around the room's perimeter, she cast an invisible thread that hovered a foot above the ground. Next she sent another to circle around Carn's unconscious body and protect him. As it settled gently in place, she sensed a pocket of energy, a trap ready to spring if she approached.

"What are you doing, Aurelia? You always were a slippery cunt."

But for all his bluster, her power stayed in place. He couldn't risk her attacking him while he investigated what she had done. But that also meant he'd been warned. She had to act fast.

She cast another two threads to lie ready behind the

one around the perimeter, then, with dagger drawn, she poured her will into them. She opened herself as wide as possible, tapping the depths of her power, drawing on all her strength, her hate, her anger, and her vengeance to take down the demon. Wave after wave rippled through her body, causing her to sway. Her skin tingled with the magic, her heart hammered, and she filled with a fresh rush of air.

The threads throbbed like blood-filled leeches until she could hold back no more. She released the first attack to find Xadrak. Before it emerged from the corridor, it struck him somewhere to her left. A spark flashed, and a snarl ricocheted around the room. Without giving him time to get away, she released the second thread, and it homed in on his location, attacking with lightning speed and burning through his defenses.

She stalked towards him; her hand clenched around the enchanted dagger. Although he stayed invisible, her magic created a display of white and blue light as it battled with his power. His shield didn't fall, but it weakened. She'd break through soon. Coming closer, sulfur burned in her nose and soured her stomach. His grunts drowned the hissing sound made by her attack. She waited, crouched, watching. She was still tied to the attack she'd released, her magic still being drawn down, and before long she'd be too drained to do much else, but she ground her teeth and kept focus. Xadrak would not get out of here alive.

There.

Xadrak became visible, his attention and energy focused on maintaining his shield rather than masking his presence. Air punched out of his nostrils. She remained hidden, but if he'd wanted to find her, he didn't show it. His attention was fixed on a point ahead.

On Carn.

This had to end now. She sucked in her breath, her whole body freezing as she shored up a greater power, then she released the third thread.

It struck with such rapid and deadly force that Xadrak's body buckled in the middle. He slammed against the wall. Freed of his protections, she sprinted to him, thrust her left hand forward and grabbed his throat. Dazed as he was, she pinned him against the wall. Her invisibility fell away and he saw her at last. Those same evil eyes, that curled lip...

She plunged the dagger into his heart and buried it up to the hilt. His hands sparked but they caused her no harm. The fire in his eyes died and the glassy sheen of death passed over them. Now a dead weight, she released him, and he tumbled to the ground, the dagger still protruding from his chest.

She stumbled back; her magic spent. Exhaustion dragged her down to the ground, and she crawled towards Carn.

"Look at you," Xadrak said.

She started and looked over to see the ghostly form of the demon beside her.

"Next time you'll die before you even get a scratch on me."

She formed a white pentagram and hurled it towards him. Weak though it was, Xadrak shrieked as it stuck to him, and he vanished in a whirl of stinking air.

She collapsed onto her side and rolled onto her back. Never before had she poured so much of herself into one working. Never before had it been necessary. She thought she'd be strong enough to defeat Xadrak in whatever human form he took, but this time she'd been underprepared and blasé.

You're alive. That's what counts.

Hame's voice came to her, slipping in cautiously, knowing her defenses were down.

Come home. Then he left.

She staggered to Carn. She waved away the last of Xadrak's traps. The final enchantment, which had kept Carn in slumber, dissipated. He stirred, his eyes blinking, then he recoiled when he saw her.

"It's all right, Carn. Xadrak is dead."

He frowned at her, and for a moment she wondered if Xadrak had done something to the boy's mind. But then he sat up, his expression unreadable. He rose and walked over to Xadrak's body. She staggered to her feet and joined him, sagging against a column to stop herself from falling.

"You lied to me, Aurelia. You said you'd given me all the power that was possible."

"What are you talking about?"

"Xadrak. He mocked me, said I was weaker than his lowest disciple. I was no match for him, none." Carn reached forward and pulled the dagger from Xadrak's chest and wiped the blood on his trousers.

"Even with every last ounce of your potential power, you could never beat him."

He spun to face her, pointing the blade at her. "You admit you held back?"

"I admit it, and with good reason."

"What reason? Envy? Revenge?" He waved the dagger around.

"Your best interest." She heaved herself away from the pillar, standing upright, ready to protect herself if he lunged at her. She'd fight him with her bare hands if she had to.

"Only I know what my best interests are, and they are not to go into a fight crippled and blind." His eyes narrowed.

"I would have increased your power eventually, but I needed to be sure."

"Sure of what?"

"Sure I could trust you."

"It seems I am not the one who cannot be trusted."

Apologize, said the voice inside her head. *Ask for forgiveness; say you were wrong.* But those words stuck in her throat, trampled by the harsh ones that marched out.

"You are a child in this, Carn."

His fist tensed around the dagger's hilt. "And you are an arrogant general who cannot see that her soldiers need strong weapons. I will not go anywhere with you until you grant me my full power."

"I have not the strength for this now."

"You will find it," he said through his teeth.

"Do not order me around. Especially not after what I went through to rescue you."

He took a step towards her, the weapon held by his side. "I would not have needed rescuing if you had been honest."

Carn was a fool if he thought he could stand up to Xadrak and win. "I give you my word that——"

"Your word isn't worth shit."

"It's all you're going to get right now. I have barely the strength to argue, let alone release your full potential—which, I might add, is not that much greater than what you have now—so you either accept I will do this soon, or we will part ways now."

Another few steps closer and he'd be within striking distance. She refused to cower even as she had to fight not to sway. The fatigue had to be endured and suppressed.

He stared at her for a long time, and though the weariness threatened to make her knees shake, she returned his gaze.

He put the dagger away, sliding it through his belt. "I swear, you so much as try to weasel your way out of this and there'll be hell to pay."

"You'd be wise not to threaten me, Carn."

"And you'd be wise not to double-cross the one who's fucking your oracle."

XXII

After Aurelia dumped Carn in his arms, Hame begged her to stay, but she vanished before he'd finished speaking. She looked ragged and worn, and he hoped she only needed rest.

He hugged Carn tight, but the witch stiffened. Worried Carn was injured, Hame eased back, a hard feat when he wanted to hold him close.

"Are you hurt?" he asked before seeing the thunder in his eyes.

"She almost got me killed," he growled, then marched into the cottage.

What had happened?

He reached for Aurelia, but she swatted him away. She was weaker than he'd ever known her to be, and although he wanted to push, although he needed answers, he wouldn't force her.

Hame entered his home to find Carn leaning on the table, his back hunched and head low. A dagger lay on the table. He approached warily, sliding his hand up Carn's

239

spine, but instead of soothing him, it enraged him further. Carn shoved him away.

"She's a liar. How can you trust her?"

His stomach dipped. He knew what had happened, not because of any prophecy or *knowing*. He simply knew Aurelia. But he had to hear it anyway.

"Tell me."

Spit flew from Carn's mouth as he gestured and ranted, relaying his confrontation with Xadrak and the puny power Aurelia had given him. The more he spoke, the greater Hame's own anger became. She had nearly cost Carn his life. His warnings had all been for nothing. He'd told her not to ignore Carn, not to treat him badly, but she'd done exactly that.

When Carn finished, he stormed out, not wanting to be calmed. Hame didn't have it in him anyway. He bombarded Aurelia until she let him in.

I need sleep, Hame. Leave me be.

No. What you need to do is come here and give Carn his full power.

He told you, did he? Might have known he'd run crying to you.

I TOLD you not to ignore him, but you seem to think I say these things to amuse myself. I'm an ORACLE, or have you forgotten?

What did you see?

He didn't want her to know about Carn's vision. She'd be too rash, too quick to snuff him out. *It doesn't matter what I saw; it's what I tell you that's important.*

What does Carn do?

Nothing. He doesn't do anything. But that'll change if you don't start listening to me.

You're lying. You've seen something. He's going to do something bad.

I give you my word he will not cause harm. But I cannot give that guarantee if you treat him this way.

She kept her thoughts quiet, but she stayed, mulling over what he said.

I will come tomorrow.

Then she locked him out. A chill stole across her mind, matching the one growing inside his chest.

Lying to Aurelia had always been hard.

SHE CAME GRUDGINGLY, BUT SHE CAME, SWEEPING INTO HIS house the next morning without knocking. But Hame kept an eye on her. He knew her tricks. And when she entered, he and Carn were awake, dressed and waiting.

"You should rise earlier if you expect to catch me unawares, Aurelia." He laughed, but she was not amused. Neither was Carn, and his sullenness worried Hame more. Carn had eventually returned before night fell. They'd made love and fallen asleep in each other's arms, but when Carn woke he still fumed.

The two witches glared at each other until Aurelia crooked a finger for him to come closer. Carn stopped two steps away from her, within arm's reach. She stretched her hand and touched his chest. His shoulders tensed momentarily.

"Don't make me regret this." Her power surged into him.

Carn's jaw tightened but he couldn't stop his grunts escaping. He lowered to his knees. Hame made a move to help him, but Aurelia glowered, and he stepped back. Then she closed her eyes.

Carn writhed, and Hame saddened to realize she wasn't above making Carn suffer more than necessary. He moved to intercede, but as he did so, she withdrew her hand. Without her to keep Carn upright Hame rushed forward, hooked his lover's arms and hoisted him into a chair. Sweat plastered his hair to his head, but he was alive, and his eyes lit with joy.

"He'll be groggy for a while," she said, her voice flat. "I'm sure you can care for him." She turned to the door.

"Wait!" Carn called out.

She stopped.

"You still need to teach me. And I still want to help you."

She glared at him. "What makes you think I'd *lower* myself?"

Hame's heart squeezed. "Please, Aurelia, don't leave. Remember what I said."

Neither her head nor her shoulders drooped, nor did she sigh, but he felt her sag, as if his plea anchored her when she'd rather sail free. He didn't regret having Carn in his life, but he admitted a crack had appeared between him and Aurelia the day the blond witch had arrived. He wanted her to know she remained in his heart, but the way he held Carn must have been a cannonball to her chest.

But at least she agreed to return.

"Tomorrow."

XXIII

CARN APPROACHED THE DUKE ONE WINTER'S NIGHT IN A Bavarian inn. The gruff and hollowed out man sat wrapped in a thick coat in front of a dying fire. This was not the first time he'd seen the Duke. Months before, he'd accompanied Aurelia to a castle and aided her in establishing a protective shield over it. Once the shield was erected, she went in search of someone, leaving him behind to witness the Duke embark on his mission: vampire hunting—Aurelia's brothers, to be exact. He'd stored that knowledge away until it came in useful.

Tonight he had cause to act on it.

The Duke had torn across the country, hell-bent on finding the fiend who'd murdered his son. Though he began his crusade with a band of men, they eventually abandoned him. He became a lost figure, rampaging from town to town in search of vampires and witches. Many called him mad, but those who did met a bad end. He'd left a trail behind him as bloody as those he sought, but he'd learned the skills of an assassin during his mission.

The Duke didn't look up when Carn sat opposite him,

243

but his nose wrinkled as if perhaps he could scent the magic coming off him. His hate of witches was no concern to Carn.

"You're looking for a vampire, am I right?"

There was no movement, but the Duke listened.

"As strong as you think you are, you won't be able to kill him yourself."

The Duke ground his jaw. His eyes became slits.

"How would you like some help?"

"I suggest you get away from me before I gut you." The Duke's growl was more bear than man.

"You are welcome to try, but you will fail, and then I will kill you. Your son will die unavenged."

"What do you know of Wolf?"

"I know a vampire slaughtered him."

"And what is that to you?"

"I want the vampire dead too."

The Duke gave him an appraising glance, then curled his lip. "You are weak. He'd pick his teeth with your bones."

He smiled. "I am more powerful than you think, but I would prefer you to be the weapon. Your thirst for vengeance is greater than mine."

"How could you possibly help me?"

"I can give you strength, speed, immortality."

"I do not wish to live forever."

"You would rather die before your mission is complete?" Carn said. "The vampire merely has to wait, and time will take care of you."

"You are a consort of the Devil. I will not ally myself with you." The Duke looked conceited enough to fail alone rather than succeed with the help of a witch. But Carn couldn't allow that.

He leant forward and stared into the Duke's shadow-rimmed eyes. "Wolf demands justice, and without me you'll never get it."

The Duke's lips tensed, but other than that he didn't move. The hard wall of his glare pressed at Carn, yet it could not budge him, so they stayed locked together until the Duke spoke again.

"Tell me what I have to do."

❧ III ❧
HE WAS AN ORACLE
NO MORE

Present Day

I

"You're sure about him?" Aurelia asked.

"As sure as I can be about anybody."

They sat inside Mira's lakeside house. A blizzard raged outside but inside they were warm and snug, seated on plush sofas like two old friends chatting over coffee.

"He's powerful, Aurelia. More powerful than I'd expect." The Canadian witch with the auburn hair and mismatched eyes—one green, one brown—had a knack for finding the magically gifted. Fifty years Mira had been doing this, ever since Hame had found her. Perhaps he knew what troubles lay ahead for them and had wanted her to have a confidante. The idea stung that he'd cared for her enough to not see her alone, but not enough to repair the damage between them.

"Worried?"

She released the ends of her hair, unaware her fingers had begun twirling them. She dispelled her thoughts of Hame. "If he's powerful, it usually means Xadrak has already got him."

"Only one way to find out." Mira couldn't know for

certain whether the witches she'd located already used what they possessed or whose side they were on. She tracked the power—weak or strong—wherever it sparked. To find out what was in the witch's soul required the personal touch.

"Any others?" She had been amassing an army for more than a century and she always needed more allies.

"There are a couple with mid-level strength. Xadrak might get them before long. Do you want me to ask one of the others to check them out?"

"Yes, though make sure they can handle what we're asking."

"Do I ever disappoint?"

"Remember James?"

Mira's eyes widened to the size of golf balls. "The *one time* I pick a serial killer!"

She laughed. Eventually, Mira did too. James had been easily dealt with.

"You should smile more often, Aurelia. It looks good on you."

Her smile softened with gratitude. "I must go." She walked over to the witch and kissed her cheek. "Thank you. For everything."

"Please be kind to this one. He's going to go through a lot with those brothers of yours."

She chuckled. "He'll need more than kindness to survive them."

THE NEW WITCH WAS A WORK OF ART. OBERON OPENED THE door wearing only a pair of sweatpants, but his chest wasn't bare. A large thorn and star tattoo splayed across his sternum and pecs. He had *30 April* with twenty-two crosses beneath inked on the right side of his lithe abdomen, and more symbols and words adorned each arm.

"I didn't expect to see you again so soon," he said.

Aurelia hadn't delayed in tracking him down. She'd approached him the day before and given a moderate display of her power. Enough to intrigue. She'd shown Oberon hers, and he'd shown her his. Mira had been right. The young man had quite the ability. He was weaker than her, obviously, but still strong enough to make her sit up and pay attention, and he had more discipline than Carn did when they'd first met.

She entered his apartment, closing the door behind her. He offered her a drink, but she declined.

"I said yesterday I'm the head of a coven of witches that stretches across the globe. Today I'm offering you a place within that coven."

"What's the catch?"

No 'thank you', no blush at the flattery, just straight to the point. She liked him.

"I'm sure I don't need to tell you that you have a lot of strength, more than I'd actually believe possible. But still—and I don't say this to boast—you are much weaker than me. I'm willing to unlock more power within you."

"But there's a price. What is it?" he asked in that cut-through-the-bullshit Australian accent.

She sighed. "There's a war raging between my coven and a group that follows a demon called Xadrak. Their numbers grow, and mine must do the same."

He sat on the arm of the leather sofa. "I'm not looking to get involved in any war."

"You might not have a choice. If I've found you, others will too, and while I'd let you walk away with your life, they won't."

He looked at the door and folded his arms over his

chest. The thumb of his left hand rubbed the tattooed *Ó* on his bicep. "What do you need me to do?"

She smiled. "I need you to protect someone."

"Who?"

"Two vampires."

His eyes bulged. "Vampires? Two of them? Are you insane?" He shot up and paced around the room, putting distance between them as if she were the vampire.

"Sadly not."

"Why do two vampires need protection? Surely they should be exterminated."

Most of the witches she knew had the same aversion, but they eventually rationalized their feelings away. She hoped Oberon could do the same. "Not these two."

"What's so special about them?"

"Without them, we will never get rid of Xadrak."

"And you want me to protect two murderous psychos? From what?"

"To use your phrase, another murderous psycho. We call him the Duke." The man was a permanent reminder of how she'd ruined everything with Liesel. She wished him dead, but according to Hame he had his uses, such as something to do with the ever-elusive key. Wherever the damn thing was.

"The vampires, Olivier and Thierry, will be coming here to Perth soon. The Duke will follow. I have extreme confidence in them that they will not come to serious harm, but I would appreciate another level of security. And aid if they require it." No doubt Thierry chafed at being stuck with his brother once more, a necessity Aurelia had had to orchestrate.

Oberon gave her a pained smile, his brow furrowing at the same time. "It's one thing to stop a demon, but to help a vampire? You do know they drink blood, right?"

"I'm well aware. Whatever your moral qualms about the issue, I need you to ensure they don't die. If you want to stop them from killing innocents, then be my guest but I'd advise against it. As strong as you are, Olivier has much practice killing witches. In fact, he takes a lot of delight in doing so."

She had lost a number of her followers to his fangs, though thankfully not as many as Xadrak.

"And what do they look like, or should I follow the trail of blood?"

She pulled a photo from her pocket and held it out to him.

He looked at it as if she'd offered him fruit from the Tree of Knowledge. Perhaps in a way, she did. He took it nonetheless.

His brows flicked up and appreciation flashed in his eyes. "Which one is this?"

"They're identical twins. Though that is Thierry."

"How can you tell?"

"He's the one who *doesn't* grin like a raving lunatic. Do you accept?"

He stared at the photograph for a long time. The offer held allure: more power for a simple surveillance job.

"I accept." He put the photo down on the coffee table.

"Excellent. And if you do come into contact with them, please leave my name out of it, especially if you're talking to Olivier. My brother gets a bit...itchy when he hears it."

"Wait. Brother? Does that mean you're...?"

"No, just a witch. Are you ready?"

He picked up the photo again and peered at it then her, trying to spot the family resemblance. Apart from the black hair, he'd find none.

"Nothing will go wrong," she said. "Trust me."

He bit his bottom lip, looking from her ready palm, to her face, to the picture in his hand. She wasn't worried. The decision had been made the moment Oberon let her into his apartment, but she allowed him to think he processed it now. Some people valued free will and all that tripe.

"Do it."

II

THE DISHWATER COFFEE SLIPPED DOWN CARN'S GULLET, leaving behind a greasy residue. He usually transformed it into something palatable but today he hadn't bothered.

His stomach was unsettled by more than what he drank. Ordinary people would say it was the guilt getting to him and making him paranoid, but ordinary people were idiots. Having part of a demon inside him was what did it. That and his concern for keeping Hame alive.

He didn't know whether Xadrak saw into every part of him. There were sections he'd locked far behind many shields so that even he struggled to find them. But to think a demon could see into his thoughts and desires, while Hame could only see the surface, froze his blood. Still, that was his own fault.

He sat in the café window, watching his grown son play with his young daughter in the playground across the street. But far from being a distraction, the sight made his stomach pitch even worse.

He did not know his son in any meaningful way. His name was Peter. He had been born nearly thirty years prior, the offspring of a calculated move. Carn had provided monetary support to the mother but was otherwise absent. He did not belong in their ordinary lives. He did not concern himself with *how* his son lived—just so long as he lived.

Peter owned a three-bedroom house in Hampstead, close to the Heath so that he and his wife, Jane, could take Diana out to play. He did not care that Peter could make pasta from scratch, that he read to his daughter every night (often the same story day after day before Diana suddenly threw it aside for something new, much as Peter used to do as a child), or that Jane and he were happy. He knew these things without caring, because to care would make him interfere in what had to happen.

He lingered longer than intended, staying until Diana tired and Peter put her, laughing, on his shoulders, then pushed the stroller, with its stuffed elephant strapped into the seat, back home. He waited until they were out of sight, put down the half-empty cup and exited the café to answer Xadrak's summons to the astral.

III

HAME WOKE ALONE. EVEN SO, HE REACHED TO THE OTHER side of the bed, and his hand touched cold, crisp sheets. He sat up and peered into the rest of the empty and silent house. Had Carn even come home during the night? Surely he would have noticed someone moving around out there. The house sat in the middle of a large block of forested land on Vancouver Island. He could have screamed murder and only disturbed a few birds, perhaps a deer or two.

But he kept the screams chained inside his skull, where they were so loud his ears rang. Only *his* bellows resounded in there, the tortured and prophesized howl of the masses having deserted him. Now he was lucky if he could predict the weather. His connection with Aurelia was brittle too, and he dared not touch it for fear it might shatter completely. He didn't have that kind of link with Carn, but their bond was just as fragile.

He had little reason to get out of bed. His limbs drooped, weighing him down, and he almost rolled over and went back to sleep, but he cringed at another day spent feeling sorry for himself in a king-sized bed.

With a harrumph, he stamped into the bathroom. He showered and dressed, pulling on a pair of grey sweatpants and a hoody. He gave himself a cursory glance in the mirror, his red hair hanging limp around a soured expression. He avoided his own gaze. Barefoot, he walked through to the living area with its floor-to-ceiling windows that gave the impression of welcoming the forest indoors. Yet it was an illusion, and he needed the real thing.

He slid open a side door and stepped onto the path to his sanctuary. His feet tingled at going from wooden floorboards to damp earth. The air had bite. He inhaled for what felt like the first time that day, the wet scent of life and decay suffusing his lungs, but it would take more than a few deep breaths to make him feel better. He exhaled in a hard huff and continued along the path.

They had built the sanctuary when they'd moved here. Thirteen stones surrounded the grassed area, about fifteen yards across. Each rock protruded from the earth, forming a jagged ring. Taken from many places around the world, no two were the same. In the west he'd placed a hunk of sharpened black obsidian, with a column of amethyst opposite. Here stood basalt from Iceland, and there, iron ore from Australia. In the center loomed the dolmen, aligned to the rising sun on the summer solstice. A chair sat at its base, with a purple cushion on it. As always when he saw that cushion, he heard Loic chide him, cheerfully, for how soft he'd become.

How he missed that voice.

Building the sanctuary with Carn was meant to repair some of the cracks that had appeared in their relationship. But while he'd enjoyed the physical work—of the velvet soil caressing his hands as they delved into the Earth—

Carn didn't have the patience. He'd threatened to use magic to complete everything in a matter of seconds. It became one more thing they'd argued about before Carn had stormed off, leaving him to finish alone.

But he couldn't do it all by himself.

Unable to lift the dolmen in place, in a fit of vindictiveness he'd called on Aurelia's help. She'd come, giving him grief about the whole thing, then raised the three stones into position as if they were a child's blocks. Once settled, he'd realized his error and bid her leave before Carn saw her. She went, eventually, but not without telling him—yet again—exactly what she thought of Carn.

Serpents had twisted inside his gut while he'd waited for Carn to see and start yelling. But he hadn't shouted. He took one look at the stones and never came to the sanctuary again. Even today, Hame's stomach turned whenever he looked at the dolmen. At times he considered abandoning it, but it was the only place he called his own, as sad as that was.

He knew what was happening but forced himself to not believe it. The visions had lied before or told half-truths. Carn was not in Xadrak's sway, but with every passing day, he wondered if that truth still held.

Sitting beneath the dolmen, he tried to meditate, quelling the thoughts churning inside him. He could tell Aurelia, but he believed he could keep Carn from falling too far. He was meant to be his lover's guide along this path, but was that still the case? Had Carn stumbled long ago and now Hame followed into dangerous territory? He had to know for sure.

But when he stretched for a vision, his mind fizzed. Images flashed inside his head, but they cut into one another and he twitched.

Meaningless. It's all meaningless.

He retreated and tried again, fighting to hold his desperation in check, but nothing clear emerged. He stayed for hours until his ass ached, and his stomach rumbled. Until the truth hammered at him.

He was an oracle no more.

IV

HAME'S DISTRESS PUSHED THROUGH THE WEAK BOND, turning Aurelia's mood to toxic sludge. They hadn't spoken in so long that sometimes she forgot the connection still existed. His sadness leached into her, a bone-deep grief that made her cry out and reach for the wall. He was in pain and she was powerless to help.

No, I'm not powerless.

Though things had not been good between them for a while, she couldn't let him suffer. But could she show up uninvited? No, he'd reject her, embarrassed and enraged that she'd spied on him. She'd be lucky if he didn't spit on her. And yet...

She craved him with a need that rocked her.

She cast a guarding spell before stepping into the ether. All of the coven took such precautions. Xadrak hadn't been heard from or sighted for some years, but his followers patrolled, hoping to find new recruits and kill members of her coven. Many a witch on both sides had been snared and slaughtered.

She jumped through space and came to form without

incident at the edge of Carn and Hame's property. A protective shield ringed the land, which kept out any who attempted entry by supernatural means. Carn had always been good with such magic. The one he used to hide himself from even her skilled eye proved extremely effective.

Her stomach fluttered with each cautious step along the mossy, slippery path. Their home was nestled among the tall firs and cedars, far from the road. As she drew nearer the building—wood cabin one side, all glass on the other—Hame walked up from his sanctuary.

To see him again in the flesh! That head of fire even more brilliant than the first day they'd met, his body still muscled and alluring, and like at their first encounter, he looked every bit the troubled young man. With his head lowered, he almost bumped into her.

"What are you doing here?" He hooked his hand beneath her arm and turned her from the house. "If Carn sees you, he'll flip."

She resisted his rough handling and removed herself from his grasp. "I came to check on you. Can we go inside?"

He looked away.

"Please, Hame, it's important."

He sighed heavily. "Fine."

Once inside, he motioned for her to sit. He stood by the window.

"Carn's not here?"

"Correct."

She nodded with a weak smile. "I'm worried about you, Hame."

"You stopped worrying about me a long time ago."

His accusation stung like a wasp's barb. "Not true."

"Then you stopped showing it."

She leant forward. "What's happened? I sensed *something*. Is it Carn?"

He glared at her. "Stay out of my head, Aurelia."

She stood and slowly approached him. "I wasn't snooping. We share a bond. I still feel you."

She was sure he felt her too.

"There's nothing you can do. You are not responsible for me. You should leave." He brushed past her, heading for the front door.

"Don't shut me out again. Our duties extend beyond simple friendship. We are weapons forged for war, and neither you nor I can cast that aside. We've both tried and we keep getting sucked back in. The best we can do is cling to each other while we're dragged into the maelstrom."

"You don't understand."

"I used to."

"No, you didn't!" He stabbed his finger at her. "Not about me. Not about Carn. Not about us."

She went to him and took his hands in hers. "Then show me, because from where I stand, you are in pain. I can see it on your face. I can feel it in my head. You're not who you once were."

He shied away. "That's because I used to have energy for this, but now…"

"Let me help. Why are you being so stubborn? Out of the two of us, I never thought you'd be the bull-headed one. Is it some future you've seen? Does Carn—?"

He threw off her hands. "He has nothing to do with this."

"If you can't see that, then you're blind."

He fixed her with a baleful glare. "You don't know what you're talking about."

But she did.

Then the bastard opened the door and entered.

It had been years since she'd seen him in person. He appeared oily. His blond hair was slicked and tamed, his mouth creased into a sneer. Magma bubbled inside her; a feeling usually reserved for when she faced Olivier.

"You!" she growled, stalking over to him. He was taller than her and thought he could intimidate her by crossing his arms over his chest and smirking down at her. "And where have you been while he's here in torment?"

If she'd expected some remorse from him, some concern for Hame's wellbeing, she might have capitulated.

"As if you care, Aurelia. Now get out. You are not welcome here."

She spun to Hame. "Do you agree with this?"

"I think you should go," he said, his voice soft and quiet.

"You can't see, can you, how much misery he causes you? Carn doesn't deserve you."

"I care for him more than you ever did, Aurelia," Carn said. "You treated him like a lapdog to answer your beck and call, much as you wanted me to be. And now you can't stand it that we don't need you."

"This was never about you needing me, creep. This was about something bigger than all of us."

"You use that as an excuse to keep us all under your power. Xadrak has been silent for a long time now. He isn't worth all this trouble."

She couldn't have been more shocked if he'd punched her. "You don't believe that, do you? After what you've been through? After all you know?"

"All I know is our lives are better when we're not running around after your every whim."

She turned to Hame. "Tell him. Tell him how real this is. Tell him what Xadrak did to Elaine, to Loic."

"Don't speak his name," he said, unable to meet her eyes.

"Go ahead," she snapped. "Stick your head in the sand. You're both fools, but mark my words, I won't be there to protect you when the final battle comes."

"We don't need your protection. Now get out." Carn held the door for her.

She shook with fury and stalked out. Power flowed through her, fighting for release. She needed to get away from them as quickly as possible. Carn's shield blocked her but then, without a moment's hesitation, she unleashed that energy into it and burned her way through his fortifications. The forest lit with lightning as she roared her frustrations into the dome. Sheer brute force cracked its surface and, seeing Carn's work undone, she pumped more magic into it until it fell, and she vanished into the ether.

A jet-fueled anger propelled her. She prayed for some evil thing to sneak up so she could obliterate it, but nothing came. She traveled, the world shifting below her in a smear of faded color. Landing would bring it all back into sharp focus, harsh light cutting through this miasma of painful emotions to reveal the hurt at its center. If she stayed here, time would pass and perhaps she could lose part of herself as well.

"You have to go back sometime," a voice said behind her.

She pivoted, ready to defend herself, but the blow struck fast and deep.

V

THE DOOR CLOSED. HAME PREPARED HIMSELF FOR THE latest diatribe against Aurelia, but it didn't come. The forest lit up with the blazing light of Carn's crumbling shield, and Carn hurried outside to see it fall. There'd be more shouting because of this, the thought making him droop and seek his bed.

Carn came in some time later. "You think she's such a friend now?"

He didn't have the energy to speak. Aurelia coming had added another worry to the load.

"Why was she here?"

Because I'm blind.

He stared at the ceiling, letting the rant about her meddlesome ways wash over him. He wished he could see past this like he used to and find a happy future for them all.

"Are you deaf?" Carn glowered by the bed. "I'm talking and all you can do is stare at nothing. What's the matter with you?"

He looked at Carn. Still so beautiful, or at least he

would be if not for that aura hanging around him, and that pitying look as he tried to be more. Carn had always been enough for him, a perfect fit, or so he'd thought. Things changed quickly after they'd first gotten together. A vision made it easier to allow Carn into his heart, but it had always been an excuse. He wanted the witch, so he'd had him.

And now he lived with two people: the man he loved and this stranger in front of him.

He rolled onto his side. Carn touched his shoulder. He shrugged away from his lover's hand, half expecting to be struck.

Instead, Carn left him alone.

VI

AURELIA STOPPED AND THE ETHER SHUDDERED TO A HALT. Elaine stood before her, looking the same as the day she'd died. Except for the begging smile. The rest—sooty hair, strong nose, big eyes—was all so familiar.

And painful enough to cut into her heart.

"Why here? Why now?"

"You need me," Elaine said in her familiar scratchy voice. It crackled but the usual note of scorn had been smoothed away.

"I needed you then. *With* me. Do you know what it's been like without you?"

"I've been without you, too."

"But still you kept your distance."

"I did it to protect you."

Aurelia almost laughed and would have if not for the sodden lump of clay jamming her throat. Slick and heavy, it dripped into the hollowness of her chest and gaping emptiness in her belly. Seeing Elaine made her all too aware of how alone she had become.

"Show me who you really are."

"What?"

"My mother is dead. I would rather look at Sinara."

"I know you are in pain, but—"

"You left and I require no comfort, never did. Instead I want to talk to the demon who I have devoted my *life* to."

Her mother sighed. "As you wish."

She steeled herself against Elaine's transition, not wanting to admit how much it hurt watching her mother leave again. But it had to be this way or else she'd have a breakdown.

Sinara emerged. She was as white as Xadrak was black. Her wings opened and resettled behind her back, such beautiful things that she immediately thought of angels. Two white horns crowned her hairless head. Her body was powerful and lean, muscled yet feminine. She wore a white tunic, and a gold belt cinched the waist.

Aurelia's eyes watered, despite herself.

"Is this better?" Sinara asked, her voice ethereal.

Aurelia forced herself to speak. "Yes. Why are you here now of all times?"

"Hame has lost his visions."

Her stomach seized. "I must return to him."

She'd been a fool, arguing about Carn because that was what she'd wanted to fight about.

"Not yet. He needs time, and you're in no state to help him now."

"But without his visions, we're blind too."

"You can't help now," the demon said emphatically. "Let me guide you, Aurelia."

"What assistance can you lend? Do you have the key? Have you recaptured Xadrak?" The words fired from her, propelled with scorn. She wanted to wound, but Sinara was unmoved.

"No, but I have a gift that will aid you in your fight."

"What is it?"

"Xadrak imbues his minions with power, and I would do the same for you and your followers."

Chains bound her heart, their hot metal searing into the bruised muscle. She was being bought off again. As tempting as the added power was, right now she couldn't accept.

"I can't take it…maybe the others will."

"Why?"

"Because it must be given freely and taken with gratitude. Right now, I don't have any in me."

"I…understand. I hope you change your mind."

"I'm sure you do."

Sinara blinked. "I offer it because I want to give you something as a mother would give her child. You might not believe me capable of it, but I love you and always have. This power is yours by birthright but is also a gift I would like us to share. Promise me you'll think about it."

She looked at the demon for a moment longer, and for all the differences between her face and Elaine's, the similarities threatened to break her completely.

She gave a hurried goodbye and dropped to Earth, returning to her home inside the mountain. And that night, for the first time in centuries, she entered her mother's tomb.

VII

ANOTHER DAY AND NIGHT PASSED WITHOUT MUCH SAID between Hame and Carn. Animosity grew like algae on a pond. While before they might not have talked a lot, there would still be a touch, however fleeting, or a look, sometimes even a smile, to stir in some kindness and disrupt hatred's spread. Now light and oxygen couldn't get in. Life withered, leaving in its wake a dead indifference.

And still his visions remained beyond reach. He sat in his sanctuary as long as he could, running through exercises Loic had taught him and methods he'd since developed to bring them forth. But nothing came, except a frustration that gnawed on his sanity. He stayed until chill air splintered his concentration.

When he walked back inside, his head pounding, Carn bumped into him on his way out the door. He didn't stop or apologize.

"What the hell is wrong with you?"

Carn swung round. "It speaks."

"Too right I fucking speak. This is what we've become, is it? Something to be ignored?"

"You started this whole silent treatment thing."

"Bullshit. You've only been too happy to ignore me."

"How could I do anything different? You look at me with such hate. You think I'll just take it?"

Xadrak's name hovered on the tip of his tongue. He wanted to say he knew what Carn was doing. He wanted Carn to know he could help restrain the evil that had latched onto him. But he didn't dare now he was so unsure of the reason. What if Carn followed Xadrak because he chose to?

"What has happened to you? You're not the man I fell in love with."

"I'm the same, but you expect to see someone else." Carn stormed out the door.

"Where are you going?" he called after him.

"You're the oracle. You tell me."

Then he was gone, vanished, and Hame roared until his throat bled.

Aurelia met two of her witches inside a London pub at two in the afternoon. They occupied a leather-seated booth in a back corner, bought a couple of drinks, and she cast a warding spell. Zach and Zoe, a brother and sister from Liverpool, with matching twinkling eyes, had requested to meet her. They had news about Carn.

"You're sure?" she asked.

Zach nodded, rotating the half-full pint glass in his hands. "We both saw him. He was talking to the witch Mira sent us to investigate."

"Maybe…" She was about to say maybe Hame had sent Carn to the potential witch's home, but Hame's ability had ceased working. "Did you confront him?"

"No," Zoe said, "there was something sketchy. How did he know about the witch?"

"We thought he was out of the whole recruiting gig anyway," Zach continued. "He's certainly not been of use lately. When was the last time he helped exterminate of one of Xadrak's lot?"

Despite being close to it all when he'd first joined her, Carn had gradually removed himself from their operations. And after their latest confrontation she assumed he wasn't helping anyway. Hence the need for witches like Zach and Zoe. They were also far more agreeable.

"We tracked him afterwards."

"Carn? How? He's shielded. Even I can't get a fix on him."

"Sometimes a bit of human tech helps." Zoe flashed her brilliant white teeth. "We put a tracker on him." She pulled out of her pocket a round disc, extremely thin and small, and placed it in Aurelia's open palm.

She held next to nothing. If Aurelia had been given it blindfolded, she'd doubt she held anything.

"You put this on him? That's incredibly risky." But that was Zach and Zoe. They exuded youthful recklessness, despite having lived for more than sixty years. They maintained connections with the mortal world, and still buried themselves in the rapid changes in technology that made Aurelia's head ache.

Zach shrugged. "It emits a beacon, but its basic components are material, so it doesn't show up when testing for magic. Of course, we used some, but it's inverted. Makes it untraceable, which is ironic. We're pretty pleased."

And they looked it.

'How did you stick it on him without him noticing?"

"A new recruit bumped into him when he walked out.

She slipped it in his coat pocket."

She dreaded to ask what they'd discovered, hoping there'd be no more to tell, that Carn's appearance at the potential's door could be explained away in their favor, that he'd gone home, or somewhere boring. But Zach and Zoe wouldn't have bothered her if that had been the case.

"Where did he go?"

"Hampstead. He's watching someone."

"Who?"

"His name's Peter. He has a wife and daughter. He's totally ordinary."

"You're sure you have the right guy? Maybe it was just a coincidence."

Zach shook his head. "He's returned twice already. The only thing that's the same is this guy. Different locations, once at a playground, once while Peter was at work. We've asked Mira, but she hasn't picked up a thing. He's completely normal."

"Then why is Carn bothering?"

Zach and Zoe's shoulders rose in unison.

Xadrak. A stone lodged in her throat. Surely she'd know if the demon had returned. Hame would have told her. Or perhaps he'd told Carn and he was now trying to be a hero. She needed to find out more.

"How long will the device last?"

"Until we destroy it. It has a built-in self-destruct function. He might find it, but it's innocuous enough he shouldn't think much of it."

"Let's hope so. I saw Carn recently and he's barely holding it together."

"He could be in love." Zach laughed.

"If only." Because then Hame might see things had changed. Perhaps it would be better to show Hame what Carn was up to. "How do you trace him?"

"The signal beams straight to us. We can hook you in."

"Do it."

Zoe reached forward and touched her fingers to Aurelia's temple. A spark shot into her mind then came the awareness of a friendly and welcoming consciousness. She connected to Zach and Zoe and slipped into the tracker.

She finally knew where Carn was.

"I'll follow Peter. Can you keep an eye on the witch Carn visited?"

"Already on it. No sign yet whether he was there for us or…"

"Let's hope there's some innocent explanation."

"Meanwhile we prepare for the worst?"

She considered how many of her coven Carn had encountered. In the beginning, when out of necessity she had discarded her dislike at enlisting new witches, he had almost rock star status among the allies. He was the good-looking blond with the dreamy oracle on his arm, and a talent for shields that left most of them gasping. He'd been charming and personable.

Now he was unapproachable and acerbic. She'd stopped introducing him to recruits a while ago, but regardless, he knew too much. If he had gone bad, his knowledge of her coven would prove disastrous.

"Tell everyone to ensure their shields are secure but try not to spook them."

"You don't want us to warn everyone to stay clear of him too?" Zoe asked.

"Not yet. There's a chance he's on our side."

"But if he's working for Xadrak?"

Her heart stopped and fell into a yawning emptiness.

"He'll have to be assassinated."

And that was going to destroy Hame.

VIII

"COME WITH ME, HAME," AURELIA PLEADED AS SHE
barged into his sanctuary.

"For God's sake, I don't want you here." He struggled
yet again to force even the easiest of visions. Tomorrow's
lottery numbers, who'd win next week's football match:
easy things that usually required such minimal effort they
were laughable. But now, he might as well attempt to
predict how the world would look in ten thousand years.

"I have to show you something."

"Whatever it is, I'm not interested. Besides, Carn will
return soon, and if he sees you, there'll be hell."

He was bluffing, of course. Carn hadn't been home for
nearly a week.

"I know where Carn is."

"You…what? No one knows where Carn is. Even I
can't…well, I didn't…couldn't see him if he didn't want to
be found. And you're telling me you can? How?"

"It's not important. You need to see this."

"Why? What's he doing?"

"I don't know."

"If this is some sort of trick to show me Carn at his worst, I won't go. I'm not surprised you'd think up such a spiteful thing."

"God damn it, Hame! Open your fucking eyes."

His stomach sank. What was she trying to show him? Carn with someone else, someone he wanted more than him? No, that wasn't possible. There had only ever been him and Carn, no one else, and he wasn't likely to start cheating now. Yet where had he been all week?

"I'm sorry, Hame. I know…I know you've lost your visions."

His head snapped up. "How do you know that?"

"Sinara told me."

"Sinara…Sinara knows? And she told *you*?"

She ignored his pointed remark. Aurelia talking to Sinara was as baffling as him losing his visions.

"I want to help you."

"But I don't want your help. I can sort this out by myself. Me and Carn."

"If he's meant to be helping you, then why is he in Hampstead right now?"

Hame opened his mouth to fire some rebuttal but he had nothing to say.

Carn's in Hampstead?

"Please, Hame, come with me and we can help each other, like we used to. Carn is up to something, and I want you to see this because I'm not sure what I'm looking at. If we don't uncover it, I'm worried there'll be trouble."

He didn't want to see anything; he'd tried for so long not to. He thought that by being there for Carn, giving him as much love as he could, then he could be the anchor he needed to stay good. The future was not fixed; things changed. But he was forced to see this tactic hadn't been working for a long time.

He held out his hand and Aurelia, with awful pity in her eyes, took it. They ripped through the ether and landed in a park. She hurried them along.

Despite the time of year, the air was dry and crisp, warm for winter, with a bright, clear blue sky. The good weather brought out the crowds and smiles. Lots of people strolled through the parklands.

Aurelia took them down a dirt track until they stopped at a lake. She pointed across the water at a park bench. Though his back was to them, Hame recognized Carn instantly.

Momentary relief swept through him at finding him doing something so innocuous. But Aurelia wouldn't bring him there if it were to watch Carn soak up the sunshine.

"So what? He's sitting in a park."

Why pick this place? They had acres of natural land at home, and Carn had never been the social type, yet families and knots of friends were everywhere.

"He's not sitting. He's watching." She raised her finger and directed his sight to a man, a woman and a little girl on a picnic blanket. The man and the woman talked, heads close together, bodies towards each other, while the girl played with a set of toy cars. She'd then lift one to her parents, and they'd bend and smile and laugh. A more perfect picture of familial bliss he'd never seen—aside from the saccharine portrayals on television that substituted for actual visions.

"Who are they?"

"Peter, Jane and Diana. But we know—"

"We? Who else is following him?"

"That doesn't matter. But we know Carn is only interested in Peter."

"You think there's something going on between them? That's ridiculous."

I would know if Carn was fucking someone else, wouldn't I?

"No, as far as I can tell he's not romantically involved. But he's watching him for a reason."

"Maybe he's another witch in waiting."

"We've checked. He's practically a table when it comes to magical potential."

"Well, there are plenty of other possibilities."

"Like Peter is Xadrak?"

"No," he said decisively. "Xadrak hasn't returned."

"But how do you know?"

He didn't. Not with any certainty. Just hope. He couldn't look her in the eye.

"Did you send Carn to meet a witch a few days ago?"

He shook his head. "Why?"

"He was seen talking to a potential. We were going to recruit him, but Carn got there first."

"Maybe he was acting on your behalf."

She shook her head. "If he was, he hasn't told me or anyone else."

"Perhaps it was a bust. It happens."

"We're concerned he's working for the other side."

He didn't speak, couldn't confirm her suspicions because he'd buried the truth six feet under, covered it in dirt and allowed the grass to grow. But the dead had a way of coming back to life. He swallowed hard.

"I'd get some proof before you make those sorts of accusations."

"I know. And I'm hoping it's all a misunderstanding. But if not, you might be in danger."

"If he belongs to Xadrak, don't you think he would have hurt me before now?"

"You're already hurt."

Her words got into the wounds over his heart and

279

stretched them wide. He had to get away before he broke. "I've heard enough. Take me home."

She hesitated but he ignored her. Instead he switched his focus between Carn and the man who held his lover's attention, until finally, thankfully, she took him away.

IX

Aurelia brought him home. She hovered and fussed, trying to convince him to sneak away with her, but he refused.

"You aren't safe with him."

He'd never felt safer, in fact. "Lucky he's not here."

"You don't have to face him alone."

"I'll be fine. Please go."

"But what about your visions?"

"Later. Please go."

"Promise me you'll contact me the moment you need help."

"Aurelia—"

"Promise. Me."

She wouldn't go until he'd given his word. She gently nudged his mind, the link sturdier than it had been in years. Kindness tripped along it, concern and empathy, too —everything he craved. He returned grudging gratitude, and the connection thickened. A grin bloomed across her face like petals unfurling in the morning sun. He wasn't the only one suffering withdrawals.

DANIEL DE LORNE

They hugged, though the worry of Carn catching them together hardened his joints into rusty hinges. He withdrew. "You should go."

She kissed him softly on the cheek and left him to await Carn's return.

Whenever that will be.

Having already been absent for a week, was he ever coming back? If he did, would he offer an explanation, even if it was a lie? After more than two centuries Hame deserved that at least, but with the way things stood, he'd likely get silence. He simmered over the possibility of enduring such contempt. Hadn't he done his best to protect the witch and provide safe haven?

Rage steamed and bubbled through the next day until Carn's reappearance that evening.

"Where were you?" The hairs on the back of Hame's neck bristled.

Carn walked past him and into the bedroom, as though Hame had never spoken.

"Well?" Hame followed

"Out." Carn threw his jacket on the bed and unbuttoned his collared shirt.

Although acting cool, he couldn't hide the small telltale signs of his aggravation—the lips pulled taut over his teeth, the cheek twitching just beneath his right eye.

"Out? For a week?"

He put on a white T-shirt that molded to his body. "I needed some space."

"Who's Peter?"

He paused in the middle of picking up his jacket. "Who?"

"You know. Has a wife called Jane, a daughter called Diana?"

Carn faced him. Slowly. "How do you know about them?" he asked quietly.

"Take a guess," he said, glad he hadn't confided his blindness.

Doesn't that sum us up perfectly?

"What did you see?" The hate drained from his eyes and was replaced with blank fear.

You thought you could lie to me.

"You, looking at Peter. Who is he and what does he mean to you?"

The muscle in Carn's cheek jumped. "It doesn't matter."

"It matters to me!"

"Leave it, Hame."

Carn slipped around him and out of the bedroom, but Hame snared his arm. "You can't walk away from this. You disappear to stalk another man, and I deserve to know why."

"You want a reward for your snooping? For your prying?" Carn hissed.

"You of all people know what the prophecies bring, and you dare say I'm nothing but a nosey fishwife?"

"You're certainly screeching like one."

Hame balled his hands to stop them ripping through Carn's hard shell. "Tell me who Peter is!"

"He's my son."

A sucking hole opened in Hame's chest. "Your...your son? What do you mean? Since when...what?"

"Peter is my son."

"You say that like it's some kind of answer. When did you have a son? Who with?"

"It was a mistake."

"No, a mistake is using salt instead of sugar. This is a major fuck-up."

"I'm not talking about this."

"You are." He shoved him against the wall. "*Tell me.*"

Carn's eyes searched his, darting around before locking dead on center. Hame's mind tingled under the scrutiny, and they were frozen together for one second. Carn's shoulders relaxed for a moment before they rose up again. Tensed once more, he spoke.

"I'm sure you can figure it out."

"I want to hear it from your lips."

"Fine. Thirty years ago, I fucked a woman, and she gave birth to Peter. I didn't tell you because I didn't want to lose you."

He blinked, picturing Carn with *her.* The image drowned in scarlet. "Then you shouldn't have fucked someone else. And now you have a son? And what? He calls you dad?"

"He doesn't know who I am," he said, scratches in his voice.

"Then why visit him?"

"Because it's nice to know I've done something good in this world, something that has a place in it."

Hame's heart seized at the rawness in Carn's voice. "You have a place. *We* have a place."

"No, we don't. We exist beside the world; we're not part of it. We became immortal and that severed us from everything. I wanted to live through him a little."

"Then you should have told me. Why keep him a secret?"

Carn bit hard on his bottom lip and studied him before his voice came out flat. "Because I was frightened you'd leave me."

"You should have trusted me. You owed me that."

"It happened one stupid night when I went searching for something to make me *feel*. Then time went by and it

284

was fine but…I saw her again and there he was." He shrugged; his eyes unreadable.

God. When did I stop being able to read Carn?

"I thought I could forget him."

"Is that where you were? Watching Peter?"

His eyes fluttered closed and his breath came out forced. "I have nothing else in my life except him and you."

"What makes you think I still want you?" His voice caught, and he clenched his jaw. Pieces of his heart splintered into the storm.

"I have to believe that," Carn begged. "Because even with this distance between us, even considering what I've done, you're the reason I'm still here. You're the reason I've survived."

Carn took Hame's hand, and the block on his visions crumbled.

X

"WHICH DO YOU WANT FIRST: THE GOOD NEWS OR THE BAD news?"

From Zoe's expression, Aurelia doubted she wanted to hear any of it.

"Just tell me." Worrying about Hame had burned up all her patience. Even so, she'd welcomed the siblings' summons as it got her out of the mountain. The tunnels had never helped her escape her thoughts.

The brother and sister lived in a three-bedroom apartment overflowing with electronics, hard drives, wires and all the other paraphernalia of the twenty-first century she loathed. So now she added annoyance of flashing lights and whirring fans cooling god-knows-what to her troubles. She should have met them in the pub.

Zoe frowned. "Are you okay?"

"It's nothing. What did you find?"

The sister folded her arms, raised an eyebrow. She leant back in her ergonomic chair. Waiting.

"I don't have time for this." Aurelia turning to Zach sitting opposite her.

He hesitated, perhaps considering who'd berate him more. His eyes darted between them, then he closed his mouth. Apparently, Zoe was the bigger bitch.

She rolled her eyes. "Fine! I'm fine. I'm better than ever. Now will you please get on with it?"

"Liar," Zoe said. "Anyway, the witch Carn visited a little while ago, his name is Roland. We met him."

Aurelia's nostrils flared. "You had no idea what you were walking into," she said through gritted teeth.

"Carn hadn't returned," she continued unperturbed. "No one of interest had approached Roland since that first meeting. It was an acceptable risk."

She nearly told them how stupid and reckless they'd been, but Zoe held up her hand.

"Please save the yelling for later. The good news is he's still only a moderate-level witch."

"And the bad news?"

"Carn definitely wasn't working on our behalf."

Her heart kicked inside her chest. "I have to warn Hame."

I've left him in danger.

Zach asked her something, but she didn't hear him.

"Aurelia!" he barked. "Don't you want to know about Roland?"

She sighed. Hame would have to wait a little longer. "Why is he still alive? If he said no to Xadrak, he'd be dead."

"He's smooth," Zoe said, with a slight curve of her lips. "He bargained for more time to consider the offer."

"Or he wants you to think he did. He could already be part of Xadrak's horde." She wasn't about to let some silver-tongued Englishman hoodwink her, not after Carn had done that so spectacularly.

"We've checked him. He's clean," the brother said.

287

"That doesn't mean anything now. If Carn belongs to Xadrak, he's discovered a way to mask the infection." Maybe he'd worked for the demon from before he'd come to her. No other witch she'd encountered smelled of violets. What if that had been the sign he was not who he seemed?

No, she would have known back then. She'd scoured him deeply in search of the taint. Carn hadn't turned bad until later. But when? And why?

"Gabriela helped," Zach said.

The petite Spanish witch had an amazing ability for getting the truth out of people, a skill that made Aurelia uneasy when she was around.

"She says he hasn't fallen to Xadrak. And that he's frightened."

"He confirmed the same to us."

"Obviously." Sarcasm dripping from her tongue.

Zoe's lips thinned. "We've done everything we can to ensure he's not tainted. Trust us."

But trust was harder to find than meat in wartime. She couldn't even trust her own judgement. She'd thought she had Carn all figured out, the power-hungry bastard with his eye on *her* Hame. She had treated him tough so he'd see no reason to stick around. But Hame hadn't shared her contempt. He'd wanted the man in his bed. He'd also told her to trust him, to treat him right. Is that why Carn had gone bad?

What's done is done.

Carn made his choice and he'd be held to account for it.

But Zach and Zoe…they were hers through and through. She'd found them. She'd encouraged them and taught them, as she had the others. She'd created her coven. Perhaps there didn't have to be the rift between her and Carn, and she could have mended it years ago. But instead she sought to absolve her guilt by doing whatever she could for her followers. And, dare she think it, they had become her friends as well.

"I trust you," she forced out. "I'm sorry for not showing greater faith." Zoe looked as if she was about to hug her, so Aurelia hurried on. "Will he aid us?"

Zach smiled knowingly. "He will. For a price."

"I wouldn't have expected anything else. Where is he now?"

"We have him. He's ready."

"Good. Train him as quickly as you can, because I have a feeling we're going to need everyone ready for battle sooner than we think."

"Especially once Carn realizes we have Roland," Zach said.

Fingers squirmed in her gut, twisting and pinching. She fidgeted in her seat, but the movement did little to ease her worry. Carn could come for him at any moment, then he'd know they'd interceded. Putting Roland back was too dangerous, even with full power and training; Carn was too skilled, too strong—perhaps stronger than she knew.

Events were moving faster than she liked with too much left unknown. They still didn't have the key, and while she now knew Carn served Xadrak, she didn't know anything about his plans.

Except that they have something to do with Peter.

"On second thoughts, give Roland's training to one of the others," Aurelia said. "I need your help with something else."

XI

Hame's head pounded with the clamoring inside his skull. His vision blurred, and his stomach pitched. Knees buckling, he collapsed, but Carn caught him.

He trembled in Carn's arms. Prophecies amassed beyond his crumbling walls, ready to launch on his meagre defenses. What would be left of him once they broke through?

Carn carried him into their room and lay him onto the bed. Was he being left alone? He clutched Carn's hand, and Carn squeezed back, grounding him. The balance between his mind and body levelled, helped by the mattress's soft firmness and the pillow's gentle cradling. But the most effective thing of all was Carn's warm, fierce hold.

Pain seared through Hame's mind like a burning arrow fired across the sky. Somewhere he heard a warning that it was not wise to stay, but he lacked the strength to comply. He tumbled into darkness.

The next morning, he woke beneath the covers. The

sickness had faded, but he sat up slowly in case the pain hadn't withdrawn completely.

Carn wasn't next to him, but the sheets on his side of the bed were rumpled. He touched them. Was he watching Peter? Was he on one of Xadrak's errands?

"Do you feel better?"

Hame's head whipped to the doorway where Carn stood dressed in jeans and a navy blue T-shirt. He didn't smile, just looked as if he awaited further instructions.

There was still a lot they had to talk about, but the hard look in Carn's eye had gone, and Hame didn't have it in him to again bash his head against the past. Not when the borders of his mind were so permeable. Still, he couldn't smile and beckon him nearer. And he had work to do.

"Yes. Thank you." He returned the same neutral expression.

He threw off the covers and walked into the bathroom to shower. As he washed, he prepared himself like a priest cleansing before a holy ceremony. Expectation hummed within him, awakening his power.

He shut off the water, dried himself, and returned to the bedroom. Carn had gone. Hame put on a pair of cotton pants and a white singlet. His sanctuary beckoned, summoning him across the house and to the door.

"If you're going out there, you should put on more than that," Carn said behind him.

He stopped short as the back of his neck tingled beneath Carn's watchfulness. There was no mocking tone; instead a concern that purred against him.

You lied to me.

"I'll be fine." He opened the door onto the forest skirted with mist. Shivers rippled through the soles of his bare feet.

"At least take this with you," Carn said.

Hame looked over his shoulder and Carn held out an orange and brown blanket. Slowly he accepted it, but when he caught the little lift at the corner of Carn's mouth, he hurried outside.

The call insisted now, and he was only too relieved to comply. This was his final chance to see as an oracle was meant to see. If he refused, that was it. He really would go blind.

Cold earth and damp air chilled his legs and spine, and he was grateful for the blanket he wrapped around his shoulders. He bolted through the fog, down the path and into the circle of stones. He tumbled into his seat beneath the dolmen, but he didn't have time to properly settle himself. The visions pounded on the gate. They breeched the walls, and an endless horde surged forward, trampling him beneath their assault.

When Hame resurfaced, an orange glow smeared the horizon. The visions had held him captive until he knew and experienced everything. Only when they were finished was he released. The dying light turned the ferns and tree trunks black. The quiet echoed.

Cold seeped through the blanket and pulled his skin taut. He pushed both hands through his hair, scraping his fingers across his scalp. He stared into the forest. He'd been shown so many things, some as clear as if they'd been X-rayed, others as opaque as ink.

A rustle of leaves turned his head, and a shadow rose. He was pleased he had a guardian, even if that guardian was going to hurt him.

Not yet. He won't harm me yet.

He stretched his arms above his head, and the blanket fell. He leaned forward, easing his body's stiffness. He jiggled his legs and cut off the rush of pins and needles. All the while he felt Carn watching.

"How long have you been there?" He arched his back. His spine cracked, releasing a flood of satisfaction.

"Long enough to worry you'd never return," Carn said quietly.

He smiled. Remembered visions flashed. He sucked air through his teeth and pressed his hand against his temple.

"What did you see?" Carn asked, nearer this time.

When Hame opened his eyes, his lover was almost inside the stone circle. He wished Carn could take those final few steps.

"Nothing." His knees popped as he stood, and he walked stiffly past Carn.

"You're lying." Carn's voice slithered out of the darkness.

Hame stopped. He still couldn't see Carn's eyes, but he had seen Carn's deal with Xadrak: his servitude in exchange for Hame's safety. But the act hadn't been as self-less as Carn wanted to believe.

"I saw us."

Carn stepped close enough for his body heat to spread across Hame's chest. "What happens?"

He couldn't give an answer, not one that would do any good. If he told the truth now, there would be no hope for them or anyone. Xadrak would win. He held on to the pieces of himself that had splintered through Carn's deceptions—Peter the biggest shard of all. He gripped it, drawing blood. He would hold his tongue, but even as he winced from the hurt, it wasn't enough to subdue the churning need in his ribcage to hold Carn for what could be the last time.

He closed the gap between them, his chest pressing against Carn's. His hand slid up the side of his lover's face. Carn jerked back.

Don't leave.

If he left now, that would be the end of them. But Carn leaned into him, hands coming up to Hame's face, and he guided him to his lips.

They barely touched, but after meeting no resistance, Hame pressed harder, and that old hunger broke like a thunderstorm over a desert. His heart thrummed, ripples shooting along the surface of his skin. His hands gripped Carn's hips, and he moaned into his lover's mouth as a blaze ignited in his groin. Carn's lips broke from his but then they were on his neck, sucking hard enough to mark.

Gripping Carn's hair, Hame tugged it, provoking a feral groan, then he wrenched harder to break the suction. Hame gasped as he was let go, the air tickling his wet skin, and pulled Carn up the path to the house. He tried to slow at the door, but Carn rammed him from behind. They stumbled through as the door opened and they rushed into the bedroom. Hame's body burned as they fell onto the mattress, the blond giant pinning him, eyes wild, mouth ready to bite.

This is worth saving.

They ripped the clothes from each other. The sight of Carn's naked chiseled body made his cock throb painfully and the fire swirled low down in the pit of his stomach. Hame's fingertips scraped down Carn's chest, over hard nipples, and down his stomach. He curled his hand around Carn's erection. Held in his palm, he gently moved his hand up and down, the feel of it hard and silken. Carn's back arched and his eyelids fluttered.

Hame studied as much of Carn as he could see, banking every memory of his lover's body: Carn's locks the color of late-harvest wheat, the curve of his chest with its dusting of hair, his nipples firm in the middle of large, dark areola—all part of the man he hoped to rescue.

Down his gaze roamed, stuttering over the uneven alignment of his abs, the *V* along his groin, and the familiar sight of his shaft. Before the night was done, he'd trace his fingers over the triangle of moles on his back, but now, as the slickness of Carn's arousal wet his wrist, his need to feel Carn inside him howled.

He raised his hips so Carn could enter. Eyes of blue slate locked onto his, and he found his way with certain aim. They had always been good at this. They had always fit. And as Carn pierced him he cried out and squeezed his eyes against tears that weren't for pain.

This had never hurt; not with Carn.

Instead it was a spear through them both, staking them together until they either survived or tore each other apart.

XII

A CLAW WRAPPED AROUND CARN'S THROAT, CUTTING OFF his breath. Gasping, he struggled against the phantom, but there was nothing to fight, only an endless crushing black. He woke when the last bit of air had been torn from his lungs. His chest expanded, grateful for the ability to breathe, but the grip on his windpipe lingered. Looking at Hame's sleeping body, it tightened again, urging him to commit such a heinous act that it forced him from the bed. He grabbed his clothes and scurried out of the room.

Fog covered everything outside the windows. Carn dressed, vanished, and hurtled through the ether, unsure of where he wanted to go but knowing it had to be far and quiet and open. Xadrak tugged inside him, a summons he normally wouldn't ignore, but right now he was too fragile to answer.

Wresting himself from the demon's command, he landed in a Tanzanian savannah. The sky opened above him. The grass waved at the stars. He fought against the pounding of Xadrak's will and roared, the sound galloping up his chest and out his mouth to trample the night's stillness. He fell to his knees, his cry continuing until he ran out of air. Xadrak retreated and he detected a hint of pleasure.

And why shouldn't the demon be pleased?

He was its creature.

And it wouldn't be long before his shields shattered completely, revealing all he didn't want Xadrak to know. He lay back and lost himself in the swirl of the Milky Way. Endless stars, an expanding universe.

All mine, Xadrak snarled, then speared him with his jagged claws. He writhed as thick nails stabbed his nerves.

He didn't know how long the torture lasted, only that when it did end, his face was wet with tears, and his lip bloody.

Xadrak slashed his mind.

You will come now!

WAKING ALONE, HAME'S BODY TINGLED FROM THE LONG night before. They'd made love three times until they'd finally fallen asleep in each other's arms. Reluctantly, he pushed away the memories of Carn's body pressed against his and got out of bed, showered, dressed, and summoned Aurelia.

She flew into his arms when he opened the door. He held her as tight as she held him. He breathed her in, that rich aroma of bergamot, the sign of her magic, the essence of her. It filled his nose and warmed him.

"I can see again."

She hugged him harder. "Oh," she said, her voice a sigh heavy with relief.

He grudgingly let her go, took her hand in his, and led her to the couch.

"Is that why you called me? You saw something?"

He nodded. "I need your help."

"Is it Carn?" she said in *that* way.

"Yes, but before you say, 'I told you so', please listen to what I have to say."

"I'm not going to like this, am I?"

"No, but I need you to hear it all."

Her eyes brimmed with all the suspicions and assumptions salivating for Carn's demise. His grip tightened. He'd hold her down if he had to.

"Of course," she said starkly.

"A part of Xadrak is inside Carn."

"What?" She shot to her feet, but he wrestled her back to the couch.

"Sit down!"

Her skin grew warm, a warning to let her go. But he couldn't. She was wild enough to find Carn now and flay him.

"You promised you'd listen."

"The rest can wait until he's captured and contained. How long have you known this?"

He didn't answer. His palm sweat from the fire in her arm. He squeezed, and the pressure forced her to look at what she was doing. She winced and the heat stopped, replaced with a coolness that spread through his body and unwound his muscles.

"Thank you," he said. "Are you going to listen?"

"Will you be honest with me?"

"I may not have always told you everything, but I've always been honest."

"Bloody oracle and your tricks," she muttered. "Very well, I will stay, but it's my decision what I do with what you tell me. And if Carn has…" She shook her head, not in disbelief, but in…

Sympathy.

His teeth clenched to stop him from smiling. "Thank you, Aurelia."

He removed his hand from her wrist, but she quickly reached out and took it back.

"When he was taken by Xadrak, the demon left a part behind in exchange for power."

"He's been infected that long?"

He nodded.

She sniffed. "He was always power hungry. No matter what I gave him, it never would have been enough."

"But if you'd been kinder to him, valued him, then maybe he would have told us when it happened."

She scoffed. "He made his own choices, and he'll have to die by them."

"He's not going to die." His arms clenched like a warrior preparing to enter the fray. "You're going to help me save him."

She blinked at him. "You've got to be joking."

"Your jealousy has blinded you."

"Your lust has clouded your visions."

"For the first time in centuries, I'm seeing clearly. It's not lust but love."

"*Pssh.*" She rolled her eyes. "Love makes us all fools."

"Then I was a fool to follow you for so long."

"That's different." She rose from the couch.

Blood thundered in his veins, spurring him towards the battle. He wouldn't let her escape from the truth. "How? I love you. I always have, and it goes deeper than what I have with Carn—"

She scowled at him. "All the more reason to be rid of him."

He rode over her scorn. "But you both give me strength. We will never beat Xadrak if the two of you can't stand firm together. I need both of you. Without one, I cannot survive for the other."

"I can't forgive him for what he's done."

"Then we're doomed."

"I can kill Carn."

He shook his head. "Not in your current state. Xadrak is *inside* him; imagine the power he has. And if you front him now, he'll best you, and with your death Carn will be lost forever."

"Why?"

"Because it will break him. Xadrak's triumph will surge through him and destroy his remaining resistance. He's already weakened."

"Then why doesn't he ask for help?"

"If he does, he'll fall. It would signal his failure, that there is nothing left to defend against Xadrak. He can't even bring himself to tell me."

When they had made love the night before, he'd understood how deeply Carn's despair ran. He'd fucked him at first, a hard, fast pounding, and he took it all, because Carn needed some release. He couldn't talk about it, couldn't admit it, because the shame had eaten away at him and Xadrak had filled the gouges. He'd come with a shout like the cry of a wounded beast. They laid together for a while before Hame rekindled the flame and entered him. He'd shown him his love, shown him that there was good worth saving. When Carn took him again, there'd been tenderness and communion.

For a while, they had been whole and as one.

He wanted that back with a ferocity that hollowed his chest. His face must have shown his sorrow and his need because Aurelia squeezed his arm.

"What can I do?"

XIII

CARN RECHECKED HIS DEEPEST HIDDEN SHIELDS, THEN cloaked himself to mask his presence on the astral. He set his course to Xadrak, drawn by the part of the demon that had spread its contamination throughout his body. The beauty of the savannah faded as he descended to the darkest levels of the astral. He itched to illuminate his way, but Xadrak would see it as a weakness, and he was already out of favor for making the demon wait.

Slimy things shimmered as he dove into a cave. As the demon's influence dragged him closer, the light turned murky grey and revealed Xadrak. His red eyes shone like a beacon, his madness leeching out and staining the air crimson. Part of Carn buzzed at being so close to the source. The rest of him turned quiet.

"Hail, my lord Xadrak." He bowed.

The demon grabbed him and hoisted him up to within inches of his lined and leathery face. Carn swallowed hard.

The demon snarled. "I sense you are unhappy with my plans."

"No, my Lord. I live to serve."

Xadrak's lips moved into something that could have been a smile but could also have been in preparation for biting off his head.

"You forget I see and feel everything within you."

"I am honored to be one of your chosen."

"You lie; yet you still have your uses. Otherwise you would not be alive now." Xadrak ditched him like he was nothing more than a doll.

He skidded across the cave's floor, his skin scraping and peeling. He winced but knew better than to fuss. He hurried to his knees and bowed his head again.

"I am unworthy, my Lord."

"Too right you are." Franz emerged from the shadows, his singsong voice tickling Carn's ear.

The witch was Xadrak's head acolyte, the only one to escape Aurelia's slaughter in Salzburg. The grey-haired man's eyes half-protruded from their sockets, and his mouth bore a rictus. But he had little mirth. Only when he destroyed one of Aurelia's followers did he show joy. Carn had himself to blame for those deaths, until he'd removed himself from her coven's operations.

"You cannot be trusted and should be exterminated."

"Do not be so hasty, Franz." Xadrak's voice rumbled like a barrel of bones tossed down a hill. "I have learned that speed leads to mistakes, and mistakes often lead to failure."

"Of course, my Lord." Franz's head cocked to the side. "I only meant he should not be privy to your plans until he has shown his loyalty."

"My loyalty is without question," Carn snapped. "I have brought the Lord followers. I have slain his enemies. I have created for him a vessel through which he may return to Earth in glory."

"Ha!" Franz surged forward. "You do only that which you cannot avoid. You are an eel, Carn, slippery in the extreme. What of the witch I sent you to recruit? I have not seen him yet."

He had forgotten all about Roland. He'd asked for time to think about it, and Carn had agreed.

"I was going to bring him to you today."

"How convenient. You want to prove your devotion? Kill the oracle."

Carn's body cracked like a whip. He scrambled to hide his terror, but it was too late. Xadrak had tasted it.

"Yes, the oracle must die," the demon said.

"But my Lord, he is of use."

"Not anymore. When was the last time he gave a prophecy of value? Kill him, and your loyalty will not be questioned again."

His heart sprang into his throat. "This is a mistake, my Lord. A decision made in haste."

"Do not lecture me!" Xadrak swooped down on Carn, forcing him to cower. "I allowed you to shield his visions from seeing the scope of our plans while he still gave prophecies that would benefit *us*. But too much time has passed since he gave anything we could use. Your toy is broken, and now the *only* worth the oracle has is to prove my benevolence has not been misguided. You will kill him today, or you *and* the oracle will be dead by morning."

He didn't care about himself, but if he were dead, he couldn't protect Hame. Aurelia wouldn't save him; to her, he was simply another soldier in the war, an acceptable casualty.

Xadrak's gaze bore into him, waiting for a response, and not just a verbal one. The demon had to *feel* it. He put his racing pulse to use, seeding it with a fanatic's love until his whole body purred.

Before he even spoke the words, he knew Xadrak approved.

"As my Lord commands."

XIV

AURELIA SETTLED HERSELF IN HER MOTHER'S SANCTUARY. Heart thudding in her ears, she struggled to find the calm she needed to ascend into the astral. Usually she could do it with as little effort as drawing breath, but now…

This must be done.

After many attempts, she finally slipped over and appeared in a replica of the chamber. She stood, gazing around the sanctuary. The stones in the wall appeared too sharp and grey. The obsidian in the altar looked as deep as space. The candles burst with light. The place had been carved into the astral.

"You haven't been here much, have you?" Sinara's disembodied voice preceded her arrival through the stone wall. The white demon, wings resting at her back, tail alert, smiled.

"No, not much. It reminds me too much of Elaine."

"I come here a lot." She walked over to the altar. Her fingers touched the athame and the wand. "I come precisely because it reminds me of my life back then."

"Do you miss it?"

Sinara looked up. "Of course. Not for who I was, but for what I achieved."

"Oh."

"Do you know what my greatest achievement was?"

She shrugged. "Managing to contain Xadrak?"

"You." Sinara changed into Elaine.

Aurelia's spine turned to lead. "I asked you not to appear as her."

"I am her." The demon's synthesized voice changed to her mother's familiar huskiness. "I never meant to treat you the way I did."

Frost blew through Aurelia's lungs. She held up her hands. "Please don't make excuses. What's done is done."

"Do you remember before I left you with Henri?"

A few memories surfaced, one of her father giving her knucklebones and she begging her mother to play, which she did and let her win every time.

"Barely. I was too young."

"Then you can't remember how much I adored you. How even Henri loved you."

She shuddered. Whatever he had been, he'd tainted the moment he'd raped her.

"But you left me behind." She turned away, eyes stinging.

"I was frightened. At that time Henri was the lesser evil."

Aurelia's stomach squeezed and bile rippled up her throat, making her gag. She shook to dispel the memory.

"But you could have taken me later."

"I know. And for that I'm sorry. But you survived. You've lived longer than I ever had a chance to. You have persevered."

Hot iron spiked in her, and she spun round like a

baited tiger. "I didn't want to survive. I wanted to live. I wanted love."

Elaine attempted to get near her, but she backed away.

"I do love you. It might not be the way you wanted, but there was love. I have watched all you have become and kept my distance because I didn't want to cause you more pain. I know you fight for me, for us, for the world, but still you must know I would change everything if I could."

She didn't want to hear any more. Hame would have to find another way…

"Do you remember the night I died?"

Aurelia's hands trembled. She clenched them but her arms shook. "You died because of me and my foolishness."

"No, no, my darling, I died to save you. Because if Xadrak was going to take anyone, he was going to take me. You had to survive. Nothing else was—and is—more important to me."

Aurelia wiped at the tears blurring her vision. She refused to give in. If she did, she'd drown. But the closer Elaine came, the less she wanted to run. Warm arms circled her, causing her to stiffen, but it passed, and sobs racked her body. She cut away the hate she'd carried like a boulder around her neck. She slipped into her mother's comfort. It had always been there, beaten and bruised, yet everlasting. Elaine's hand brushed her hair, the gesture so familiar, so ancient, that more tears broke free.

She closed her eyes and drifted in her mother's embrace. Unfettered, she sailed above the pain that had tied her down. The memories remained—the times she'd lost and found her mother, the scalding pride that stopped her from seeking her out, the substitute Liesel had provided, the wasted years—and they'd shoot her down if she let them.

No more.

"I'm sorry," she said.

"There's nothing to apologize for." Elaine kissed her hair.

She unpeeled herself from her mother's embrace.

"Are you ready?" Elaine asked.

She opened her mouth to object. She didn't want Sinara to think she'd only done this to get power, but then she looked at her mother's face, at the soft, kind smile, and the understanding eyes.

"Willingly and gladly."

Elaine's fingers rushed up to hide her widening grin. Her eyes glistened before she closed them. Her breath quaked as it rushed out through her fingertips. Then she reached forward with a shaking hand and placed it on Aurelia's chest.

Her back tensed. She'd given any number of witches hell when increasing their gifts; she expected all seven circles of Hell from this. Her heart thumped faster. She gritted her teeth and screwed her eyes shut.

It started.

But it wasn't anything like she'd expected.

Warmth spread from Elaine's hand, through Aurelia's chest and into her heart. Power suffused her like tea steeping in a pot. More energy flowed and Elaine's full essence unfurled, and with it came the truth of her mother's love. Knowing it had been one thing, but now she felt it completely.

She saw through her mother's eyes, felt her mother's heart blaze with fierce love for her children, the pride of watching them grow. She bore the agony of leaving them behind, the horror of Olivier and Thierry's downfall, and her sucking guilt.

She gasped at Sinara's love for Xadrak before he'd fallen.

She took it all in, opening herself fully and accepting it freely.

Elaine's hand pulled back, but the power continued to flow inside her. It twinned with her own and pulsed with her heartbeat. She smiled at the buzz.

"So much strength," she whispered.

Elaine laughed. "You're going to need it."

Then Hame beckoned.

XV

CARN SHUDDERED INTO HIS BODY AND TRAVELED THE moment his eyes opened. Xadrak lurked inside him, waiting for him to slay Hame, deep behind shields in a part of himself even he struggled to pinpoint. He buried his true intentions, but meanwhile he cast a spell over his mind to fool the demon into believing he'd returned home.

Instead, he landed outside Peter's house. It was early evening, but at this time of year the light had already gone. Damp air clung to him. Through the window, he watched the family eating dinner at the table.

Diana made a mess of the spaghetti, using her hands more than the fork she wielded. Jane attempted to get her to eat, but Diana was having none of it and squealed when her mother came near. Peter laughed, and his wife glared before cracking. Diana giggled, thinking it was something she'd done. Peter, taking advantage of his daughter's good mood, proffered food, and she opened her mouth without fuss and ate properly. She gave him a sauce-covered grin, and he smoothed strands of hair out of her face.

His son.

And a vessel for Xadrak to enter the world with all his power.

He knew this day would come. He groaned at having created this life just to destroy it. The weight of his shame nearly crushed him. How could he tear this family apart?

Coldness spread throughout his body. He wished he could do this without Jane and Diana present. He walked up the brick path and knocked on the blue door. He heard Peter say he'd go see whom it was, followed by the scrape of wooden chair legs across the floor.

"Daddy!" Diana called.

He chuckled. "I'll be back in a minute, sweetheart."

Carn summoned his power and held it invisible.

The door opened.

"Yes? Can I help you?"

Until now, he had never received that generous smile or seen up close the twinkle in his son's blue-grey eyes. He recognized himself, except after harboring Xadrak's pollution for so long he had lost that joy. He realized how much he'd shut away.

Fractures splintered his chest.

"I'm sorry," he whispered and released his attack.

Peter's eyes and mouth widened, and he stumbled from the blow. Carn watched him fall. Jane screamed. He forced himself to bear witness. He had no right to look away.

But her shrieks cut midway and Peter vanished. Carn stepped inside. Diana and Jane had disappeared as well. What the hell had happened? That blast had killed his son. No one could have survived such a thing, not unless they were Xadrak himself.

Or Aurelia.

His breath stopped.

Illusions.

Hame must have told her about Peter. Or perhaps

she'd known all along. But where had she taken him? Did she know who Peter really was? If so, why bother with these tricks? She could have killed him outright.

He searched the house, thoughts tumbling, heart beating fast and control slipping. Xadrak's claws unfurled and tore down his outer defenses. The demon's touch burned him, and he clutched his head. Xadrak broke him apart, and his mind was consumed with an ungodly roar.

XVI

ROLLING CLOUDS TURNED THE FOREST DARK AND A cutting wind whipped the undergrowth. The ferns fluttered like frightened doves. Hame crouched, waiting for Carn.

Then, between one moment and the next, he appeared. Only it wasn't really him. Carn's mouth twisted into a grimace as he advanced. Hame stood firm, but Carn raised his hand and levitated him off the ground. Claws sunk into his flesh. He cried out, squirming in the phantom grip, but his thrashing was for naught.

"Where are they?" bellowed Carn in a voice that wasn't his.

"Go fuck yourself."

Carn growled and his nails burrowed deeper. Hame screamed.

"I'll ask you again, *where are they?*"

"You'll never find them." He gasped.

"If you want Carn to live, you'll tell me."

"You've always been a terrible liar, Xadrak."

Carn formed a fist and Hame's femurs shattered.

Splinters shot up his body and he howled. His legs dangled useless beneath him.

"Carn hates to hear you scream," Xadrak said in mock-concern. "He's weeping, *pleading* for mercy on your behalf. It's pathetic. Just like Loic."

Hame started at his teacher's name.

"Ahhh, I see you haven't forgotten him," Xadrak said, with an unctuous grin. "Did you know he lusted after you? Hungered to have you in his bed, even when you were a young boy. Oh, how he hated himself."

Lying, he's lying.

"I sucked that shame clean out of his head. He wanted you to serve him on your hands and knees. He dreamed of licking your thighs and fondling your small cock. He wept when I finally killed him, happy to be rid of you."

A dull ache oozed along his nerves. He didn't believe it of Loic. Xadrak told lies to get what he wanted, the more sickening the better, but that wouldn't work here.

He glared at the demon.

"Be blind, you worthless oracle," Xadrak spat. "It must sting to know I've been here all along, fucking you while Carn fucked you. I'm in him deeper than you could ever be. I know all his secrets. I know how much he *loathes* you and Aurelia. He's mine completely, and you mean nothing."

If Xadrak had said it with Carn's voice, he might have believed him. If black eyes didn't shimmer in place of blue-grey ones, he might have withered. And if Carn and he hadn't made love the night before, he might have succumbed.

But this was not Carn. And the demon could not sway him.

Hame closed his eyes and fought the swamping nausea. Ignoring Xadrak's snarls and demands for Peter, he searched. He shoved aside the poison of the demon's words and clamped the pain in his legs. He just needed a little peace.

"Look at me!" Xadrak shouted.

Hame's arms snapped, and sick gurgled up his throat. His eyelids fired open. He heaved great breaths as his bones crunched. He held back his screams, but his neck stiffened, and the strain caused his nose to run with blood. But he compelled himself to seek some calm. Forcing his eyes shut, he grunted through the agony in his fractured body. He sought that fragment of solitude.

Xadrak's hot breath heated his face, but by then it was done.

He smiled.

"Insane, like all oracles," Xadrak snarled. "Your only worth now is to help punish Carn for his disobedience. But don't think you'll meet him in the afterlife. I'm going to keep him alive and in torment for eternity."

"Not if Aurelia kills you first."

Xadrak roared with laughter. "It's a pity you won't be here to see her fail." The demon pushed him up and away, high above the dolmen. His palm opened to the sky.

"I hope Loic finally gets to rape you."

Xadrak flipped his hand and drove it down, and Hame hurtled towards the Earth.

XVII

AURELIA'S POWER BROKE FROM HER, SEVERING CARN'S
spell and grabbing Hame before he smashed against the
dirt. A rabid snarl turned her head, and she shielded
herself. Even so, a wave destabilized her magic, and Hame
was thrown into the scrub. She blocked most of Carn's
power but not enough to stop her propelling backwards
and slamming into the dolmen. Her spine and skull
smacked against the stone, and black spots darted across
her vision.

Thick claws grabbed her, their icy touch scaring away
unconsciousness, and she lashed out. Carn unleashed a
torrent of blows, each coming from a different direction.
She defended herself with a force-field stronger than any
she'd ever summoned. She marveled at the mass of energy
she poured into it, yet still had plenty to spare. Sinara's
power shone through her.

"I see you've whored yourself out," Xadrak sneered
through Carn's face as he advanced towards her. His
stench tanged at the back of her throat.

"I am your daughter, after all, Xadrak."

The muscles around Carn's eyes tightened. "So you figured out Carn's merely a puppet, did you? Took you long enough."

If only she could take the credit. But that didn't matter now. She needed to get rid of the demon, and there was every chance Carn would die in the process.

Don't kill him. Hame's voice burned inside her head.

Thank God, he lived. But relieved as she was, if she had to, she'd destroy Carn.

If he dies, you can stick a knife in me too.

She banished Hame as Xadrak snuck a swipe beneath her shield, taking advantage of Carn's knowledge. It merely scratched the skin, but it drew blood.

She shot lightning towards him, crashing into the protective bubble he'd cast, ricocheting into the forest where it exploded tree trunks. Xadrak smirked at her, but his straining jaw revealed how her retaliation had rocked him. She couldn't be sure how much Xadrak had given Carn or how much he could channel, but she was confident he'd never give all of himself. The demon was too selfish and too terrified of usurpers. Meanwhile, all of Sinara flowed through her.

Blue light streamed out of her hands. She connected with earth and sky, her demon-mother and the universe beyond, drawing such massive power that her body hummed. It roared in her ears, and the vibrations warmed her. Her strikes were too much for Xadrak to withstand and he dove away. She chased him, firing bolt after bolt to crash into his shield. He vanished, but she spun in time to divert an assault aimed at her back, then disappeared.

She materialized beside the stone circle, shields strengthened, and an orb hovered over her palm. Xadrak lobbed a thousand spears at her, but she melted them with a swat of her hand. She fired a volley that drove him scurrying backwards. Gone was the smirk on his face. He grunted as he retreated, defending more than attacking, and she savored his fear.

"You've lost, Xadrak. Better luck next time."

———

CARN SAW IT HAPPEN BUT COULDN'T STOP ANY OF IT. HE railed against the prison Xadrak had created for him inside his mind.

Hame's torture had nearly wrecked him. Though he hadn't been the one to break Hame's bones, he'd felt them snap like sticks of chalk. It had sickened him, while Xadrak had relished it.

Unable to save his lover, Carn had waited for Aurelia to obliterate him. He deserved it. The demon would have killed him when they'd met if he hadn't begged and seized the first offer of safety. Only later did he build the lies to justify what he'd done in Xadrak's name.

He would subvert Xadrak's plans.

He would bring about the demon's downfall, and Hame would consider *him* the hero.

He'd submitted so Hame would be saved.

That last reason stabbed. Of all the excuses, it was closest to the truth.

Yes, he'd been a coward. Yes, he'd been hungry for power, but he loved Hame with every scrap of his tattered being. Keeping him safe was the only thing that stopped him from becoming a burned-out acolyte. And if he had any hope of proving his love, he must fight, even if it meant his own demise.

Aurelia followed up attack after attack, which Xadrak deflected. Carn searched for a way out.

It's just a shield designed to block me from controlling my body.

With that realization, he groped around the jail's edge, testing here and there, then surged forward to strike a weakness. He rebounded and writhed from the shock. He shook the pain before attempting again. His brain lit up, the jolt worse than a taser to the balls, but he muscled his way through.

Then he understood.

The shield was constructed with every lie, every shame, every bit of guilt he'd ever experienced, from leaving his village without saying goodbye to his family, to failing Aurelia's first test. He relived Xadrak's defilement and suffered again the despair of having to hide his secret. Worst of all had been his violation of Hame by building those shields around his ability. At first it was just to hide himself, but then Xadrak, then Peter and Diana and Jane and everything else. And every time he looked at Hame, he was reminded of his betrayal, and that led to neglect and contempt. Even when he couldn't keep the shields together any longer and they'd crumbled, it hadn't made up for the past. But now he saw his deliverance.

He merged with the worst of himself, and the prison vanished.

Xadrak spotted him the second he was free. Aurelia bore down on him with a murderous glee in her eye. Xadrak growled, both inside and out. Carn lunged, wrapping around the weakening and frantic demon, and held on with every ounce of strength. His body fell to the ground. This was it. Aurelia would have him now, but he didn't dare relax. The demon tore at him like a wild cat, slashing and shredding his mind.

"Now!" he yelled.

Aurelia's might blazed through him in a brilliance of white, green, and blue, then all went dark.

XVIII

Aurelia burned into him. The attack pushed him to the ground, and she forced her hand against his sternum. He thrashed as her magic delved and hunted Xadrak.

She spied the fragment of the demon as it was about to slip from Carn's grasp. She surged forward and wrapped around the shard. Barbs punctured her, but she brushed aside the pain and enveloped him.

Let go, Carn.

Weakened to the point of death, his grip slackened, and he tumbled into the abyss. She held Xadrak while he flipped and flailed, stinging her but unable to break free. Her energy intensified, expanded and scalded him. He screamed and punched her. She increased her power and Xadrak shrank, squeezed into a dense ball. The piece of Xadrak shriveled to barely a speck, then ceased completely. He wasn't dead, but this conduit had closed.

And he'd lost one of his greatest weapons.

She saw the damage the demon had left behind. Carn's mind had partly eroded and protruded with stalactites and stalagmites. Some were recent; most were old. She didn't know if she could fix him.

She retreated from Carn's consciousness. When she opened her eyes, he didn't wake but at least he breathed.

Thank you for not killing him.

She dashed to Hame. The sight of him lying against a tree trunk, his legs stuck out at odd angles, his arms limp and disjointed, and his face bruised and bloody, stopped her cold.

"You think you have it in you to heal me?" he groaned.

She dropped to her knees and laid both hands onto his legs. She inhaled, hoping this wouldn't leave her in a coma, and accessed the well of her strength. She released the healing energy.

His back arched. He grunted and ground his teeth together.

Her tears leaked and panic skittered down her arms, accelerating her power. She felt the bones in his legs knit together with a crunch, then he was whole. His chest heaved, sweat sticking his hair to his scalp. She didn't budge; her body locked, waiting to check he was okay.

He lifted his head from the tree, shook it a couple of times, then flexed his arms and legs. He grinned wide, his eyes finding hers, then he grabbed her.

She sagged into him, a long sigh coming out of her mouth.

He's safe.

But he stiffened, and she scurried back.

"What is it?" she asked, before noticing his faraway look.

He blinked rapidly five times. "Danger. We have to get out of here." He jumped to his feet with no sign of the trauma he'd suffered and sprinted to Carn.

Her heart pinched at seeing him hurry to his lover.

"You're a dolt, you know that?" He scooped Carn off the ground and carried him to her.

She frowned at him. "Why?"

He chuckled. "Yes, I love Carn, but who do I have floating around in my head all the time?"

She shrugged. "It's convenient."

"You think I have such a connection with you purely for *convenience*?" He nudged her with his shoulder. "You're there because I love you, Aurelia. And I'm inside your head for the same reason."

"It's just—"

"I know, it's not everything you'd hoped for. And believe me, if I were different...but honestly, you think what we have is somehow inferior?"

She sighed. "I guess not. But it would be nice to have the whole package."

"No one ever gets the whole package." His gaze fell on Carn.

He was right. What did she have to worry about? However, one thing was certain. Hame had enough love for her *and* Carn and losing either would devastate him.

"Enough of this touchy-feely stuff. Get us out of here," Hame said. "Xadrak has ordered his lot to hunt us."

She hesitated, considering remaining behind to obliterate whoever attacked.

He caught the thought. "Not now, Aurelia. You'll overextend yourself, and you've got work to do."

"You never let me have any fun." She smiled.

He rolled his eyes, and she laughed. She placed one hand on Hame's arm and the other on Carn's head. For better or worse, she was bound to them. Her relationship with Carn required work, but she'd do it for Hame. She exhaled a deep breath and took them home.

CARN ROSE AND FELL ON WILD SEAS. AT THE CREST HE
heard familiar voices and tried to signal them. He had to
warn them. But then he tumbled. The waves swelled,
blocking the light, and they crashed on the deck so hard he
almost shattered. Eventually the storm calmed, the sea
leveled, and he sailed into harbor.

A weight rested on his chest, and he peered down at
Hame's fiery hair, half his body slumped across him. When
he repositioned his arm to drape it over his beloved, Hame
startled and sat up.

"You're awake," he gasped.

Carn didn't have a moment to respond before Hame's
lips fastened on his. He absorbed the desperate relief in
Hame's kiss and mixed it with his own. They'd both
survived. And—he searched—Xadrak was gone.

But that didn't mean everything was fine.

He pushed Hame back. "Wait, wait."

"What is it?"

"Where's Aurelia?"

"You've woken up after three days and you want to see
Aurelia?"

"Where is she?"

"She needed to stop her brothers from slaughtering
each other again."

"The Duke?"

"Dead. Your doing?"

Carn cringed. He didn't relish having to explain that
one to Aurelia. He didn't much enjoy the idea of
explaining any of it to her, but he'd have to bear down and
take it.

"Lucky I told you they could never be killed by anyone
except each other, wasn't it?"

"More like lucky I listened to you."

Hame took hold of his hand and lay beside him.

The Duke had been a risk. He was never meant to succeed; not only for Aurelia's sake, but Xadrak's as well. He didn't know all of the demon's plans, but Aurelia had to hear what he knew.

The skin on the back of his neck prickled.

"Where's Peter?" he asked.

Hame tensed. "Aurelia has him and his family. They're safe."

Peter would never be safe while Xadrak lived, and that truth gnawed on his bones.

"You don't have to worry about Aurelia." Hame looked up at him.

He peered into emeralds and saw for the first time in a long while they were unguarded. Like they'd been at the beginning.

"I'm sure she's itching to tear strips off me."

"She wouldn't be Aurelia if she didn't want to do that." He laughed. "But she let you live. Even helped heal you. Me, on the other hand…" Hame's finger stabbed him in the ribs.

He crunched his side. "Ow!"

"You keep any more secrets from me, there won't be anything left to bury."

For all the humor in Hame's voice, Carn's blood turned to ice. "I…I'm so sorry." Tears bit his eyes, and his breathing stuttered. Hame moved but, Carn couldn't bear to see the accusations. How could he ever expect Hame to love him after what he'd done?

Lips pressed his and he tried to escape them. He didn't deserve them. But the kiss came again, and he couldn't resist. He opened his eyes and saw everything he needed to see.

Hame broke away, his thumb wiping Carn's tears. The rough touch of his skin sent a shiver up his spine. "You're mine, Carn Gwyn. Ain't no demon going to take you from me."

Hame kissed him quickly and snuggled beside him, his arm heavy and reassuring across his ribs. Carn breathed deeply, the scent of earth wafting from Hame's hair. There was a lot to talk about, and although Hame might have forgiven him, he still had amends to make and demons to slay. But, for now, he held tight to the oracle in his arms.

Because if this was all there was, it would be enough for him.

EPILOGUE

"Maybe I should have kept you locked up from the beginning."

Manacles slid around his wrists and ankles and pinned him to the stone wall. Of course the cunt had a dungeon.

Olivier didn't struggle, not while she was there. He wouldn't give her the satisfaction of seeing him howl and holler. Instead he watched her jugular throb. The way he hungered now, even her stinking blood would suffice.

She sneered and scuttled away, taking that rotten stench with her, and bolted the door, plunging him into darkness.

Certain she'd gone, he rattled the chains. How dare they treat him like this? His shaking became more violent, but the shackles held.

If it weren't for witches…

Slaughtering the Duke had weakened him, allowing his once-beloved brother to betray him and make him a sacrifice so his slut-whore could live.

Hunger leached strength from his bones, making his head droop and body ache. All that paled compared to the ice-cold rage thundering within. Aurelia might think she had him trapped, but he'd escape.

Then he'd wipe her whole fucking species off the planet.

And drown the world in blood.

ABOUT THE AUTHOR

Daniel de Lorne writes about men, monsters and magic.

In love with writing since he wrote a story about a talking tree at age six, his first novel, the romantic horror *Beckoning Blood*, was published in 2014. At the heart of every book is a romance between two men, whether they're irresistible vampires, historical hotties, or professional paramours.

In his other life, Daniel is a professional writer and researcher in Perth, Australia, with a love of history and nature. All of which makes for great story fodder.

And when he's not working, he and his husband explore as much of this amazing world as they can, from the ruins of Welsh abbeys to trekking famous routes and swimming with whales.

You can contact Daniel through his website or sign up to his newsletter to receive all the latest news on releases, giveaways, cover reveals and more.

Connect with Daniel and get a FREE short story. Be the first to know about new releases, cover reveals, giveaways and more.
www.danieldelorne.com

ACKNOWLEDGMENTS

Thanks to my good friend, Nikki Logan, for the many hours she spent critiquing this book, providing untold feedback to bring it up to a publishable standard. I'm so grateful to have someone like you in this business.

And thank you to my family, friends, and fans, who enjoyed *Beckoning Blood* and wanted to see what happened next. My husband, Glen, gets extra marks on this front.

Printed in Great Britain
by Amazon